√2

D1372763

AUNT LUCY

DATE DUE

Underwood			
M. Porter			
2/00	MRF		
Johnson			
Wilkins			
Hamby			
Humphrey			
Wester			
D Jenkins			
GAYLORD			PRINTED IN U.S.A.

AUNT LUCY

Pamela Hill

Chivers Press • G.K. Hall & Co.
Bath, England   Thorndike, Maine USA

This Large Print edition is published by Chivers Press, England, and by G.K. Hall & Co., USA.

Published in 1999 in the U.K. by arrangement with Robert Hale Ltd.

Published in 1999 in the U.S. by arrangement with Robert Hale Ltd.

U.K. Hardcover ISBN 0–7540–3535–2 (Chivers Large Print)
U.K. Softcover ISBN 0–7540–3536–0 (Camden Large Print)
U.S. Softcover ISBN 0–7838–0358–3 (Nightingale Series Edition)

The text of this Large Print edition is unabridged.
Other aspects of the book may vary from the original edition.

Set in 16 pt. New Times Roman.

Printed in Great Britain on acid-free paper.

British Library Cataloguing in Publication Data available

Library of Congress Cataloging-in-Publication Data

Hill, Pamela.
    Aunt Lucy / Pamela Hill.
        p. (large print) cm.
        ISBN 0–7838–0358–3 (lg. print : sc : alk. paper)
        1. Large type books.   I. Title.
    [PR6058.I446A96   1999]
    823'.914—dc21
                                                    98–36967

CHAPTER ONE

'Hubert, do you like my new red stockings? Papa sent them to me from Italy. I think they're pretty.'

Lucy Meggett, who knew perfectly well how pretty they were, plucked up her skirts high enough to show a shapely calf encased in bright scarlet hose with white clocks. She didn't tell Hubert about the silk garters Papa had sent as well, because Lady O'Hara would only say that that kind of thing wasn't proper. Next year, when they were married, she herself would be able to tell Hubert anything she liked and the old witch could go back to her husband at Liskey. Meantime Lucy laughed, showing her pretty teeth and flaunting her legs and her petticoats. Hubert, her cousin, whose mind was straightforward and not too strong, ran his big square hand up and down his betrothed's calf and ankle appreciatively. Lucy was turning out all right. When she'd come over first from England she'd been a skinny little thing, but game even then. Now, the sight of her gave him continuous pleasure; fair curls tossing as she seized him now and whirled him about in a sudden joyful dance, long hooded hazel eyes dancing likewise, in a disturbing manner, beneath their creamy lids. Her mouth smiled as always, red and inviting and full. Her little pert breasts beneath the sternly laced bodice interested Hubert even more than the stockings. They were comrades; it didn't matter that the engagement wasn't formally announced yet, it soon would be. It didn't matter either that his own movements were clumsy, his feet big and awkward and square, like his hands. He knew that he could do nothing gracefully, but again it didn't matter, there was hunting, Lucy and Clonough, in that order. Hubert, fourth Viscount Meggett of Clonough, seldom looked in the glass except to shave. Had he done so more often the sight might have given him pause; he had a great hook nose, bad teeth, curly chestnut hair and the squat ungainly body of his mother's family. All this was compensated for by an immense exuded charm which allowed Hubert to make friends with everybody; the hunting confraternity, the county, the tenants. There wasn't the ill-feeling at Clonough that was still to be found elsewhere in the south, left over from last century and earlier. Everybody could be as they chose, Protestant or Catholic or nothing at all; Hubert's younger sister Cathy had become a Catholic herself three years ago, but that was understandable. He, Hubert, didn't care much one way or the other about anything except, as stated, riding to hounds; his elder sister, Isobel O'Hara, saw to the estate as she had since their father's death when Hubert was eight. He cared now, of course, also about

2

Lucy, who looked well on a horse as she did everywhere and would soon—Hubert was beginning to look forward to it avidly—look well in his bed.

A shadow darkened the doorway as they were still breathless from the dance. Lady O'Hara herself stood there, wearing her narrow dark crinoline and long black peaked hood and cloak as always, drawing off her gloves after having walked to the cottages for rents. She was frowning; it occurred to both young people that she had never been known to smile, taking life much too seriously as she did. She was a prudent childless creature married to a passive husband much older than herself. In her father's lifetime she had been old Lord Meggett's right hand, and since then, and following the death of his young second wife at poor Cathy's birth, had reared the two children as though they had been her own instead of half-brother and half-sister. Perhaps, however, the lack of closer relationship had led her to accede to Cathy's cruel arranged marriage, planned in her father's lifetime to prevent the Meggett-Clees cadet line from inheriting should anything happen to Hubert. Cathy and that great lazy idle cousin of theirs, Arthur Meggett-Clees, were, predictably, childless also. It had been known from the look of Cathy at her birth that she would never bear a child, and had killed her mother: and there had been enough money

3

then to bribe Arthur's widowed mother to agree.

The marriage of Hubert and his cousin Lucy had also been arranged by the prudent old lord, who could not have foreseen how his estates would run into debt despite Isobel's careful management: it was partly Hubert's fault for his extravagance, which, since he came of age at eighteen, his half-sister could no longer quell. In addition, the intended marriage had itself been a hoped-for mending of the old breach between the Aylors branch in England, where Lucy's widowed father still lived when he was not abroad—he was not, on the whole, a good influence on Lucy, who knew far more than a young girl should—and Clonough itself, where, two generations before, there had been a duel between brothers over a beautiful oyster-seller from Dublin whose name was Hetty Torke. Hetty was said to have borne a son to one or the other, but nobody knew what had happened to him: in any case it was unimportant. Lucy herself, whose dead mother had been the heiress of Fermisons, five miles off, had been sent to be brought up by Isobel at Clonough with the prospect of becoming Hubert's wife, thus adding to the estate although, truth to tell, there was no money with it. Any of that that was left after Lucius Meggett's meanderings abroad and his expensive habit of buying whatever took his fancy there, and sending it home, would go to Jeremy, Lucy's twin brother who was about to finish school and, probably, go on to Oxford, though judging from his infrequent letters he would need a crammer first. Jerry was so handsome he was disinclined for work, as Lucy herself admitted; in fact she had seen a great deal less of her brother than she had of Hubert, though Jeremy would come over for the occasional stay in the holidays, and they would all hunt together.

Meantime, prudent Isobel had guarded and maintained everything as best she could, her husband old Pat O'Hara interfering in no way whatever.

Now, Isobel had herself come to the door. The two young people stood respectfully still. Lady O'Hara's long face disapproved in any case of their romping; Lucy was aware that she herself was considered a trifle unladylike. Perhaps it was true.

In any case, also, this was evidently a moment for gravity; Lucy repressed her laughter and lowered her cream-lidded gaze to the floor. What was wrong?

'There is bad news from Meath,' Isobel told them quietly. 'Alan Fox-Strangways, whom you both knew, has been killed in a carriage-accident in London, foolishly racing against a rival in a crowded street. There is mourning at Mackens and there will be black worn here by you both. The funeral is to be on Thursday after the body is brought home. Hubert, I want

5

to speak to you privately.'

*   *   *

Dismissed to the garden—no doubt Isobel wanted to make arrangements with Hubert about going up to Meath—Lucy wandered about by herself. She was always happy to do this at Clonough; she loved it better than anything in her life and looked forward to becoming its mistress, especially the garden. It had been raining lately and the earth still smelled of soft Irish rain. Lucy knew every plant and flower, had helped to put in some of them, for once getting on well enough with old Isobel O'Hara as they grubbed in mutual dedication at the beds with their gloves and trowels. Now, by this time of year, the work had been worth it; pink and white anemones nodded with golden hearts on long stems; the clove carnations and irises and burnet roses had been there since the old lord's time, before Lucy had come. In a corner, a great mock orange, a philadelphus, dripped with the rain and Lucy turned her face up to the creamy soaked blossoms to savour their returning scent. She rubbed her face against the wet dark leaves; it was one more way of saying to Clonough how much she loved it, how greatly she would care for all of it after next year, when she had become Hubert's wife and had her own say in everything. She herself would

6

decide then what should be planted and where; Isobel could go back to her old Pat and get the roof mended for herself at Liskey. They were all crossing over, at any rate, to England in a few days' time to watch Jerry captain his school cricket team at the end-of-term match, and afterwards there was to be a dance in the pavilion. A great many girls would be after Jerry, as always, and she herself would enjoy dancing with him; he was by far a better dancer than poor Hubert, and knew it. Nevertheless Lucy loved Hubert, her future husband, not only because one ought to try; there was something appealing about his reliance on her, the way his eyes would look at her lately like a beseeching spaniel's that wanted to be taken for a walk. They would be happy here together, at Clonough, and life would go on as it always had; Jerry would come over, and they would all three ride out in the early morning to the meet and come back much later laughing and splashed with mud and soaked to the skin, with stories to tell about jumping the low grey walls and, maybe, meeting again the strange darkly beautiful Empress of Austria who rode better than anyone, sewn into her habit, and jumped the drystone walls with serene courage. Her English escort Bay Middleton was very handsome.

*   *   *

Hubert came towards Lucy presently down the stone path. His face was no longer cheerful, as it usually was at the sight of her; he looked crestfallen, almost sly. He did not take her hand as usual, but stood before her, eyes on the ground. It was no doubt the mourning for Alan Fox-Strangways.

'Sir Pat and I are to go up to the funeral on Wednesday and stay,' he said. 'You and Isobel—England, I don't know—she said—maybe she'd better tell you the rest herself.'

He tailed off uncertainly, looked at Lucy once, passed his tongue between his lips, and turned away. It was hard to tell pretty Lucy what Isobel had, in fact, quite firmly said. Evidently Annis Fox-Strangways, the dead man's motherless sister, was coming to stay here at Clonough for a time after the funeral. Isobel had already arranged it by letter. She said it wouldn't do for Lucy to be here as well. Hubert felt depressed; he'd seen Annis already at hunt balls up there in Meath; she was a bad dancer, like himself. She wasn't pretty either, not like Lucy. However, there was the money, a great deal of it, now Alan was dead, and Isobel had flatly stated that they couldn't go on here at Clonough as they were. The bird in hand, she'd said, her prudent pale eyes fixed on his face; soon it would be realised that Annis was a rich heiress in her own right, and others would get there before himself. This challenge had spurred Hubert on a little, and the rest had followed. 'You know it costs a lot to keep up the place here,' Isobel had said. 'I've done my best. I was not at all sure how the pair of you would manage on your own without giving up the hunters altogether. If there was money from Annis, you could build new stables and add to them. As it is, Fermisons itself will bring in nothing; the house is in bad repair and nobody lives there. You are of an age now, my brother, to think of such things for yourself.'

Hubert had thought, or thought he had thought; trying not to recall that Annis Fox-Strangways was pigeon-chested and had nothing to say, and he'd miss Lucy a lot. He'd promised not to say too much, however, and it was best anyway to keep out of trouble. Isobel would see to everything. She always had.

*　　　*　　　*

Lady O'Hara kept her own silence on the matter till the voyage to England was undertaken a few days later by the two of them only, herself and Lucy Meggett; the men, her husband and young Hubert himself, were up at the Meath funeral. Pat would keep an eye on Hubert in case he tried to slip across afterwards. She herself would return Lucy promptly to Aylors, her father's house in Buckinghamshire, and then come home at once; she wanted to be there when the plain young heiress arrived, as it was unlikely matters would progress by themselves. Meantime, she fastened a considering gaze on Lucy, who did not travel well and was therefore lying down below decks. Isobel, who travelled excellently, now regarded the prospect of the grey sea churning between the Irish coast and Fishguard with equanimity. Knowing the tides, it would be worse on the way back; but Lucy Meggett did not yet know that she would not be coming back to Clonough. It was perhaps time to break the news while her physical weakness made her mind receptive.

Watching the pale exquisite heart-shaped face, its fair curls tangled by hazard and the wind at sea, Isobel felt what she herself admitted to be a somewhat customary irritation. It was perhaps due to the fact that Lucy Meggett appeared constantly, by reason of the full curve of her lower lip, to smile, and that her creamy eyelids seldom opened themselves fully. The effect was that of a sleepy and rather sly young queen bee about to engage in a nuptial flight: and that business of hitching up her skirts the other day to show Hubert her Italian stockings was no more than had been expected for some time. Altogether, apart from the pleasing prospect of the Fox-Strangways money, it would have become increasingly difficult to maintain one's mastery over Clonough once Lucy herself had begun to

10

reign there. It had been, in its way, providential that young Fox-Strangways had chosen, at this particular moment, to break his neck. His sister Annis would make a biddable wife for Hubert, who himself, poor boy, would always need guidance from some woman or other. She, his sister, would meantime of course be at hand to supply it, the more willingly as the prospect would now recede, with Lucy's going, of the loss of what was in fact a most comfortable diet of Clonough home farm produce, not to mention properly hung game. Dear Pat was too old now to provide many birds himself, or in fact to do very much else. As for Liskey, with its leaking roof, Isobel had no particular desire to return there.

'Lucy, my dear.'

The long lashes—they were darker than the hair, an advantage not commonly possessed by such extremely blonde young women—raised themselves. Isobel O'Hara saw for once the colour of Lucy Meggett's widely opened eyes. They were not blue, as should properly have been expected, but hazel, almost moss-agate, flecked brown on green. The bee-stung mouth continued to smile in the girl's pale face, framed as it was by the dark contrasting collar of the heavy felt travelling-cloak.

'Would you prefer that I sat up?' Lucy asked the older woman respectfully. 'It's really safer not.'

11

'There is no need,' replied Lady O'Hara calmly. 'Lie still; I have something of importance to say to you.'

She set about it at once; it was best to be ruthless in the circumstances. 'You will not be returning to Clonough, at least for the time.' Not ever, she was thinking, to tempt Hubert from his duties as would most certainly happen in the event. Lucy's face had meantime grown whiter than before.

'Not—' She struggled up, then asked curiously, 'Is Papa taking me somewhere?' It was, perhaps, she thought, the explanation; it was like old Isobel to make it sound doleful and dutiful. One never foresaw what Papa would do; he would appear suddenly, mysteriously, out of nowhere, from foreign lands and far places, where he collected goddesses' statues and broken pillars from ancient temples, and fragments of marble friezes and pottery, and carved stones from a time beyond telling. He would talk about them with his long fine hands waving, his prematurely white hair long also, and as usual wild. It was all of it no doubt a comfort to him after the death of Mama, long ago; they had loved each other. If he was to take her, Lucy, somewhere or other for a little while now she would be pleased, of course, like the time they'd gone together to Bavaria, without Jeremy, and looked at churches. Papa, however, was more of a stranger than Hubert,

12

and Aylors itself, where he sometimes sojourned briefly like a perching stork, wasn't the same as Clonough; nothing could be. A sudden longing took her for Hubert's squat familiar appearance: the funeral must be over.

'Not that I know of,' replied Isobel, folding her lips judiciously over the matter of Lucius Meggett, of whom she had never approved. 'He will of course be present at the cricket match, or so he says. One can never be certain.' She then took the plunge.

'Lucy, you are old enough now to understand what I have to tell you,' she vouchsafed gravely. 'You are not, after all, to be married to Hubert. He is to marry elsewhere.'

'Hubert—marry—but he loves *me*.' The beautiful face had paled long ago to the colour of bleached linen; afraid that Lucy would faint, though it had never yet happened, Isobel continued quickly. 'There is not enough money from the combined estates to make such a marriage practical,' she said firmly. 'You are a personable young woman and must take yourself to market in England. It will not be difficult for you to find a husband, preferably with enough money to repair Fermisons, which as you know has always been considered your own property as it belonged to your mother. As for Clonough, it needs money also; Hubert's habits are extravagant and he could never live like a poor man, as he would have to

13

do if he married you. So—'

'So you are trying to marry him to Annis Fox-Strangways instead,' replied Lucy shrewdly; her sharp brain was one of the factors that had caused Isobel, on the whole, not to prefer her. 'He may not want to,' she added. 'Annis has bad breath. I'm going to be sick.' Tears rose in her eyes at this additional, and rapidly pending, humiliation and she leaned sideways, preparing to vomit unbearably on the lower deck. Lady O'Hara bent swiftly and ferreted in her reticule, producing a small basin; one was always prepared on these sea voyages. Lucy grabbed at the basin and used it, tears mingling with the vomit. If Hubert were only here she'd persuade him, but as it was she knew very well what would happen; she would be kept at Aylors, not allowed to make the crossing again, her letters not allowed to reach Hubert, and anyway writing wasn't the same—and of course she *would* be sick in front of Isobel O'Hara just when the latter had managed to get her at a disadvantage. Poor Hubert would never stand up to that woman, the way she, Lucy, usually could for herself; the way she would certainly have done if all this had happened at Clonough, dear Clonough of the grey walls and the remembered flowers and the famous portico. Ugh, it was all coming up still. But Hubert himself might have warned her; he'd known, that time in the garden. He'd known,

14

and hadn't told her anything. That was what she, Lucy, really felt sad and hurt about, almost more so than about losing Clonough. After all, there was still Fermisons; some time, she'd go back there. In the meantime, Aylors itself, which belonged to Papa and would go to Jeremy, would have to do. She'd take herself to market, as Isobel put it, from there. She'd marry the first rich man she met, it didn't matter which.

She handed the basin back fiercely to Lady O'Hara. 'You never liked me from the beginning,' she said, wiping her mouth with her fist. 'It isn't only the money. You never liked me because you're old and ugly, and I'm as I am. You knew I'd manage Clonough as well as you ever could, and Hubert with it. You knew, and you arranged everything as you've told me only now. Papa will never forgive you, and neither will I.'

'Pray do not talk like a child,' said Isobel coldly, going to dispose of the basin's unsavoury contents over the ship's side. The wind was blowing in a convenient direction, and the Welsh coastline was approaching with its familiar blur of buff and green. She turned with composure to Lucy.

'It is time to tidy yourself,' she said. 'Shortly we will be ashore.'

CHAPTER TWO

Jeremy Meggett bowled overarm, a Discobolos in immaculate white flannels, watched adoringly by a dozen or so young ladies and their mamas, seated as these were in provided deck-chairs at the annual county match against the school eleven. Batting, and noticed till now by nobody except his parents, was Sebastian Maule Wint, who had joined the school prefects' year only last autumn, hopefully to acquire a smattering of English manners; he had formerly had a private tutor in Boston. Sebastian's batting, like most other things he did, was not very successful as his pince-nez slipped at the wrong moment and he was in any case short-sighted. Jerry however was in top form, running like a god, white shirt gleaming in the sunshine and almost, as had once been said of Henry VIII in gilded youth, showing the rose-flush of his fair skin through the snowy linen. He was eighteen years old. The fond mamas, and a few fathers who had come to watch their sons excel themselves on this special day in all the year, enviously observed Lucy Meggett, seated in a spread white dress with the sun glinting on her fair hair beneath her hat, and recognised her without any doubt as the handsome bowler's sister. It had been permitted to Lucy today to wear white, which after all was French mourning, and Ireland was in any case far away. Lucy smiled on, and the miserable Wint heir noted her meantime mostly as a gold-and-white blur against the shaven grass. Already his timid mind however stirred with the hope of meeting her afterwards, perhaps at tea in the tent, or still later on at the dance. He had been of course taught to dance correctly in Boston. He had in fact been extremely well educated there, but somehow it didn't matter in this place of shaved and fragrant English grass, superior young men and the hallowed and hated stumps. Sebastian glanced in guilty fashion towards his parents, and his mother Mehitabel smiled at him encouragingly; she knew very little about cricket, but had come today because it was her duty.

Mehitabel Wint, born a Maule of New England, was a plumpish woman with wistful grey-green eyes behind pince-nez like her son's, a pronounced double chin and fair hair turning grey beneath her prosperous hat. Mehitabel might not understand cricket, but she knew the art of shipbuilding backwards, in particular the lately introduced carbon treatment of steel. She had kept the books herself at her own works at Quinty until, of late years, when she wasn't quite what she had been, her husband Luther K. had taken over. He, his fat body planted squarely now in the next chair but one, was with her for this occasion, an unusual circumstance nowadays.

Luther K. Wint's dark jowl, which needed shaving twice daily, was raised in expectation of the outcome one way or the other of the game; at times he grunted aloud in assent or dissent, nobody was sure which. Sebastian was making a fool of himself as usual, Luther K. had decided; that had been evident. It wasn't certain what would become of the business once that boy was left in full charge; his bookkeeping was no doubt adequate and he had been allowed to spend a part of his rather slowly maturing years in the Quinty office to practise it. However all that was a long way off and this was England. Sebastian's second sister Sabine, who had been brought over initially for a year at a London finishing school, sat now between her father and mother, her dark and lovely profile intent on the bowler. Wint himself did not spend further thought on the vexed question of Sabine, but his wife did, remembering everything from the beginning. It had all been most unfortunate; before they themselves returned unencumbered to the States, they had been asked to remove Sabine from the élite London finishing establishment, where it had been hoped that her manners would improve after paying out all that money. However she was, the headmistress had clearly stated, quite uncontrollable, a bad influence on the other young ladies, did exactly as she chose, would listen to nobody, and must go. It was in fact difficult to know what to do with

18

Sabine next. At home in Boston, everybody of course knew by now what she was like, and this was the trouble; timely advice, even the occasional judicious caning, had failed, and Mehitabel was in despair at ever finding the girl a husband despite her undoubted looks and all the money. Sabine, in short, had the passions of her father without, so far, the opportunity to indulge them.

Mehitabel glanced past the exquisite, if intractable, sight of her daughter to where her husband sat, still intent on the game—Luther always liked to know all about everything—his thrusting beagle's nose raised to sniff the matchless smell of newly scythed English summer grass. Sadly, his nose was not the only thing about him that thrust, as Mehitabel, who had as a rule not much humour, reminded herself. Luther Kelly Wint, whom she had married long ago as a prop to the business, was as unfaithful as a tomcat, probably had been so from the beginning; although for the first few years, when she'd had her own looks, he'd been attentive enough, in fact too much so. Almost at once there had been Susan, married last year to good, steady Nathaniel J. Passmore and duly expecting her first in the autumn. Then there had been two dead babies, then Sabine, all much too promptly one after the other; then, after all the rest, the delight of his mother's heart, out there now wielding that very heavy-looking wooden bat; she hoped it wouldn't bring on one of Sebastian's breathless attacks. Mehitabel had watched, with the anguish of Hecuba, as her son did something or other with the bat he shouldn't, and his glasses had slipped and the crowd howled in sudden execration about whatever it was. Sebastian wasn't used to games, they weren't good for him, no exertion was so. After his birth at last Mehitabel herself had had trouble with her kidneys, and by now was in general a trifle blurred at the outlines; that didn't matter. Soon Sebastian, her darling, would be back with them, away from this unkind place and these disapproving people, safe home again in the Quinty office, learning the aspects of the business only she herself could teach him, whatever Luther K. might say about it. She, a Mayflower Maule of Philadelphia, had succeeded her father long ago in what was then a mere log-felling concern, steam not yet having become important; Mehitabel could remember the great swathes of felled logs floated down the bay from the redwood business culled from the thousands of Maule acres of forest maintained in the south. It continued still in a small way. However she, Mehitabel, had seen for herself the way things were going to go, with the first crossing of the Atlantic by steam and that that would soon replace sail altogether. She had, on her own initiative—and it hadn't been easy to get anybody to take a young woman seriously—

started a small metal-plate plant after reading up the Bessemer steel process. All this had shortly brought her in touch with a young dark-haired engineer named Luther Kelly Wint. They had married, no doubt, partly as a business proposition, but at that time—

'Mother.' It was Sabine's husky voice; her great grey eyes, the brooding colour of slate, had been staring from the beginning at the handsome cricket captain who had lately attracted all eyes with one celestial arm whirling round above his head, on whose bright hair the sun still shone down favourably. Jerry Meggett was certainly worth looking at, a darling of the gods. If only Sabine would behave herself they might somehow, afterwards in the tent at the dance—after all it was useless back home except for fortune-hunters—

'Mother, see that bowler?' Sabine announced. 'I want to marry him.'

*   *   *

That was how it had all started; and afterwards, in the tent, it was evident that Sebastian, who'd never looked at a girl before in his life, was greatly taken with young Meggett's pretty sister Lucy. Hadn't there been a Lord Meggett sometime? One remembered looking it up. Asked, young Jeremy replied politely—his manners were really excellent, it was certainly a good

21

family—that that had been his grandfather in Ireland, and by now a cousin there; and he then smiled in dazzling fashion at Sabine, who amazingly enough kept quiet. Afterwards, Luther K. murmured to his wife that these Meggetts didn't have any money; his nose always ferreted out such things immediately, but it didn't matter. Sabine still failed, unusually, to push herself forward; she didn't really have to, she was the loveliest girl there, both at tea and the dance afterwards, where a band played on the grass outside the tent and some young couples wandered by themselves out on to the grass. During the evening, having watched Sebastian vainly trying to obtain Lucy for a dance among all the other clamouring young men in white flannels, Mehitabel invited Jeremy, with his sister and her chaperone, a silent dark Irishwoman in a peaked old-fashioned hood, to luncheon with them all in London at a very expensive hotel indeed, two days afterwards. It meant delaying their own sailing or, as one supposed it would soon be called, their steaming meantime. That didn't matter either: Nathaniel J. was coping at Quinty. There was certainly, on all sides, sudden hope. Luther K. said it would be good for Sebastian to marry, and although she herself didn't altogether like to think about it, there was no doubt Sebastian was still extremely taken with young Lucy Meggett, who seemed well-bred and healthy as well as

22

pretty. The luncheon, in short, was a success.

* * *

The double engagement was shortly announced in the papers, to the disapprobation of certain mothers of hopeful daughters, and of the disappointed daughters themselves; it was generally agreed among all such persons that Jeremy Meggett was too young to marry; his sister was a different matter and nobody knew her in any case. Lucy herself noticed another paragraph in the papers about then; Hubert's engagement to Annis Fox-Strangways of Mackens, County Meath, Ireland. She pursed her lips in a manner that was not typical, and shed no tears. Isobel had of course gone back as soon as possible to Clonough, to make sure it all happened; well, she herself, Lucy Meggett, would take care of her own life from now on.

This ambition was complicated by the fact that with the departure of Lady O'Hara, there was nobody left to chaperone Lucy. Mehitabel had gladly therefore agreed to take on the task, especially as it seemed politic to take Sabine well out of the way until the wedding despite the latter's fierce desire to remain at all costs near Jerry. She was bribed by the promise of a Paris trousseau, and why not, decided Mehitabel, take Lucy to buy one there at the same time?

23

This suited everybody, even Sabine, who was not beyond considering her own appearance. Luther K. Wint went back by himself to the States meantime, intending to return briefly for the wedding: Nat Passmore couldn't be expected to hold things down at Quinty forever. Mehitabel sighed, with compassion for the Boston housemaids and worry about her pregnant eldest daughter; but for the present the thing to do was to keep Sabine occupied and also, perhaps, to get to know one's future daughter-in-law. Lucy seemed both sensible and graceful, and would certainly pay for costly dressing: as for Sabine, she must at all events be kept apart from Jeremy till they were firmly married, lest the young man find out meantime how extremely difficult his future bride could be. For the present, had Mehitabel known, all Jeremy had seen was a beautiful dark-haired girl in an expensive dress, had mentally undressed her at once and, as her mother was invariably present when they met, left it at that meantime. He was glad the old lady would go back afterwards to Boston; life at Aylors could proceed after his marriage as usual, only with a great deal more money to spend, which prospect was pleasant.

Meantime, Mehitabel and the two girls departed for Paris. On the train after the crossing, Sabine began again to behave badly and Lucy tried tactfully to interest her in talk about Jeremy, which held his betrothed's attention as nothing else except his actual presence would have done. Mehitabel meantime thought fleetingly of certain advice she had received from a friend of hers who had married into the English aristocracy and had told her some time before of a Belgian finishing school which was virtually a prison, with a certain creeper-covered tower thought by all concerned to be impregnable until the latest recalcitrant subject had eloped out of the window with the postman. The young woman in question had been rumoured to be slightly lacking in her wits. Fortunately, there were bride-clothes to interest even Sabine from now on. Mehitabel nodded brightly to where the girl sat sullenly in silence, Lucy having meantime exhausted her reminiscences of Jeremy; after all there hadn't been many to relate, except about hunting. 'You can,' said Mehitabel, reading her daughter's thoughts, 'write to him, darling, after all, every day from Paris.'

Sabine did so devotedly, from the discreet hotel where they all stayed in intervals of arranged visits to M. Doucet the famous couturier. That luminary swore that both mesdemoiselles possessed figures to ravish, and that it was a pleasure to dress such young ladies as they should most certainly have been dressed long ago. Lucy was on the whole more greatly interested in this situation than Sabine, who had always had enough money and the right clothes. After Clonough, where one wore any old thing, it was enchanting to be draped and expertly fitted out in tulle for the ceremony, satin for evenings, muslin for summers, velvet for the winter with a deep fur trim. There was also a great deal of convent-made underwear so fine it would slip through a wedding ring once the latter was put on. Lucy had almost forgotten the existence of Sebastian, who in course of their brief encounters had remained tongue-tied and had merely gazed at her beseechingly from behind the pince-nez. She had treated him kindly, as one might be kind to one's dog.

Sabine's daily letters brought occasional brief replies from Jeremy, who was not by habit a letter-writer. His eagerly awaited missives, seized upon and torn open at once and only later shown to Mehitabel as duty demanded, showed little evidence of passionate devotion. They contained, for the most part, news of healthy male pursuits: Jerry had been to Leicestershire to hunt with the Quorn, and to some other shire to a house-party; there had been a shoot up there and he had brought down a good bag. Back in London, he and two other chaps were taking boxing lessons from a worthy named Buck Mullins. This news alarmed Sabine, who wrote back by return 'Don't spoil your precious, precious face.' Mehitabel, who was of course careful not to post them all, posted that one;

the continuing evidence of Sabine's searing passion *in absentiam* alarmed her slightly and might well alarm the bridegroom when actually encountered. She herself, in the early days with Luther K., had never gone on like that or, for that matter, he with her. However if Jeremy Meggett really did smash up his handsome face, Sabine was capricious enough to call off the whole thing: and by now no other outcome but marriage seemed possible for the almost exhausted director of Quinty Maule Associates, Inc. Doucet's bill would naturally be enormous, but worth it: after all he dressed the Empress Eugénie. Altogether Mehitabel put in a cautious little note of her own to Jeremy Meggett to be sure to be careful during the boxing lessons. He promised to obey.

*   *   *

All went well for the time being, and the double wedding took place at last in the presence of a returned Luther K. and of Lucius Meggett himself, recovered from his understandable fury over the Clonough betrayal. He had most unexpectedly married a wife again, an Italian whom he had obtained as part of a bargain over a Pompeian vase he greatly desired to possess. Caterina spoke no English and was entirely unobtrusive, standing in black, which she always wore, as the two exquisite brides on each of their fathers' arms

27

approached the altar behind their respective veils, no doubt inflaming the passions of the two waiting grooms commendably. The vows were exchanged, the two engagement rings—a small diamond was all Jeremy had been able to afford, but Lucy's from Sebastian was magnificent—were removed meantime to alloy for the slipping on of gold wedding rings upon slender fingers, and the exchanged nuptial kisses appeared entirely proper and did not alarm the watching Mehitabel, herself stately for the occasion in wine-coloured bombazine and a sealskin peignoir. If only Sabine continued to behave till after the reception, it should be perfectly all right.

Sebastian Maule Wint himself could hardly believe his luck or, in fact, totally understand its implications: he was still in a state of pristine innocence, having been too self-effacing even to have been seduced at school like everybody else: in fact no one had thought of it. Sebastian Maule Wint was, as often happens with a second generation, completely lacking either in the constructive enthusiasm of his mother or in the business flair, let alone the tremendous physical presence and intelligence, of his father. Had he been born in less affluent circumstances he would without doubt have ended as a clerk in some counting-house, given satisfaction over forty-odd years, and retired on any savings he had managed to accumulate in course of a blameless existence.

As it was, after cutting the cake together, Sebastian found something quite remarkable happening to him physically. His bride, with her exquisite face, her glorious hair, her eyes that concealed laughter, had her little plump breasts clearly outlined by her white boned bodice; one hadn't been able to help noticing them even in church. Sebastian felt an unwonted stirring in that part of his anatomy which had never stirred before, despite the earthy instructions issued shortly prior to the ceremony by Luther K., which at the time had made Sebastian feel slightly uncomfortable. Now, it was different. He had only just begun to live: and with Lucy, life itself would be like heaven.

*   *   *

'You've done well, Lucy, my girl; never mind that business of Clonough. This is far better; plenty of money, and that's what we all need. Can't take to old Luther Wint myself, but that's of no importance. You'll have everything you need, a carriage, town house in Boston, society—suppose women want it.' One bright-blue eye swivelled towards Lucy in the disconcerting way it had from beneath Lucius Meggett's mane of thick unruly white hair. Probably her own hair and Jeremy's would turn the same colour when they were both old. One couldn't remember the colour of Mama's;

she had died too soon, and the only portrait, hung by now at Aylors, showed her in a concealing hat and riding veil. She'd died in a hunting accident. It was strange to think of Papa's having married again lately. Caterina seemed to do nothing but tell her beads; she'd even done it at the reception, sitting alone.

'Give them an heir,' said Lucius shrewdly. 'That's what they want, especially old Wint. You'll be company for the old lady; she's a force to be reckoned with still, as much as he is. The boy himself looks kind enough, better than Hubert, damn him. The sister in Boston's due to give birth any minute, they tell me. Your son will inherit, however; get on with it.'

Papa had never concealed the facts of life from anybody: it would not have occurred to him to do so. He got up now, spread wide his upper limbs like a welcoming gander, and embraced Lucy. 'We're off to Milan,' he told her. 'Use the house when you want to; it's as much yours as Jeremy's. Expect they'll start breedin' for themselves.' He eyed Caterina with some discontent; she did not excite him, but was after all no trouble to anybody and besides the Pompeian vase she had predictably brought, had a relative who knew the whereabouts of certain Etruscan tombs hitherto never excavated. Lucy would be all right: she had plenty of sense. Lucius kissed her, and departed with the other guests in course, taking his second wife on his arm

30

somewhat absently.

CHAPTER THREE

Poor Mehitabel had to put off her wine-coloured bombazine almost at once and to discard her fond remembrances of Doucet. A telegraph message had come that very night from Nathaniel J. Passmore in the States, now a widower; his wife Susan Wint had died in premature childbirth. The child, a boy, still lived. It was necessary to order immediate mourning for everybody and to make arrangements to return to Boston at once. Meantime, they stayed quietly in the London hotel.

Lucy was mildly irritated, although of course sorry about the news from Boston. She had looked forward to wearing her pretty clothes, having just come out of mourning, or half-mourning as it had latterly been, for Annis Fox-Strangways' brother, whom she had hardly known. Now, here again was a black dress, granted, this time, of the best material, and with wide velvet bands which suited Lucy's fair hair. Sebastian still gazed at her adoringly. He hardly seemed to grieve for his elder sister, who had evidently been like him in nature, quiet and biddable. He told Lucy that a passage had been arranged at once by way of the British and American Royal Mail Steam Packet Company, leaving Liverpool for New York. 'We will go up by train,' he remarked thoughtfully.

Lucy accepted the information, as she had accepted his shy attentions on the night before; they had been somewhat inept, perhaps because Sebastian hadn't been wearing his pince-nez. She had stared above his finally jerking head at the oil lamps decorating the walls and at the night pressing dark against the windows beyond the half-drawn curtains; it had been too hot in the hotel room to draw them fully. The flutterings commonly supposed to afflict brides had not assailed her. It was Sebastian, in the process, who had burst into tears; Lucy had put her white arms about him and tried to comfort him. 'Keep trying,' she had told him. 'I expect it will be all right; it's probably the same for everybody.' She had wondered, at the time, how Jeremy was faring with Sabine: one couldn't of course ask.

Sebastian, having again beheld her only as a beautiful blur, was in fact torn between his father's advice and his mother's: the latter had told him lust was sinful and not to let things go too far. 'Tell me about Boston,' Lucy had intervened helpfully. 'There hasn't really been time to find out anything, and I'd like to know more.'

He told her, rather miserably, as much as he knew, about his mother's weekly sewing-circle and his tutor, and the Quinty office; and by then had tried again, and this time found it much better. In fact, to enter Lucy was delicious, and the first thing he'd ever really done for himself; the oftener it happened the more Sebastian found he liked it. In the morning, after they had both slept, he turned to her, rose-flushed on the pillow as she was, and managed it yet once more; the necessity of dressing and going down to breakfast at last was unwelcome. His father and mother were of course waiting, coffee having been poured and eggs and bacon kept hot in a covered dish. Mama had red eyes behind her glasses; the news had come about poor Susan last night or early this morning. Jeremy and Sabine had not yet come down. Sebastian found that he could hardly think of his dead sister. He continued instead to watch his bride, placidly eating scrambled eggs. Luther K. Wint continued in his customary worldly and observant silence, and later that day, the mourning-clothes having duly arrived, they all four departed in these in a closed carriage for the Liverpool train. Jeremy had come down to convey polite condolences and to see them off: the brother and sister kissed one another goodbye. Sabine had elected to stay in bed awaiting Jerry's return. Her mother went up briefly to say farewell and then came down mopping her eyes with a black-bordered handkerchief, several of which had been thoughtfully

33

included in the packages delivered at once by Peter Robinson's store.

*   *   *

Mehitabel's acquaintance with the directors of Cunard, who were in the process of acquiring rights in the existing steamship company and already owned them in the railways, meant that no tickets had to be purchased: Luther K. Wint merely waved signed vouchers and they were all conveyed with deep respect to their separate carriages. These had been reserved, and Lucy found that she and her young husband, by thoughtful dispensation of Luther K. himself, were in a compartment of their own to which luncheon would be conveyed in due course. One heavy eye winked as Lucy's father-in-law handed her in. This seemed improper in their mourning state, and Lucy primly arranged her black skirts about her in the corner seat by the window, without winking back.

She had never travelled by the new railway before, and would have liked to look out at disappearing London and whatever should follow beyond the window. She was still aware of a very slight inward discomfort from the sharp brief pain of the previous night; no doubt it would go away. However she saw, with some resentment, Sebastian pull down the blinds on either side. He then begged her to lie

34

down along the seat. Lucy demurred; Sebastian almost dragged at her, avid, flushed, and already unbuttoning his trousers. 'Nobody'll come in for a long time,' he muttered. It was a considerable speech for Sebastian. Lucy, already a little weary of him, was however anxious not to hurt his feelings in any way.

'Don't you think, dear,' she suggested, 'that perhaps you've done enough at least till we get to the ship? You don't want to tire yourself.' His mother had told her, one time when they were in Paris, that Sebastian had always been delicate, a claim which his present anxiety seemed eager to discount. Lucy however did not argue with him, merely recalling how Jerry, when he came down this morning, had had his full underlip bitten and bruised as though by an animal; evidently marriage was like that. She therefore submitted in wifely fashion, and accordingly, when some time later the steward's face appeared at the suddenly opened door with a tray, found herself still in a compromising position without having ever heard that term. Her young husband's vaguely focussed glance, through pince-nez somehow remaining secure, raised itself and he blushed, and began to fumble in embarrassment as though to try to pretend it hadn't happened. Lucy recalled how Lady O'Hara had always said embarrassment showed middle-class origins. 'Shut the door meantime, serve

35

luncheon presently, and knock before you come in,' she told the equally blushing steward, who later on remarked to the engine-driver that he had never seen the like; and by the time he humbly knocked and again brought in luncheon, which itself was not interesting, the young couple were seated decorously one on either side the compartment looking out at the view, which was not particularly interesting either. Lucy found the luncheon difficult to eat and hoped that she would not be sick on the coming voyage; the rocking of the train was enough without Sebastian as well, and the so-called Railway Pudding had been rather heavy.

In due course they beheld the long docks, bristling with masts and the brand-new funnels of steamships, some at least without doubt provided by the industrious workshops of Maule Wint Quinty, Inc. Lucy walked up and down between her husband and her father-in-law, who discoursed knowledgeably about which type of engine was which. She was glad of his talk and although at first his appearance had revolted her slightly, there was no doubt that Luther K. Wint had charm. Sebastian himself said little, being as usual in awe of his father: but Lucy was to find in any case, as the days passed, that her spouse never did have much to say. Sebastian had discovered that making love to her was the thing he liked best in the world, and he gave rise to this situation whenever they were in private. Lucy herself

36

tried to escape now and again to talk to the other passengers, but Sebastian always followed her like a dog and the others melted away, thinking that the young pair wanted to be by themselves; so things were sooner or later back where they had started. Everyone however regarded Lucy with avid curiosity behind her back: brides were always interesting, though one did not of course speak of such matters. Poor Mrs Wint senior did not appear, but had meals in her cabin. Mr Wint, of course, they all knew. It was impossible not to.

*   *   *

The voyage was smooth, and Lucy was not at first assailed by qualms unless the tide was running strong. Sebastian, on the other hand, seemed increasingly filled with lassitude after their lovemaking and stayed generally down in the cabin except for meals; when Lucy did persuade him up the hatchway to walk with her on deck, he would do so with his arm about her, his head laid against her shoulder as if his neck were the stem of a wilting flower and could not support itself without her aid; it was, Lucy was beginning to think, more and more like a child with its mother than a man with his wife. Sebastian's short-sighted eyes would watch everything she did; in the close and primitive conditions of the shared cabin, she would feel them fixed upon her as she washed, combed out her hair and duly pinned it up, and laced herself finally into her clothes. Sebastian did not help with the lacing. Perhaps, she decided, he was missing his real mother. Mehitabel still kept her own cabin, grieving for Susan and no doubt worrying about the motherless baby, who had been christened Hartley shortly after birth; a letter from the widower, Mr Passmore, had been waiting for them at the port. Now, Lucy escaped for once and went up the hatchway by herself to savour the fresh wind blowing on deck, and walked about, her hair whipped loose again beneath the pinned-on hat. She came upon Luther K. with his back turned, having just bitten the end off a cigar and thrown the end nonchalantly out to sea. Lucy hoped to pass by without being noted, but he knew she was there, the way he seemed to know everything; and turned, his teeth still showing against the newly lit cigar. The teeth were strong, yellowed slightly, but his own. Lucy was already aware of the immense physical power of the man; he came over now and drew her arm through his, walking up and down with her firmly against the wind. It was early and there were few others on deck.

'Does Sebastian know what he's doing with you, Lucy?' she heard him ask. 'Does he give you pleasure? That's the main point with a woman like you; most women can't contemplate it, maybe don't know they need it. If he does as he ought to do the right way, you've felt it already; if not, you haven't. I can speak to Sebastian if you'd like that.'

She was angry; it was as though he'd stripped her naked in public. For some reason his touch disturbed her. He gripped her wrist now with his free hand, the other still holding her arm, and the pressure of the hairy-backed flesh against her own roused strange feelings in Lucy. Why should he speak to Sebastian? What would he say? He had no right to interfere in such things. She smiled on, but shook her head silently. Wint moved his arm so that it pressed against her breast, and she made herself move away a little; both breasts had grown tender over the last day or two, and this morning again she felt queasy. She knew more about marriage in any case than most young women: Papa and Hubert hadn't minded what they said.

'Make him give you a son,' said Sebastian's father in a low voice. 'Encourage him all you can. Whether or not Susan's baby dies, and a delicate premature child can do so easily, yours will inherit Quinty. Without you there's no certain hope: remember that. Mehitabel's worried about Sebastian exhausting his strength. I tell her not to fret, it makes him happy and is of more use to the firm than he's ever been. That sounds cynical, I dare say, but I'm a man who knows the world. You're silent,

Lucy. Nobody much knows what you're thinking at any time.'

The small brown eyes, full of irony and yet appeal, turned to survey her. She would have answered in some fashion, but Sebastian himself climbed up then out of the hatchway near the base of the ship's funnel, hair flat like an emerging merman's. His eyes sought hers in mute appeal behind their glasses. 'Go down with him,' said Luther K. 'Go down now, and get on with it. Remember what I said.'

For once she was sullen; would they never leave her alone? She wouldn't have minded going to lie down by herself, in the cabin, for an hour; she still felt sick. Luther left her and she turned away unwillingly towards Sebastian, who came to her at once, his eyes full of tears.

'Oh, Lucy, don't be angry with me. I love you so much. I—I want us to be together always, one flesh, like the Bible says. It says a man should cleave to his wife.' They stared after the departing figure of Luther K., who had gone back to the ship's stern. 'Soon we'll be home,' pled Sebastian, 'and they'll want me at the office all day. Please, please come down this once more.'

She turned to him, recalling how he'd burst into tears on their wedding night and at times since. He was more like a sick child than anything; one must be kind to him. Lucy kissed her own fingers and laid them on his cheek.

'Whatever you want, Sebastian,' she told

40

him, adding 'I'm glad you love me.' Nobody, after all, had loved her much at Clonough, judging from what had happened there after all those years. They went down together.

*   *   *

They had made love. It struck Lucy, watching afterwards coldly, that Sebastian was in fact less exhausting to her than exhausted himself; his breaths came too quickly still and he was flushed, as though he'd been running. Even so, he tried almost at once to enter her again. She was feeling increasingly sick, but the bell to summon the steward was out of reach above where she lay. Sebastian was kissing her naked breasts all over as he often did; their pearly round shapes thrust up like twin globes and Lucy turned her head aside. She could hear Sebastian groaning, as often happened; then suddenly he gave a great gasp, and his head lolled against her as it so frequently would, the glasses perched lopsided on his nose the way they'd been at the cricket match. Why remember that now? Why wonder if she and Jerry would ever meet again, just as she was about to be sick on to the floor? She turned and was so, recalling how last time it had happened Isobel O'Hara had been there, with her basin. It was useless to expect Sebastian to provide anything as practical. He lay limp and heavy now upon her, no longer thrusting in her

41

at all. It was some time before Lucy realised
that he lay quite still, and was dead.

*   *   *

She could not remember screaming. She had
in some manner freed herself; perhaps the
body lying on hers had already begun to grow
cold. She heard herself calling out for help
above the throbbing of the ship's engines, a
constant sound which had become so familiar
she scarcely noticed it as a rule. Now, it took
some time for them all to come after she had
rung the bell repeatedly for the steward: the
man himself, not glancing at Lucy where she
stood half naked, with a wrapper thrown over
herself, came at last; then both Wints, he heavy
and silent, Mehitabel a grey-faced mask of
grief, flinging herself down where the dead boy
lay, tears rolling down behind her glasses.
  'Sebastian. My only boy Sebastian. He's
dead. He's dead and you killed him. You killed
him sinfully with lust.'
  The word rose in a wail. Mehitabel had
begun sobbing, and kissing the corpse; she had
not looked at Lucy. The girl stood there
shivering; it seemed suddenly cold although
the cabin was by now full of people. Someone
took Mehitabel away. Someone also came and
put a blanket round Lucy. 'You mustn't catch a
chill,' she heard; the voice sounded like Wint's.
Then Sebastian's body was taken away also,

42

and put somewhere or other; there would have to be an autopsy, they wouldn't bury him at sea, there were five days to go till they reached port. It was unspeakable to think of what might happen to it before then.

Amid all the horror, the chaos and questioning, one thing stood out in Lucy's mind; sympathy for Sebastian's mother. She herself hadn't meant to kill Sebastian, of course, but it had happened. Perhaps she could after all comfort Mehitabel Wint, who had so lately lost a daughter and now a son. But on enquiry, she was told Mrs Wint would see nobody, and had already been taken back to her cabin, where she had asked to be left quite alone.

*   *   *

There was fog in mid-ocean. It drifted past in unsubstantial greyish wisps beyond the yellow light of the oil lamp bracketed against the cabin wall. Lucy lay listlessly and stared at the dark porthole, beyond which nothing at all was to be seen, no ships' lights, only miles upon miles of unknown and heaving sea. She closed her eyes; in fact she felt better and less queasy now. It was best, as she already knew, to keep lying down. Earlier they'd brought her a stone hot water bottle, but it had grown cold long ago and she'd laid it carefully on the cabin floor. She hadn't wanted any dinner. Some of

43

the passengers had sent messages of sympathy and one woman had tried to come in; Lucy had sent her away. She had wanted to be by herself, for almost the first time since leaving Clonough. Clonough was in another world and in this one, everyone no doubt blamed her for killing Sebastian.

She had begun to be frightened, a state which was new to her; she had never been afraid of anything, not the highest jump over a drystone wall, a hurtling gallop over boggy ground, a ride back in the winter dark. This was different. It was the shock of the death, and being left alone now in the foggy cabin with the pounding engines' echo. Sebastian's body would be down in the hold, without warmth of its own any more. His pince-nez still lay nearby; they'd forgotten to take them. They gleamed balefully, and Lucy could no longer endure it. She got up, wrenched open the porthole so that the chilly fog drifted in, picked up the pince-nez gingerly and flung them out to sea. Wherever Sebastian was now, he didn't need them any more. If they asked about them, she would say she didn't know.

She shut the porthole, climbed back into the bunk and tried to get warm. The engines still pounded relentlessly, bearing them on to wherever they were going; New York, Boston. It wasn't certain what would become of her now in Boston, or anywhere. A widow's life was supposed to be finished. Hers hadn't really begun.

She shivered under the blankets. On embarkation at Liverpool, while the rest were reading the hasty message from Passmore, one had come for Lucy and she had managed to read it by herself. It had contained an engraved invitation to Hubert's wedding to Annis Fox-Strangways in a few weeks' time in Meath. She wouldn't have wanted to go in any case. She'd send Hubert a gift of some kind from Boston, perhaps made of leather; that was light and wouldn't spoil in the post. Hubert seemed already to have turned into someone she had known vaguely, long ago, instead of all her life.

Her life now, what was it? What was she to become? Where was she to go?

The ship's siren hooted: it was the fog. There must be other vessels nearing, to be told that they themselves were passing by, unseen, measured by sound only. The captain would be up on deck. He was a pleasant, reliable middle-aged man. She and Sebastian and the latter's parents had sat at his table, and today he had sent down a courteous little note with condolences, among the rest. Not everybody had sent word; perhaps they had done so to Mehitabel. Perhaps, also, more notes would come with the steward when he brought her night tea. They had seldom heard him coming because of the constant engines, deadening the sound of footsteps and all other sounds. Engines turned nowadays by means of a screw

45

called a turbine, not paddles any more like the old ships had used to have. Jerry had told her that. He took an interest in such things now and again, then forgot about them. She wondered again how he was faring with Sabine and if she bit his underlip every single night. The thought made Lucy give way to nervous laughter.

The lock turned now with the steward's key; she herself had of course locked the door from the inside. She turned her head expectantly, then drew a breath. Her father-in-law was standing there alone, his solid form leaning inside against the shut door. How had he got the key?

Lucy pulled the sheet up higher against herself. At home, it wouldn't be proper for a man to be here alone: perhaps Americans were different, more free in their manners. She still didn't like it. She—

'Don't be afraid, Lucy,' she heard Luther K. Wint say reassuringly. 'They can't hear anything in any case.' He smiled, and the engines pounded on. 'I have come,' Wint continued, 'on behalf of my son.'

*   *   *

He had advanced purposefully towards where she lay. The sound of the engines continued to roar in her ears; he was right, nobody would hear if she called out, it had taken long enough

46

earlier, when she was in here trapped alone with Sebastian's body. What did his father mean now? Perhaps he had come to comfort her. He was leaning over her now, his presence filling the cramped space in the cabin; the thick jaw, blue with a half-day's stubble, was close in the faint yellow light. She saw his hands, fleshy, powerful and covered in the now familiar way with black hair along their backs; they'd touched her earlier. They reached out with decision now, closing about her shoulders.

'I have to find out,' Wint said, 'if you are pregnant by Sebastian. I think you may be; I've thought it for some days. Maybe it happened on the wedding night, maybe not. You're not a fool or a prude, Lucy. Let me feel you. There are ways of telling, even so early.'

She steeled herself not to shrink away; undoubtedly he meant well. 'Why,' she heard him say, 'you're as cold as a little frog. Let me get you warm.' He began to chafe her hands, then her arms below the linen chemise; his hands were knowledgeable, rubbing, persuading the blood back again slowly. While he rubbed her, Lucy lay bewildered and half lulled; how could he tell whether or not she was going to have a baby before she knew it herself? She was always queasy at sea. She must think of Wint now as a kind of doctor, trying to find out in whatever way it was they could. No doubt Mrs Wint would have come with him if she'd been able, and not exhausted

47

with grief. As it was, she'd no doubt left it to her husband.

Lucy closed her eyes and turned her head away. 'That's right,' Wint said. 'Don't tense up; lie still.' He was unbuttoning her chemise. The hands examined her breasts lingeringly, as though he knew what to look for. At the end he gave a grunt, whether of assent or dissent Lucy did not know. She had begun to have sensations she had never felt before.

'Lie still,' he told her again, adding 'It's not certain.' The hands continued to assess, feel, explore ever more intimately the lower parts of her body as well; he'd folded down the blankets now and pulled up her chemise. Lucy began to feel hot with confusion. 'Please,' she said. 'Please stop.'

He was so close to her by now that it was only a slight movement until he lay upon her in the small space; he had by now penetrated her so subtly that she had thought, still, that it was his invading hands. She cried out as his mouth came down on hers, silencing her. Lucy lay helpless, pinned beneath him; his great belly began to jerk, overflowing the bunk and her conquered body. His entry was swift, confident, assured, and ended in a completion Lucy had never before experienced. When it had happened Wint began to talk against her throat, lying meantime secure within her. She was still too shocked and amazed at her own pleasure to try to free herself from under him.

48

Despite herself, her mind took in what he was saying.

'Hear me out, Lucy; don't be angry. If I'd said why I came, you wouldn't have let me do this, and it had to be done. It had to be. Sebastian was inept; I was fairly certain of it, and now I know. You like this that I've just done: it surprises you; you've never known it before. It's for your good; you must believe me. It's possible that you have after all conceived by Sebastian; a man can become a father, and a great many do, without knowing fully how to make love. If there is no child at all, what are you? A penniless young widow of no importance. If there is a son of yours, to inherit Maule Wint Quinty, thousands of redwood acres to the south, contracts promised across the ocean, all of that and more, you are maybe the most important young woman in North America. Does that mean anything or nothing to you?'

He had begun again to caress and kiss her; strange things were happening, she felt her mouth open, as if without volition, against his. There came the flavour of cigars. 'If my son has not given you a child, I may be doing just that this minute,' Wint said in a low voice. 'No one's to know which, and by now, you won't be ringing the bell for that steward, the way you would have done at the beginning. Maybe anyhow he wouldn't come.' He smiled, and thumbed her. 'You like what I'm doing well

49

enough, Lucy; you've forgotten already how ugly and old I am. You're my girl. I knew it when I saw you at the cricket match. You remember the match, and Jeremy bowling, and you in a white dress. You're lovelier without any dress at all, and we have four nights left. Tomorrow night, don't wear that damned chemise.'

Her body's full response had come, and had astonished her; she had sweated and trembled, feeling his warm seed flood her agreeably. He was still talking softly, irresistibly. 'You're warmed now,' he told her. 'Remember I said at the beginning I'd make you warm? I guess I know how to handle any woman. When I married Mehitabel, she was running the business. She was my employer, for a while. That wouldn't do.' He fondled Lucy's upper arms, then plunged his fingers in her hair. 'My blood is as old as the Maule blood, but you won't hear as much about that in Boston, only maybe up further north.' He began to thrust in her again a little, then withdrew. 'I got Mehitabel pregnant on the wedding night, not a doubt of it, and every year after that I gave her a baby. By the end she had her hands so full there was nobody left to run Quinty works but me, and I've run 'em ever since. I'm my own man, and her master, and now yours, Lucy love. We have four nights, like I said. I'll come again tomorrow, and the night after, and every night after that until New York. After all of

50

that's over, we'll know for sure where we are. We'll know for sure, one way or the other.'

She was soothed by his voice, hardly even resentful of the situation any longer; she was in fact growing sleepy. It was after all pleasant to lie in a man's arms; a full man, not like poor Sebastian had been; she was warmed, as Wint said, and comforted for the first time since her marriage.

*   *   *

Next day, she woke to sharp recollection and reproach. What had she permitted to happen? She was an unspeakable person, her dead husband's father's harlot. One had read about harlots in the Bible. Lady O'Hara hadn't allowed the word to be mentioned at Clonough, and Clonough wouldn't be the only place not to mention it. What would Lady O'Hara, even Papa, anyone, say if they knew what had taken place here, in this very bunk, last night? It mustn't happen again. Four nights, he'd said. It mustn't be allowed any more, tonight or any other.

Lucy swung her legs off the bunk, found that they were shaky, clung to the bunk's frame and steadied herself: she was feeling sick again. It might be the tide or it might be a baby. Lucy huddled the wrapper about her naked body; her chemise was still lying on the floor and the sight aroused shame; to think she'd let him

51

take it right off her in the end! The rest . . .

She had hardly pulled the wrapper together when the door opened and the steward came in bearing her breakfast; it had of course been understood that she wouldn't eat upstairs for the rest of the voyage. Lucy closed the wrapper angrily; it was like that time on the train, only worse.

'You should have knocked,' Lucy said to the man. 'If it happens again I will complain to the captain.' It wasn't the kind of thing she said as a rule, but there had been, there must have been, an arrangement about the key last night; he'd given it to Wint, probably for money. She saw his tongue pass swiftly over his lips like a snake's. He was a small man with a lean, spiteful face. The eyes regarded her without respect; he knew it all. She felt herself blushing.

'You won't complain, not likely,' he answered in a thin Cockney voice. 'I can tell the old lady what's gone on, can't I? You keep quiet and so will I.'

He turned to the door and Lucy watched him go, feeling as if she had been punched in the stomach. This kind of thing had never happened to her before. Later she realised that there was no need to trouble; it was as much as the man's job was worth to say a word against Luther K. Wint. He'd been in here with her last night for an hour or more, and the son's body lying down in the hold under a tarpaulin. The Wints of this world took what they wanted. Outside again, the steward spat. The young woman was a fine piece, out of his class; it was laid on for tonight again, the whole thing, and the night after, and more nights till they docked. Old Wint had tipped him handsomely in accordance; there was no complaint there. He closed the door carefully, leaving Lucy staring at its panels.

*   *   *

She made herself swallow some coffee; she could still eat no food. Dressing herself, lacing her stays with fingers that still trembled, she had the fancy that they wouldn't fasten as tightly as usual. That was ridiculous, so soon: but her body felt swollen, her breasts more tender than ever and chafing against her bodice. She knotted up her hair and put on her black veil; mourning had been bought for somebody, not Sebastian, who else had it been? Susan, his sister, unknown and dead likewise in Boston. Susan's funeral must be over by now; Sebastian, heir of the Wints, would be buried when they reached home, not buried at sea. She forgot by now who had told her, how she had contrived to know anything at all. Everything had been arranged. She herself had been shamefully manipulated. Now, she was her own woman again, and she knew what to do.

53

It was still fairly early. The determination in Lucy had quenched her customary travel-sickness; the fresh air on deck would help. If she met Wint, she would walk straight past him. She made her way out of the cabin, leaving the pervasive sound of engines she would never in all of her life forget; up on deck there was a light breeze playing on the sea, and the fog had gone. Lucy averted her gaze from the ruffled grey unending water; there was still no land in sight. Four nights to go, he'd said. She would see about that. She went down to the Wint cabin, and knocked on the door. If he was inside, it didn't matter. She knew in any case what to say.

A different steward answered, taking out Mehitabel's breakfast tray, like her own untouched. Mrs Wint, he murmured, would see nobody at all. Through the space made by the opened door Lucy glimpsed Mehitabel herself lying alone on the lower bunk, a crusader wrapped in a black cloak for warmth above the tomb. Her head was turned away and she might have heard nothing. Lucy said clearly 'Tell Mrs Wint that her son's wife is here.' Then she walked in past the man without waiting for him to speak. There was nobody else in the cabin. She heard the door close behind her discreetly; the steward had gone. Lucy went straight to the bunk and knelt down by her mother-in-law, taking the flaccid hands in both her own.

'I think,' she said, 'that I am going to have a baby. Does that give you a little hope?'

For moments, she thought Sebastian's mother was not going to answer, that there would be nothing for herself now in any case but continuing hatred. Perhaps—the possibility had already occurred to her—Mehitabel had, in some way, guessed the rest. But the puffed face, with Sebastian's own eyes in it, turned towards her slowly. The eyes held more purpose, even now, than Sebastian's had ever done.

'A baby,' said Mehitabel. 'That makes two to carry on. Everything maybe isn't in vain, everything I've done. It was kind of you to come, Lucy, after what I said. Do you feel well? You must take great care of yourself.'

So she couldn't know. One would make it one's business to see that she never did, never guessed even remotely; there would be no more reason now. Mehitabel suddenly leaned over and kissed Lucy on the lips. After last night, with Wint's thick mouth seeking her own time and again, they had felt bruised and dry. Now, this gesture healed them. Lucy found herself saying again what she had come to say. If there wasn't to be a child after all, it didn't bear thinking of: but at least she had made peace with Mehitabel Wint, who would be her friend from now on. That was important, and she herself was no longer quite alone. She said then the other thing she had come to say, knowing well enough it contained deceit like the rest.

'Mrs Wint, will you let me stay with you in your cabin for the rest of the voyage?' she asked. 'Last night somebody tried my door. They must have known I was alone. It was foggy, and I was afraid. Mr Wint could perhaps go down there instead and use my cabin.' There, she'd said it, and he could go and lie alone on her bunk, remembering whatever he wanted to. They would bring her things up here. Already she knew that she had persuaded her mother-in-law, that the other woman's strong will echoed her own, that they were allies and would soon be friends. She still chafed Mehitabel's hands with her own small warm ones; like the older woman's face the former were puffy and chilly, the unhealthy colour of dough. There was something wrong physically with Mehitabel; she was ill, had been ill for some time. She must once have been handsome.

As though she had accepted all arrangements Wint's wife began to talk suddenly, bitterly aloud. 'He'll go wherever he chooses,' she said of her husband. 'He'll go to some woman. Always there have been other women, from the beginning when we were first married; chambermaids, housemaids when we had 'em, anyone at all. Two of his bastards black the boots back home. I pretend not to notice. I'm telling you all this in time so that he doesn't try to get to you. You're going to bear a child to my son. My son, my son! That's what King David said, in the Bible. I was reared on my Bible; I've always believed in God, despite everything. Now, when it seemed as if God had forsaken me, there's your child coming, and little Hartley waiting back home. He won't have any mother of his own. We can look after him, you and I together. We—'

A shadow stood in the opened doorway; Wint, returned from wherever he had been. Lucy rose and faced him, hearing her black skirts rustle and at the same time seeing his eyes glow red and angry, like those of a bull. He thinks I've told her everything, she thought. Aloud she said, smiling as was her habit, 'Mrs Wint is going to allow me to sleep in here with her until we dock. I was frightened last night by someone trying my door. If you wouldn't mind occupying my cabin for the next few nights, I would be grateful.' Mehitabel then spoke up.

'God has consoled us, Luther. Lucy has hopes of Sebastian's child, already, so soon. It is almost as though he is to be returned to us again. We must be thankful.'

He had listened with an expression which nobody at all could have described. Now he said, smooth as a cat, 'If Lucy is expecting a child she must certainly have every care.' All the time, his glance had never spared Lucy herself. I've had you, my girl, flat on your back, legs wide open, it said, and you won't forget it

57

and neither will I: child or no child, we'll both remember. Lucy felt her knees tremble, and knew that it was true. Wint turned abruptly and left the cabin. Her things were brought up and she did not set eyes on him again until they docked in New York. Seeing the famous harbour close slowly in at last, she was already beyond wonder. It was almost certain, by now, that she was pregnant; it didn't, after all, much matter by whom.

*   *   *

A well-sprung carriage was waiting to convey them to their hotel before the last stage of the journey, when the sad coffin containing Sebastian's body would follow them to Boston by road. With the carriage had arrived Susan's widower Nathaniel, long-lipped, pallid and bland of face, clad in heavy blacks. His little light eyes surveyed Lucy with an expression no widower should so soon portray. He told them that the baby, Hartley, hadn't seemed to flourishing when he'd left. 'Perhaps the nurse's milk doesn't suit him,' said Mehitabel. She was already in a fever of anxiety to get home, but for Lucy's sake they spent one night in town before journeying on. Then they all got together into the carefully driven carriage; Mehitabel and Lucy sat facing the horses, their backs to what followed behind. The two men talked together in grave low voices opposite.

58

Lucy did not look at Wint, but was aware of his presence all through the journey. She kept her eyes down, as a widow should. The carriage made its way, and presently came to the outskirts of a great town lately gutted by fire; a few prosperous buildings still reared on the outskirts. 'That's the business quarter gone,' she heard Wint say. 'It was burned down just as we left. They're rebuilding as fast as they can.'

The business quarter was not the only thing gone. When they reached the brownstone Wint house, it was to be greeted by the news that the baby Hartley was dead. They went up to stare down at the tiny waxen face from its open bassinet. That would make a double funeral, Lucy found herself thinking coldly, supporting her dry-eyed mother-in-law; Mehitabel Wint was beyond tears. Presently, once out of the room itself, she turned to Lucy. 'Everything now depends on you,' she said gently. Lucy kept silent. She heard them carry Sebastian's coffin into the house. If it hadn't been for herself, she was thinking, and the need to rest overnight in New York, Mehitabel might have seen the baby before he died. Everything she herself did seemed to bring death and disaster. She prayed that she might at least bear this child of hers alive, and healthy. She would do everything to ensure that.

CHAPTER FOUR

Lucy's memories of Boston would always be of dust and ashes. There had been the great fire which had destroyed the entire business quarter, much of it built in the days of the early settlers; Sebastian's funeral cortège had had to drive through rubble, rebuilding and builders' dust. Beyond this desert, the brownstone Wint house, copied from one in New York and built with materials quarried at a distance, still reared unharmed, with the Quinty works not far away. The workers there had stood with heads bare, lining the road as the two coffins passed, one long and one tiny; the dead Passmore baby would be lying inside, still like a wax doll. Mehitabel sat stony-faced in their carriage behind the placid American trotters; Nathaniel Passmore, widower, wept dutifully at the graveyard, wiping his small reddened eyes under his tall mourner's hat. Lucy felt sorry for him; he had after all lost his young wife and then his child. She allowed him to take her arm on return from the burial at the Wint vault, where ashes to ashes and dust to dust had been laid, and a farewell was said to the young husband she herself had hardly known. She was glad of her black veil, which protected her from the followers' overt glances and concealed the fact that she shed no tears. It was sad about Sebastian, sad about the baby, sad about his mother Susan whom she had never met: but she herself, Lucy Wint, held hope.

They went back to the house, where a collation awaited them; the Presbyterian minister who had taken the service, and several of his congregation known to Mehitabel rather than her husband, who seldom attended church, stayed on to condole and to drink tea. Lucy sat listening to the high, almost English accents of polite Boston society. The black-clad company smelt of mothballs. She herself had glimpsed, on their return journey, a great space of green grass, with riders cantering on the oddly pacing saddle-horses they bred here, tails nicked to curve high and disposedly. It must be like riding a camel; the horses paced quite differently, one side moving first and then the other following, not like the hunters at home. She asked Passmore about it all. 'That is the Common,' he replied discreetly, not enlarging on the artificial elegance of the horses. 'There are several parks in Boston; we are fortunate.' All of his statements were precise, informative like a guide book, and delivered in the flat nasal voice of elsewhere. He told her that he came from Michigan as a boy, had found work for himself at Quinty, and Mrs Wint had noticed him and had paid for him, later on, to go across for a year to Clydeside in Scotland to learn the new steam engineering under a former blacksmith named Robert Napier, who had made his name sufficiently at last to attract Admiralty charters from London. 'How did Mrs Wint come to hear of him?' Lucy asked. Passmore allowed his flat pale dish of a face to grow almost animated.

'That is a wonderful woman,' he said. 'Nobody knows how she finds out the things she does. She ran Quinty for a while; she could do it again now, I guess. She has a man's mind.' He recalled that it was a funeral, that it wasn't long since he had buried poor Susan, and fell silent. Lucy did not question him further; she knew by now that he worked with Wint in the firm's office, and was greatly trusted by both partners; they had after all left Passmore in sole charge of everything when they visited England.

Mehitabel took charge of Lucy herself as soon as the others had gone. 'You must go and lie down, dear,' she said firmly. 'It is more important than anything else that you do not overtire yourself at present.'

Lucy was to find that a strict regimen had already been prescribed for her; each morning she was brought breakfast in bed, with a lace handworked fall laid across the top of the sheet first by two white-capped negresses. All of the furniture in her room was pleasant, clean and made by hand, even to the Shaker light wood furniture, beautifully turned and crafted, and the patchwork counterpane worked long ago by Hannah Maule,

Mehitabel's grandmother, for her marriage chest. Lucy would lie for hours marvelling at the tiny varied patterns of material sewn together with stitches almost too small to be seen: stripes, checks, flowers, zigzags. She had plenty of time; the afternoons were to be spent lying down, the mornings, after she had finished her breakfast, devoted first to household prayers, which the servants attended while Mehitabel herself read to them from the Bible and prayed impromptu fashion, all the capped heads remaining bowed from the rows of neatly arranged chairs which were afterwards put back in their customary places. Later, when Mehitabel had seen to the housekeeping, she and Lucy would go together for a short drive. It was usually in the same direction, past the works, where Luther himself had by then been since early morning; he did not attend prayers. Lucy had seen very little of him since they came back, and never alone: and was thankful. She knew that she herself was now the sole hope of the Wints, except of course for Sabine left in England. She resolved not to fail Mehitabel if she could help it; that woman had had enough to endure. She herself hadn't even asked about the possibility of riding on the Common on one of the strangely loping horses with high tails. No doubt, in this strict genteel city, her mourning wouldn't permit it, and perhaps her condition wouldn't either. She must resign herself to pass nearly nine months as a widow in this humdrum way, until the birth. It seemed a long time.

*   *   *

A welcome letter came at last from Jeremy. Sabine also was to have a child, about the same time as herself. He'd heard already from his friend Jack Clifton-Turner, who had been across to Clonough, that Annis, Hubert's ugly wife, was expecting a child likewise. *That makes three of us*, Jeremy wrote. *Jack says that judging from both this Clonough baby's parents it hasn't much hope of looks*. He went on, as usual, to talk about the hunt, life at Aylors, and the lack of any news at all of Papa. They were both used to this; the old gentleman would disappear for months at a time, in Greece or Italy or Anatolia.

*   *   *

Lucy found herself growing very fond of her mother-in-law as time passed. It was true that there were things she herself resented, such as having her freedom curtailed and her days precisely arranged for her, as at Clonough they had certainly never been; but this was no longer Clonough. Mehitabel Wint was an able woman who governed her house well, as might have been expected; she was strict and fair with her servants, as she had in her day been strict and fair with the workers at Quinty. Lucy found that it was she who had started a practice at first not common among employers anywhere; payment when a man was off sick and, if necessary, medical treatment for him. Mehitabel still visited the workers' families, much as a lady of the great house would visit tenants in Ireland or England, seeing to their welfare and that they lacked nothing they honestly needed; if a man here spent his pay on drink, to the deprivation of his wife and children, he was threatened with dismissal and, if he persisted, dismissed. As working conditions were good and as most of the Quinty men had long grown skilled at the job, dismissals were rare. Rows of small brick houses had been built in Mehitabel's own time behind the works, and only employees had a right to live there; the children were put to school, the girls taught to sew, the boys to cipher, so that in either case there would be work for them when they were ready for it. In no way did Mehitabel now interfere with her husband's management of the business itself, although Wint consulted her often; Lucy would hear their murmured voices in the room next her own, then Luther would go out and the sounds would cease. The couple no longer shared a bedroom. Afterwards the decisions come to at the talks would be carried out, generally with the assistance of Nathaniel J.

Passmore.

*   *   *

Passmore proposed marriage to Lucy when she was six months pregnant, making it clear that the ceremony itself should not take place until after they had completed their year's mutual mourning. 'Folks might talk, otherwise,' he put it placidly. They were walking, as they by custom did on Sundays after church, on the Common, while Mehitabel and her Highland maid and small dog walked in front. Lucy attempted to remove her own hand from Passmore's arm, murmuring that she had not considered remarriage. She had the uncomfortable feeling that the whole thing, like everything else, had been arranged.

'Give it time,' remarked Nat imperturbably, tucking her gloved hand firmly back against his thick black broadcloth sleeve. He began to talk with assurance of the protection he could be to her and to the unborn child. 'It'll be better for him to have a father from the start.'

If you only knew, he has two already, Lucy thought irrepressibly, and wondered if to tell Passmore so would shake his self-esteem: it seemed nothing else could. She herself, freed from the early sickness which had plagued her in the first months of pregnancy, was filled with steady determination: she would on no account marry Nat Passmore and no doubt become the mother of a graded procession of future assistant managers of Maule Wint Quinty, Inc. She resented the obvious planning to this end of her mother-in-law, who walked ahead discreetly with McPhail the maid, evidently intent on exercising the small long-haired terrier on its lead. Anybody looking at the party as it walked, and many did, would have perceived only a small company of well-dressed persons in mourning, a bereaved woman well known to the town, her widowed young daughter-in-law in a tactfully concealing pelisse, and her equally widowed son-in-law in his tall black hat, unsmiling. Lucy returned the formal salutes of such ladies as she had met at the brownstone house during Mehitabel's now quietly resumed sewing-parties on Thursday afternoons, on behalf of the heathen in Africa. Not only did Lucy herself suppose that the heathen looked better as they were, but the talk people made at the sewing sessions was either dull or disappointing: any that interested Lucy concerned events to which she could not properly go. The prospect of a Museum of Fine Arts had already been raised and subscriptions were being asked for; a rich sugar-refiner's wife, her plumed hat nodding, had talked with more or less knowledge of the future building of an Opera House on a site already mooted. However Lucy herself had been permitted to view only one feature of gradually reviving Boston; daringly, on a

Sunday drive when all work had of course stopped out there except for tending fires, the Quinty workshop itself. There was the little high office where Luther K. and Passmore sat daily at their accounts and held their frequent discussions: the same where, in her time, Mehitabel herself had supervised the ongoing of the great converter furnaces to be seen now from the window beyond the low sheds, wherein jets of cold water, Mehitabel told Lucy, were directed on to red-hot metal read heated by charcoal, the workers remaining naked to the waist. 'For that reason, it was never proper for me to be seen out there, but they knew I was watching them,' said the Quinty founder gently. 'I knew every worker and what he was worth. I still do. I would see that the good ones got promotion and have the useless ones fired after a second chance. Always give everyone a second chance, Lucy. I kept the business small, but it was known to be reliable. It still is. Most folks don't know to this day that a woman ever ran it.' She smiled, revealing discoloured teeth, and continued to gaze out at the tall brick chimneys, still discreetly tended by one man lest they grow cold by Monday. Seeing Mehitabel thus, Lucy could picture the handsome, forceful young woman she must have been when the clean lines of her jaw were uncluttered, her body still taut and unhampered by constant childbearing.

She herself had begun to thicken long ago. She would be now and again aware of Luther K.'s eyes, beady as a forest boar's, watching her occasionally above the cigar which he smoked openly in the house. Their cool assessing glance told Lucy what she already knew; that Luther would leave her alone until the heir was born. After that, she must fend for herself. Aware of the sexual power of Wint—after all she'd recognised it almost at once for what it was—Lucy compared him with his dead son, likewise with poor Nathan J., her tireless and unencouraged suitor. Wint's personality pervaded everything, like the scent of his cigars. He ruled the brownstone house whether or not he was in it. Frequently, he was elsewhere.

*   *   *

The months passed. Lucy had contrived to make it gently clear to her mother-in-law that she would never under any circumstances marry Passmore. 'You feel that way now, Lucy,' replied the older lady with quiet determination. 'Wait till your boy is running about, and is a handful. You'll be glad of a man to help with him by then. Nat has great patience.'

She went on knitting placidly, a shawl for the baby. Everyone seemed determined that it should be a boy. Lucy kept her own counsel

69

over the matter of Passmore and his patience, which greatly irritated her, but, after all, they couldn't force her to the altar. Nat still called daily, and was attentive. Lucy endured it.

*   *   *

Shortly before the confinement she was much heartened to receive a letter from her father. Lucius Meggett seldom wrote to anybody at all. He was doing so now, she knew, because he loved her as much as he could, since his first wife's death, love anyone. He said he wished her all the luck in the world, and a handsome boy. Caterina, he added, was praying for her. As for Sabine, she had already given birth prematurely at Aylors to a little girl, very pretty, with golden curls; mother and child continued both well. *They are calling her Maria after my beloved wife*, he finished, signing himself her ever loving father, Lucius Meggett. Lucy folded away the letter to keep and reflected that poor Caterina had small chance of any such memorial from him, having been married for a vase. However Caterina was praying for her, Lucy. That was something. She wrote to the address given, thanking them both; it would no doubt be sent on and lost in foreign parts, never reaching anybody.

*   *   *

70

It turned out that Lucy needed prayers. She went into labour on the expected date, having felt the child move in her for the past few weeks. Mehitabel and the maid McPhail walked her up and down the room between them, they said to bring on the pains. At first it was like recent walking on the Common, dragging the heavy weight which was herself. Then the pains came, sharp and, at first, regularly every so often. They put Lucy to bed and Mehitabel sat and watched over her like a plump, anxious, and bespectacled hawk. Lucy turned her head aside and wished everyone would go away. Wint looked in, then took himself off again. Flowers arrived in a ribbon-tied bouquet; they turned out to be from Passmore. Lucy, between pains, renewed the vow she had made to herself that never, for any reason at all, would she marry Nathaniel J. Passmore, flowers or no flowers: they meant he hadn't even yet taken his dismissal seriously. To have to endure this, year after year, as Mehitabel had done, giving birth and giving birth, more and more little Passmores, no doubt the same as now when it was about to be a little Wint, the probable son of its grandfather. Lucy bit her lip; that must never, never be mentioned, even in utmost agony. The little Wint was in any case taking a long time to come. The pains grew fainter, and Lucy began to cry at last with exhaustion. She hadn't known it would take as long.

'Try again,' Mehitabel kept saying. 'Bear down.'

She had borne down and borne down, half killing herself, and even Mrs Wint couldn't expect her by now to bear down any more. It was growing dark; the whole thing had started in early morning. They sent for the doctor at last; one wasn't usually needed, it was thought to be qualified in all the new skills. He bent and examined Lucy, then stood up, looking grave.

'The placenta is preventing the birth,' he said. 'It is misplaced.'

At that rate, Lucy thought despairingly, it was certainly Sebastian's baby. Luther K. Wint wouldn't have misplaced anything.

*   *   *

Luther K. himself came striding in once more, angry that the doctor had said it might be necessary to operate. 'You're not cutting my Lucy open,' he said. 'Let me get at her. I know what to do, far better than a fool like you.'

He came to the bed, bent over Lucy, pulled the covers down and her nightgown up, and began to massage her abdomen with strong, squat fingers. It was horribly like and yet unlike the cabin on the ship. Lucy gasped with pain, and Mehitabel at first protested vainly; Wint continued with his merciless massage. 'Women have been having children since God

72

made time,' she heard him say. 'No need to be afraid, Lucy love; bear down like they say. It'll soon be all over.'

He stood up from her, and she felt a last, slow and weak movement of the exhausted uterus: then a searing pain came, worse than any. Lucy screamed aloud. 'Get ice,' said Wint, and they fetched it and he packed it hard against her; Lucy gave a loud further cry. 'It's coming,' she gasped, and in a mess of stanched blood and green meconium the heir of the Wints was born at last: a boy, and dead. Lucy saw them carry off a filthy green bloodied mess in a towel, then fainted. Her last clear memory was of Mehitabel's face. She would never forget it. Wint's wife had realised everything that must have happened, and she herself would never again be forgiven. When she came to herself, weak still and flat as a board once more, everyone had gone.

*   *   *

There would never be a next time, with Passmore or anyone else. The young doctor came next day again and examined Lucy once more, then told her, gently, that the wall of her womb had ruptured and that the ice pack had saved her life, as otherwise the haemorrhage from the placenta would have killed her as the child burst through, suffocating itself in the process. 'You will never have another,' he told

73

her. 'Try to bear the disappointment. You are young, and there are other things.'

I can bear it, Lucy thought; in fact I thank God. They can't use me as a brood mare any more, with Luther K. or Passmore or anyone else. She wondered if Luther K.'s determined massaging of her was what had caused the uterine wall to rupture in the end: no doubt he had meant well, and had in any case saved her with the ice. She was glad he hadn't let them operate, though it might have saved the life of the baby; but, again, it might not.

She thought of Mehitabel, shocked, alone and desolate; this child had meant far more to her than to oneself, from the beginning. When the maid came at last into the room Lucy ordered her to take away Nat Passmore's flowers and give them to Mrs Wint. 'How is she?' she remembered to ask. McPhail replied that Mrs Wint was poorly, very sad, had taken to her bed and was reading her Bible. Lucy hoped it would console Mehitabel, but did not say so. She closed her eyes and slept at last, waking to find her body still stiff and sore, but, after all, unscarred. She supposed that she was an entirely different person now, no longer a woman; she would have to get used to it. The main thing was to make friends again, somehow, with Mehitabel. She must explain that she had been alone, cold and frightened in the fog on board that time, and hadn't expected what had happened.

*　　　*　　　*

'The Sermon on the Mount says we must forgive those who despitefully use us. I find I can forgive you, Lucy, after much prayer. As for my husband, I have already forgiven him times without number. All I ask is that, whenever and however it happened between you, it shall not do so again in this house.'

Mehitabel Wint had come at last into Lucy's room, wearing a loose quilted wrapper. She looked double her age, grey and somehow without clarity even in appearance as though no certainly of anything at all was left, even her own identity. She had seated herself in one of the wood Shaker chairs and sat with the lamplight behind her grey head; one could not see her face. Lucy, when her mother-in-law came in at first, had been afraid; now she was no longer so, only filled with pity and admiration for this great woman, who could repeatedly forgive. She heard her own voice coming timidly. There was no need to explain about the fog, the cold, the loneliness there had been; it didn't matter. She said aloud 'You told me, that day at Quinty, that everyone should have a second chance. If you will give that to me, I will do what I can to atone. I can't do more than be with you, for company, perhaps. It won't be the same as Susan would have been. I myself don't remember my own

75

mother; you have been as much to me in that way as anyone.' She stopped talking; silence after all said many things speech couldn't. It must be understood between them that she wouldn't let Wint get at her again, not in the house or, as far as she was concerned, anywhere. If there was trust between herself and her mother-in-law, that would suffice.

Mehitabel had begun to talk again and already plan, as usual: her pitiless sense of destiny, the iron certainty that things must continue somehow, were after all what had brought her long ago out of logging into steel; would help her to survive now, when all had seemed lost. 'I have sent for Sabine and Jeremy to come across,' she stated. 'They can bring the little girl Maria with them. There must be more children. Sabine isn't easy, I know; you yourself can help me with her. You can be a great comfort to me, Lucy; your beauty makes it a pleasure to watch you, and your laughter; I haven't heard you laugh often, as things were and are. Perhaps—'

Suddenly she stretched out her hands, tears running down her face. 'There is so little love anywhere,' she said. 'God wants us to love one another. Love me if you can.'

Lucy reached out from her bed to the hands, and kissed them and then Mehitabel's puffed cheek. All the time she was thinking clearly, coldly. Mehitabel Wint's husband and children had brought her nothing but sorrow. Sabine, in

76

any case, couldn't be sent for like that, as though she could be moved from place to place like a pawn in chess. Jeremy might not want to come, to leave Aylors and his easy squire's life there. Papa likewise might object; he sounded fond of little Maria. Mehitabel doesn't consider things like that, Lucy thought: everything has to be done her way.

She said nothing of it aloud, merely asking, when she was about again, to be allowed to move into the room beyond Mehitabel's own in order to sleep in there at nights. She would keep the door open. That way, Mehitabel would know there was nothing going on in any fashion with Wint. Later, perhaps, Jeremy would take her, Lucy, back to England once things were arranged in some way. Meantime, she couldn't leave this forsaken woman by herself; she must stay, perhaps for as long as Mehitabel Wint lived. From the look of her, it mightn't after all be too long.

*   *   *

Lucy's young strength returned, and brought healing with it. She was soon up and active again, and ventured to ask for a horse to ride on the Common. That would get her back into any shape she might have lost; even Boston Society would understand the necessity.

There was added bitterness by then also, which Lucy wanted to forget. Jeremy had written in due course to say he was sorry about the baby; Sabine, he added, was already pregnant again. *It's like Charles II and whatsername*, he wrote rather wearily. He added that they would certainly not be coming over at least meantime; Papa was home once more, and doted on Maria. Then Jerry added an item of news as an afterthought. Jack Clifton-Turner, whom he kept mentioning and who evidently went over to Ireland frequently to hunt, had been again to Clonough. Hubert's wife Annis had given birth to a surprisingly beautiful boy. They had called him Alan, after Annis's dead brother who had been killed in the carriage-accident. Jack had said Hubert was very pleased. Jerry ended with his love and, as an afterthought, Sabine's. Lucy folded the letter and put it away with the rest from home. She hadn't to her knowledge met this Jack Clifton-Turner her brother was always writing about. He must be one of the coterie of young men, perhaps from school, who still hunted, shot, boxed and occasionally played cricket together. It was of no importance in any case, except that Clifton-Turner seemed to go over often to Clonough.

It was at that point that Luther K. Wint made Lucy a present of a young Morgan mare from his farm in Vermont. She hesitated to accept it from him, but succumbed; to ride again was pleasant. The rest of the days she spent mostly with Mehitabel, who was fretful

78

at Jeremy's refusal to obey her commands and by now spent most of her time on a chaise-longue to relieve her increasingly swollen ankles, an afghan being placed carefully over these. Mehitabel's sight was beginning to blur and Lucy now read to her aloud from the Bible. *If I walk through the valley of the shadow of death, yet will I fear none evil.* Mehitabel was certainly near death, and there was no sign of Sabine's coming. Lucy wrote privately to Jeremy, begging him to reconsider the situation, if possible before the new baby should be born. One never knew how Sabine would react, however, she was so unpredictable; she might be glad at the thought of coming home, or else not.

Jerry, if you can, bring Sabine out to see her mother. She is all they have left after my disaster, and apart from anything else, it would be worth your while to please the Wints. There, that hint might suffice; Jerry was fond of the good things of life, and still wouldn't have enough money to indulge his tastes despite the marriage. She herself was in a similar state: at the moment, she had to ask Mehitabel for every coin, not that she herself spent much or was denied anything she needed. It was more like being an unpaid companion than a daughter-in-law, in its way. Lucy never complained aloud; no doubt it was simply that no one had thought about any money for her in the press of events. She supposed there was some sort of jointure due by law to a widow, but hadn't liked to ask.

*   *   *

Nat Passmore came to the rescue. He had at last taken her refusals of marriage as final, without doubt because he had heard there could be no more children. He duly called to condole about the baby's death, and in course of their talk admitted that a man liked to see his grandchildren. Lucy smiled on, and presently raised the subject of the jointure. Passmore slowly raised his large pale head.

'I'll see about that for you myself with Luther K.,' he promised. 'It should have been done long ago. That's one thing I can certainly do for you, Lucy. I only wish there was more.'

If he did speak to Luther, nothing more was meantime heard of it; and in the meantime Mehitabel's state continued to worsen. The time came to telegraph across the Atlantic to Sabine to say that if she wanted to see her mother alive, she would come soon. Knowing Sabine, that meant Jeremy as well. She, Lucy, would be glad to see her brother. She would never feel at home in Boston, despite the daily rides out on the beautiful Morgan mare.

But Sabine stayed on at Aylors, and gave birth to a son. They called him Lucius after Papa. The news heartened Mehitabel and she rallied. Perhaps after all she would not die

80

quite yet. There was hope again.

CHAPTER FIVE

'Your brother bowls a fast ball, but he surely can spend money,' remarked Luther K. Wint, seated with his wife and Lucy at Sunday luncheon. This was usually an informal meal, as the servants had spent the morning at church; one helped oneself on return from silver covers ready laid the night before. Lucy forked cold ham into her mouth, not replying meantime: she knew that this was one occasion when Wint and Mehitabel had already been in conference, as still happened at times: and waited to hear what had been planned between them. Certainly something would have been; Jerry's latest demand that the Wint finances cover the entire cost of his extension to the west wing at Aylors, opposite which Papa had long ago erected two crazy towers and had then run out of wherewithal to finish everything, had been frostily received in Boston. Lucy reflected once again on the somewhat fluid arrangements made at the time of the marriages; Papa could drive a shrewd enough bargain over a Pompeian vase, but had failed to attain Luther K.'s own standards of expertise in mutual dowry arrangements. In fact, as tight a fist was kept on Jeremy and

Sabine in England as it was, still, eight months after Passmore's enquiry about her tardy jointure, on Lucy herself.

Passmore was lately married again; one had after all expected it, and it was some relief that his former persistent dalliance had stopped. Lucy listened to her parents-in-law playing one off against the other before her, in the way they could still do. Mehitabel sighed, and turned her pince-nez on Jerry's sister, seated here quietly eating their honey-cured southern ham. It was merciful that poor Lucy again had her health.

'He is very extravagant, with that string of hunters, and all the rest,' she ventured. 'Luther wondered if he could be induced to do a little work for us on both sides of the Atlantic. The children will have no future at all if their father goes on as he does, living for nothing but pleasure. Luther and I earned our money, in our day; it isn't pleasant to have to watch it being squandered. I know I'm speaking plainly.'

'What sort of work could Jerry do?' Lucy asked, knowing it was her cue and that Wint would answer. He cut in at once, as expected. 'He could come over here, with Sabine and the children, and learn to run the New York office I opened two years back,' he said. 'There's nothing in the work an intelligent young man couldn't master, and he'd learn to persuade customers soon enough both here and in

Scotland, about contracts. He's good to look at, and that's an advantage, and he speaks like a gentleman. He'd get on with old Robert Napier. Napier's a millionaire.'

'Sabine and the children could live here, and Jeremy could come up and down often when he was on this side,' put in Mehitabel. She wants the children with her more than anything, Lucy thought; the whole business is only secondary to all that. Papa may however not agree.

But old Lucius lacked one essential aspect of the argument, enough money: if the rebuilding was to be paid for, Jerry, like herself, must take his handsome presence to market elsewhere. Lucy would in any case be glad to see him over here, even now and again between voyages. As for Sabine, she might have improved with marriage. One never heard, one way or the other.

*　　　*　　　*

Sabine had not, as was seen on her arrival at last. It was like being in the presence of a slumbering volcano. She was still very beautiful, perhaps more so than ever; the sight of her gave pleasure when she walked into a room; but she bullied her sick mother, repeating again and again that they hadn't wanted to leave England, they had been happy there; why should they have had to come? She

83

clung to Jeremy's arm possessively; it was difficult for Lucy to have a word with him alone. Worst of all, they had not brought the children. 'Lucius is too young to travel, and their grandparents are with them, and a good nurse,' declared Sabine, smoothing her silky dark hair with one slim free hand; the other clutched her husband as usual. Mehitabel's clouded eyes had filled with tears. 'I will never see my grandchildren now,' she remarked sadly.

However when Jeremy did contrive a word alone with Lucy, he told her with some resentment that Sabine was pregnant a third time already. 'She's insatiable,' he muttered. 'It's the only way I can get any peace.' He himself had put on some weight, despite the hunting in England, and by now drank heavily: he and Luther would sit for long enough after dinner together over their port, while a discontented Sabine walked up and down the upstairs room where Lucy read aloud to Mehitabel, who by that time was almost blind. When she could, Lucy murmured the news about the third pregnancy to her mother-in-law, who brightened at once. 'God meant it to happen,' Mehitabel said. 'The baby must be born here. Sabine must rest, not go travelling about any more. It's as well the crossing was smooth for them.' She had it all planned; Sabine now would be subjected to a regimen such as Lucy herself had been, taken care of hourly, daily, her every need met in advance, her freedom considered not at all. Jeremy went off by himself to New York with Luther K. and the house rang with Sabine's resentful cries; but Lucy knew that Jerry would be glad of the respite. It was partly, no doubt, why he had agreed to leave Aylors meantime. He seemed to accept the prospect of having work for Maule Wint Quinty, but rather as if it was a favour he himself conferred on the firm, not the other way round. There was no doubt that Jerry's charm would alone sell contracts, on Clydeside or anywhere else. He was not, however, to be considered quite ready to visit Scotland for a further year; in the meantime, New York claimed him, at first in Luther's instructive company and then alone. Luther reported that he seemed to have taken to the office work quite well. Sabine howled, but uselessly.

Sabine thickened, and time passed: sometimes Jeremy would visit them all in Boston. The visits were punctuated with the sounds of kissing from upstairs: Sabine never had the least compunction about her desires, and claimed Jerry at once. Mehitabel warned her about the safety of the baby. 'Oh, I never have any trouble in that way,' replied Sabine airily. It was true that her slender body seemed to give birth with surprising ease; Lucy remembered her own agony at such a time, and tried not to envy her sister-in-law.

Passmore's new wife Elizabeth was likewise expecting her first. She was a young rosy-cheeked obedient creature with little to say. Nat himself continued in the Quinty office as usual and when Luther was away in New York, took increasing charge. Nobody knew what he thought of Jeremy Meggett's arrival and promotion; the two men seldom encountered one another. Meantime, Lucius himself wrote from Aylors, where he seemed to have settled for the time: the reason was no doubt little Maria, on whom he still doted. Both children were well, he said, and Caterina and the nurse looked after them: young Lucius was evidently a quiet and solemn little creature who gave no trouble.

*   *   *

Sabine gave birth, in due course in her parents' brownstone house, to a lusty male infant who caused her more suffering than usual. He resembled his grandfather Luther K. Wint closely and was to be called after him. Lucy's imagination, briefly soaring to heights she knew were impractical as the child himself had certainly been conceived in England, watched Mehitabel crooning over a grandchild at last and wondered if the same thought had crossed her mother-in-law's mind briefly, to be likewise dismissed. At any rate, there now existed, large as life, Young Luther Wint Meggett. Jeremy came home briefly, kissed his wife, gave a finger to the firm and immediate grasp of his lively second son, then went off again to New York. The business there was meantime engrossing him and there was talk soon of his visiting old Robert Napier across seas with a view to an important Quinty contract involving Admiralty ironclad. It was in fact the first time Jeremy had been involved in anything approaching responsibility, except perhaps for his marriage; for the time, he took pride in the Quinty assignment. He suggested that Lucy should perhaps accompany him to Scotland and also pay a visit to the children left at Aylors. 'They'll be glad to see some of us,' he remarked airily. Old Lucius Meggett had meantime gone off again, this time to Ephesus, a place to which he was increasingly devoted. Caterina remained behind with the children.

Lucy demurred, much as she would have loved to go with her brother; in fact she still had no money, and dependent as Jeremy himself was on the Wints' goodwill she hesitated to bring him into the question of her jointure. She continued quietly as usual, reading to Mehitabel when the latter was not occupied with the baby, visiting Sabine who showed little enough gratitude from her bed; she was still fractious and poorly, and the doctors said she needed a long rest: this ruled out, if it had ever been considered, her following Jerry to New York. 'They're bachelor quarters, darling,' Jeremy stated firmly. He was becoming increasingly confident as a Wint representative, leading a cheerful life of his own. He appeared to accept the probability that young Luther Meggett would remain with his grandparents at least meantime. He was by far better looked after at present than he would be in England, and his future appeared to be already arranged for him; he would be brought up in the expectation of the Wint inheritance rather than young Lucius at Aylors, whom nobody across here knew.

All this joy, the arrival at last of an heir who would live, might have been Mehitabel's Nunc Dimittis. Her condition worsened rapidly over the next few weeks, and she died at last at two in the morning in early February, the killing month. It was the end of an era; Luther K. himself realised it, seated with bowed head at his dying wife's bedside; he did not look at Lucy, who was present. It was he, and not Lucy, who closed the dead eyes.

* * *

Sabine showed no grief for the death of her mother; she merely shrugged and remarked that it had after all been expected for some time. Lucy, who had gone to tell her, looked down at the baby Luther kicking in his bassinet. He had black hair.

'Don't touch him,' said Sabine. She sounded

jealous. Lucy straightened from the bassinet and held out her hand.

'Sabine, why can't we be friends?' she said. 'I want your son to love me. I have no child of my own and never will.'

Sabine did not take the hand and Lucy let it fall to her side. 'That's your good luck,' Sabine said pitilessly from her pillows. 'It's all I'm for, that's evident. Now they've got their heir they will try to take Jerry away from me. You're trying as well. You think now I'm laid here helpless the pair of you can go off together to Scotland. Nobody ever thought of taking *me*.' Her face darkened; it was however impossible for it to be other than beautiful. 'I suppose you know,' Sabine went on, her husky voice rising, 'that it's only my presence here that makes it possible for you to stay on in this house? Boston would gossip, wouldn't it, if you lived here alone with my father?'

She was shouting, and in her state it was in any case dangerous for her to have one of her scenes; the doctors had said so. Lucy went quietly out of the room. She had not answered about Jeremy, or about Luther K. Wint.

*   *   *

At Mehitabel's funeral, Lucy had expected to share the first carriage with Wint himself, Jeremy, perhaps Nathaniel, and his wife if the latter came. Sabine was not yet considered fit

89

to leave her bed. However after the coffin was set on its black-draped hearse and the horses nodded their plumes ready to start, Wint came to Lucy where she stood among the mourners and handed her in alone. She was aware of stares behind her back from the women of the sewing-circle, who were naturally there in force; immediately behind that again Jeremy and Nat, evidently already instructed, took certain of these on an arm and shepherded them into the second carriage. Other carriages followed, many of them private: Mehitabel Maule Wint would be buried after a long and slow procession through the town, through the new business quarter steadily rising from its former ruins, past the Quinty works which she and none other had started. As at Sebastian's funeral, the workers stood in the road bare-headed to see her pass; some, old men who remembered the Quinty beginnings, wept. Wint himself sat impassive, staring ahead at the swaying coffin; but he had begun to talk to Lucy already. Watching the hired mourners in their tall hats with long weepers, the sable plumes of the horses nodding in rhythmic pomp, he remarked 'If they're paid by the hour they go more slowly. It stands to reason.'

Once past the works, he began to say what he had meant to say; and all of it shocked Lucy, coming at this time.

*   *   *

'I'll marry again, of course,' was the first thing. The boar's eyes surveyed her. 'It can't be yourself, Lucy, or it surely would be. Boston would talk a little; but I still need an heir. That baby of Sabine's can kick and yell all right, but a lot can happen to a baby, as I needn't tell you. I've selected the young woman in question for some time; she's in the fourth carriage now, Mayflower blood. You know her well enough; she comes to sew, but I can give her other things to think about instead. Her name's Gertrude Pryde Coxon.'

'Your wife is dead,' said Lucy in a low voice. 'Can you not at least pretend to mourn for her?' She knew Gertrude Pryde Coxon slightly, and disliked her; a pallid sharp-featured young woman who kept her eyes prudently lowered. Only the workmen, Lucy was thinking, have shed tears for Mehitabel; not her daughter, not her husband, not even myself; I'm long past tears. As for this man beside her now in the carriage, he'd used the dead woman, her money, her talents, and her body as it pleased him: and hadn't even been faithful from the start. She herself wouldn't give Wint himself any grounds now, any more than she had done since it had happened, for repeating what once had: he needn't hope for it. *Not in this house.* She'd respected that, always.

'Why pretend anything?' said Luther K. 'Mehitabel was a great woman. When she was young, we were partners. Later, because she was strong-willed, I had to conquer or else be conquered. Can you understand that, Lucy?'

'It is not my business to understand. I prefer to remember my mother-in-law as I knew her and to respect her memory. I think that we should not talk any more; people are watching from the other carriages.' They were in fact rounding a turn; she could see black-veiled women's faces peering, avidly, behind them and sideways ahead. They could in fact see very little beyond the glass.

'You are become a model of propriety lately,' Wint replied in his dry way. 'We must talk now, however, and quickly, before they get us to church. As I say, I wish I was coming to church with you for another purpose, Lucy, but that's a dead duck. Listen; I have a proposition to put to you, in fact two.'

The first was what she had half expected. Having arranged with Jeremy to stay in New York, and for Sabine to remain with her son in Boston—there could be no argument, that was done—he suggested now that Lucy should go to be her brother's housekeeper and his own mistress on his frequent visits south. 'You would enjoy New York, Lucy,' Wint said quietly. 'It's a great city. Nobody knows you there yet; you would be the pretty widowed sister of Jeremy Meggett, too devoted to the memory of her dead husband to consider remarrying anybody. You would have plenty of offers, however. You could keep up as respectable a front as you chose.' He grinned, showing the strong, yellowed teeth. 'Jerry will do as I tell him,' he said. 'It's all to be done on my money. We'd find him a house in the best part of town. I'd be down often, and he'd pay visits up here to see to Sabine. She needn't know anything, neither need anyone. What do you say to it, eh?' He eyed her; it was almost, in the funeral carriage with the coffin swaying in front, as if he was ready to light a cigar and enjoy the flavour.

Lucy had not replied. '"Never" is the answer for any virtuous woman, I know,' Wint mocked. 'I daresay Gertrude'll say it at first often enough. No woman worth her salt needs that kind of pretence; and you're well worth yours, Lucy. Do you suppose it's been easy for me to keep my hands off you all of this time, watching you closeted like a nun with Mehitabel? I used to look at your breasts laced under that black dress. I'm looking at 'em now. They've grown fuller. They could fill my hands. I like your long thick eyelashes as well. I never knew a blonde woman with lashes as dark, but they're gold at the tips. The rest further down is darker, to match. Do you remember I kissed you all over, that time in the cabin? I could have done it again any day or night, back at the house, despite that open door to Mehitabel. I didn't, naturally, being the gentleman I am.'

He winked, using the eye unperceived by the

93

following carriages. Lucy had already felt shock and outrage flood her; her cheeks were scarlet. 'Put your handkerchief up to your eyes and pretend you're shedding a respectable tear,' Wint told her, but Lucy clenched her fists angrily in her lap. 'Very well, then, don't; you're a wilful young woman,' he said. 'I know what to do with wilful young women.'

His voice deepened. 'Come to New York,' he murmured. 'It's a lively city, full of sin disguised as virtue, especially for the rich. You would have furs, gowns, jewels, your own carriage, anything.' His eyes devoured her; almost, she was thinking, he would get at her here, this instant, along the funeral carriage seat. Boston would certainly talk then. She made herself answer coldly.

'You say you will give me anything. What about the money you owe me as your son's widow? I have seen not a penny of it. I have lived, evidently on charity, with you all since his death. I want it and the arrears, without conditions.'

'I thought we would come to that,' Wint said. He leaned back in the carriage. 'You're a good business woman, Lucy. I knew you had it in you; that's why I waited. I can pay you the minimum, enough to keep you in genteel near-poverty as the law demands. Otherwise, I can make you an allowance handsome enough to enable you to do anything you want, buy anything you want, go where you want, for as

94

long as you live. For that last, you must however pay me in your own coin.'

'What is that?' she asked idly, but her knees were already trembling; she knew quite well what it would be. The cortège was slowing to a halt as they neared the Presbyterian church; soon she must get out on his arm, and go in before everyone.

'I have a little place up in Vermont, in the mountains, as you know, where I breed the Morgans,' Wint told her. 'Give me a week of your company up there, that's all; we'll make the most of it together. You can't say I'm not making you a fair offer; that, or New York. This way, you'd have your freedom and I'd have my memories.' His eyes had hardly left her as she sat, heavily veiled and wearing a black hat and black gown; as always, it was as though his glance assessed and stripped her of all of it, here in his wife's funeral cortège. 'A week in the mountains, Lucy, that's my price,' Wint repeated softly. 'That, or genteel dependence for life of a kind you don't like even now. Everyone knows you can't bear another child, and no one is likely to rescue you; look at old Nat, defecting at once. Think it all over, and let me know soon; I won't wait long, in any case.'

Lucy firmed her shaking lips beneath the veil. Then she got out of the carriage and walked up to the church and inside it on Wint's arm, as though they had been any casual couple. When they were seated side by side in the pew before everyone she said, again without turning her head lest the others hear, 'You will put all of it in writing. I will not be cheated, at the end.'

'You won't be,' said Luther K. Wint. 'Neither will I.'

The service proceeded, with Mehitabel's burial following in the Maule vault at the cemetery. The handles of Sebastian's coffin and the baby's and Susan's were still bright. Life would no doubt be pleasant with enough money. She mustn't think about what must happen first: not yet.

CHAPTER SIX

The little place in Vermont proved to be near nobody and nothing except for the sight of Camel's Rump rearing in the distance among its further mountains. A river sounded not far off, between trunks of paper-birch and stout grey rearing beeches. These had shed their leaves over the years to make a thick carpet on the logger road, deadening the sound of buggy wheels. The hired buggy stopped, and Lucy got out and saw a clapboard house among the trees. The door opened and a negro servant stood there, bowing. His feet were bare and he wore a clean shirt and ragged sky-blue trousers. He took her baggage; she hadn't brought much. The driver turned and went back, his wheels lurching and creaking.

'What is your name?' said Lucy to the black man. She knew already that Luther K. would arrive unexpectedly in his own time; her reputation had no doubt been preserved by this arranged separate arrival. Boston had been told that she had gone away for a well-deserved little holiday after her mother-in-law's death. In its way, it was true.

The negro gave his little formal bow a second time and said his name was Day of Reckoning. Lucy laughed. 'That's unusual,' she said: she was always friendly and at ease with servants.

'Missy, I been brought up by missionaries after my mother died. She came from the South.' His eyes brooded, then he smiled. 'They taught me hymns there,' he said. 'I sing them sometimes.' Later she was to hear him, crooning to himself in a curiously light and honeyed voice, songs about gathering at the river and being washed in the blood of the Lamb. Meantime he said she could call him Reck for short. 'I do everything for Missy,' he said. 'I bring Missy's bath now?'

*   *   *

She was glad of the hip-bath, which refreshed her after the lurching journey and which filled the room with a delectable scent of garden herbs. Day of Reckoning came and went, carrying thick fleecy towels and a great jug with more hot water; he stood like a satrap, holding the large towel ready as Lucy climbed out naked. He seemed used to the duty and she reflected wryly that no doubt Luther brought many other women here, to be attended to in precisely this fashion. She let the negro dry her, then comb out her hair. He carried away the bath and the jug and towels, came in once again and stoked the wood stove with short chopped logs of birch, shut its doors and then asked if Missy would like supper brought in. Lucy, by then in her wrapper, nodded; no doubt Luther K. would come in at some point, but she was hungry. The hot coffee which Reck brought heartened her and she began to feel sleepy despite it; he had carried in a tray neatly set, with cold meat, a plate of buckwheat cakes and butter, a leg of cold chicken, blueberries and goats' cream and a bland pale cheese. Lucy rinsed her fingers afterwards in a small fluted bowl of old settlers' white china, wiping them on a carefully ironed linen napkin. Then she drew up her chair to the stove, and waited, not looking at the double bed. If it grew late enough, she'd get in; no doubt that was what Wint expected, to find her ready for him in bed. She'd stay meantime where she was. It was warm.

98

She heard the faint thud of hoofbeats come at last, dulled by the carpet of dead leaves outside on the path. Wint came in presently, still carrying his wide-brimmed stetson and wearing a felt cape which disguised his belly. He came to Lucy and kissed her hard; she smelled rain on the cape. She hadn't expected him to ride here, and said so, asking also if he had eaten.

'I had something in Springfield. There's a surprise in the stables tonight; a young foal, that kept me a while. Give me a moment more and I'll be with you. Get into bed and undo that hair; I want it loose.' She loosened the hair, but stayed where she was until, within minutes, Wint emerged in a Paisley dressing-gown with a tied fringed girdle. His jaw was blue with stubble after the ride, his mouth as usual thick and moist like a plum. Lucy felt revulsion rise as he came to her. He stripped the wrapper off her shoulders, letting it fall to the floor. Lucy stood again naked, Aphrodite in gold and ivory. Wint drew his breath for an instant.

'God, you're beautiful,' he said. 'I'm glad I didn't let them scar that body.' He picked Lucy up then and carried her to the turned-down bed.

*   *   *

This time, it was different from the ship. Wint

99

was less considerate, avid for her, entering her swiftly. The thick mouth travelled searching over her face and neck, his hands grew rapidly intimate with every part of her body; fingers prying into the soft secret flesh between her buttocks and thighs, beagle's nose thrust with relish in her armpits. His hands explored her breasts as if they were fruit he was assessing for its ripeness; the fat naked body, covered with black hair, lying upon her own revolted her. She closed her eyes, turned her head away and endured it, trying to think of the money. Wint lay aside for a time and then came at her again, and Lucy found herself coldly remembering a thing Papa had told her of, à propos of nothing, that time on holiday in Bavaria. Louis XV on his wedding night, aged fifteen, had achieved his twenty-seven-year-old Polish bride seven times. Perhaps Wint in his fifties would be satisfied with less, though for the moment it didn't seem like it. By the end Lucy was beginning despite herself to feel a vague pleasure, also exhaustion. 'Please stop now,' she said. 'I'm sore. Let me sleep.'

'You're slow in coming, Lucy,' he grumbled. 'I like a woman to come. It shows politeness.'

He tried once more, exacting as ever among the by now twisted and rumpled sheets. The patterns of flame the lit stove had been making on the wood ceiling had died down and as if he had been sent for, the negro came in silently to stoke the stove. Lucy blushed; it was worse

100

than that time on the train with Sebastian. 'He's used to it,' remarked Luther when Reck had gone. 'Women and horses, they're all the same to him.'

The patterns flared up again on the cedar ceiling as they lay; presently, she slept, Wint's arm possessively about her still as though she could not be physically free of him while the bargain lasted. In the morning, she was wakened by his hand slipping once more between her thighs. The night's rest had refreshed him and he took her at once, using her hard; he had evidently watched for some time while she still slept. Presently the negro came in with coffee. By now Lucy had no awareness of anything except that she was perhaps a captive nymph in the inexorable grasp of an elderly satyr in full fettle. Seven days; was this the second, or would he count it as the first? Whichever he said, she was completely in his power; they were miles from anywhere. The trees outside pressed against the windows, watching.

'That'll do for now,' said Wint presently. 'We'll go out after breakfast, and I'll show you a bit of the countryside.' He sounded complacent. Lucy felt unwilling to be seen with him alone, even up here; one never knew who would notice, and talk. Wint sensed her unease, and laughed.

'Your bottom'll wear out if I fuck it all day. Give it a bit of saddle exercise for a change.

There's plenty else to see here other than people: that's why I come up. I'm a different man up in Vermont from the one you thought you knew in Boston.'

He was, she was thinking, the same man exactly, and always would be: but she said nothing, combed the tangles with some difficulty out of her hair, and they dressed and ate. Two Morgan ponies were waiting outside, ready saddled by Reck. 'I want to show you the foal first that arrived yesterday,' Wint said. 'That's why I took a moment or two coming in, as I said.' He kept his arm about her; as on the ship after their night together, her walking was uncertain. She was confused that he had noticed it.

The foal was suckling its brown mother, legs still splayed and weak. 'A bit like you this morning, eh?' said Wint. Lucy flushed scarlet: it took time to get used to the things he said, and there evidently wasn't much he wouldn't say. 'That little mare,' he told her, 'will grow up to work for her corn, like you're doing now, Lucy love. By then you'll both stand straight enough on your own. It's a matter of getting used to it. Come, up with you.' He helped her on to the crupper. Once with a knee hooked over it, Lucy felt better and more secure. In its way, perhaps not very precisely, it was like Boston Common. Reck must have to look after the Morgans as well as everything else.

They began to walk the horses. Luther told

her he had a small farm down the hill. 'We won't go there today,' he said. 'I want to show you Camel first. However, there are chickens down there and some goats, and a herd of cows from England and a bull who knows his business, like I know mine.' The small lecher's eyes ran over her. 'I could keep myself up here if Quinty failed, which it won't,' Luther remarked. 'I like to come here, though, to get away now and then. I was born in the country. Town folks don't know what they never did learn and maybe never will.'

They rode down the logger road and towards the great mountains; he made her draw rein below Camel's Rump. 'They want to start calling it Hump now, folks are grown so proper,' Luther told her. 'I guess it's more like a camel's moving arse than its hump, but I never saw either of 'em except in pictures in some book. These mountains are older than anything in the world, seven times as old as the Rockies.'

It was not difficult to be charmed by him when he talked so, almost like a boy; she could understand why Mehitabel had married him, shrewd as she must even then have been; young, lithe, dark and filled with knowledge about engines and the growing world, Luther Kelly Wint must have been hard for any woman to resist. Come to that, Mehitabel hadn't resisted. She, Lucy, was beginning after all to bend to his will. She could feel herself growing pliant, like a willow in water. Luther turned his square head now beneath its stetson.

'Wait till we get to Lost Pond,' he told her. 'It's the end of the world, far away from everything. Not everyone knows about it even if they've lived in these parts all of their lives.'

*   *   *

They rode on. Day of Reckoning had put food ready in the saddlebags and they dismounted at one point and ate it, drinking clear water from the river that ran below a slope. Continuing the journey they came to a place where the trees grew so thickly they had to dismount a second time and walk, tying the ponies' reins at last to low branches and leaving them to nose the moss. Wint put his arm about Lucy's waist as they walked into the depths of the woods. It had been dark under the trees. Gradually she became aware of a growing prevalence of greenish light, like some strange dawn on another planet. The vista opened up suddenly to reveal an immense smooth pond, covered with flat lily leaves and surrounded by sedges and upspringing green brush. There was a contented sound of frogs' croaking. Wint led Lucy wordlessly to the water's edge, which did not slope down sharply but blended imperceptibly into mud. The oooze darkened her boots, and he drew her

104

back protectively. 'Don't go any further here,' he said. 'It's true this part isn't lethal; if you fell in you could rescue yourself, though you'd get wet.' His thick lips smiled down at her, then he turned his gaze to the near distance. 'Over there in the green brush it's deadly bog, though, and a man can sink in so far without expecting it, then call out for long enough and nobody will hear. He'll stand there sucked down by the mud till he's dead of starvation if he's a tall man; a short one will suffocate at once. It's happened, but not often; as I say, nobody comes up here once in twenty years. They say that in a century, the trees'll have crept in and dried up the bog. They'll find some strange things then, though maybe not men's bones.'

He looked down at Lucy again, and his arm tightened about her. 'Your beautiful body could stay in the mud for long enough and be preserved, maybe five thousand years if it lasted; they'd find you looking like you do now, but pickled dark green.' He laughed. Lucy drew away in terror; he could thrust her down here if he liked; nobody but Reck, who wouldn't dare ask questions, would know where she'd gone. They could search for years and never find her. Wint began to laugh again. 'Don't be frightened, Lucy,' he said. 'I value your body too much as it is. Look at the damsel-flies, mating away down there at the water's edge; you can see what they're doing, it's the same as we do, but we don't lay any young in the mud.'

She stared down, free for the time of her fear of the bog; this was clear, inhabited water. At the edge, in a serried row, were paired fairylike creatures in gold and silver, their balanced wings whirring steadily. The gold males copulated with the silver females who stayed passive, clinging to the edge. 'The frogs are mating as well,' she heard Wint say. 'They'll leave their eggs among the sedges, hundreds in each jelly. A male frog gets swollen thumbs to grasp the female, this time of year. I guess I got swollen thumbs this minute. Come.'

He led Lucy back towards the wood. She was trembling, her knees already turning to water. The sight of the rhythmically jabbing damsel-flies had had a strange effect on her; she felt one with them. She let Wint lay her down, unresisting, among the trees. As he said, there was nobody else up here in twenty years. For a time, while he used her in the accustomed way, she gazed back from where she lay at the glassy-smooth water beyond the trunks, and saw the upthrust sedges quivering, sensed the varied unseen layers of the pond full of life. She herself was fully alive; the surge of orgasm came more strongly than ever before. She heard the cries of a fulfiled woman and knew that they were her own; had she ever doubted herself, though she was by now one of the creatures Papa had told her of, the haeterae, sterilised by the ancient Greeks to give pleasure and bear no children? If she were to look at Wint, she would loathe him still; his fat belly sagged upon her, sated meantime; otherwise, unseen behind her closed eyelids, he was Pan, she Syrinx, except that Syrinx hadn't been captured and had been turned instead into a reed. A reed; sedges, frogs, damsel-flies. Wint began to thrust in her again like a great male fly. She began to laugh at the notion, then murmur once more with pleasure. 'That's better,' she heard him say. 'That's much better, Lucy. You're a very good girl. You had me worried for a while, the last day or so. I thought the birth had maybe harmed you in some way, though the doctor said not.' He lay back, still within her in their surcease. 'You know he, the doctor, told me that time you still had everything you ought to have afterwards, except for the womb's scar. You won't breed, not like those frogs. They're in it for the dividends. We're in it for pleasure. You're pleased by now, eh?'

She smiled, saying nothing. His lips came down on hers again, and at the same time as opening her mouth she felt a third presence, small and furtive, run across her hand where it lay open on last year's dry leaves. Lucy turned her head idly; it was a tiny scarlet creature like a lizard, soft and young. 'It's a red eft,' said Luther. 'It came to pay you a visit. They don't

107

often show themselves. Again, my girl. Once more, then we'll go back. I told you a trip in the saddle would do the trick. Tomorrow we'll stay in bed all day, eh? Then the day after, I've got more of the country to show you. Afterwards there's the rest.'

*   *   *

The magic left her with his incessant urgings, and in fact came no more; but she had ceased to resent him and was acquiescent now. For the rest of their time together she submitted, and learned a number of lessons. She would remember them, and the other things Wint showed her. They rode out on the ponies now and again, once down to his farm; another time to see a giant pebble the full height of four men, cast down in remote ages while the glaciers were eating away at the mountains, leaving them at a height in the end no greater than Camel's Rump. Before that, Luther said, they had been as high as the stars. 'The Rockies are nothing,' he told her once again. 'They're newcomers.' They became almost comrades on these rides together, then they would be in bed again between cool fresh daily replaced sheets which rapidly became hot once more and twisted. One day he mentioned New York again. 'Or else stay on here,' he said, 'and I can visit you often.'

She was angry, thinking he intended to go

108

back on his word. 'You couldn't keep me here,' she told him. 'I could get down to the farm and find help there, or else ride off.' She knew it was a vain boast; where would she ride to?

Wint laughed, but the eyes stayed hard. 'Old Cassidy down at the farm, whom you saw the other day, wouldn't let you get far,' Luther said. 'He's as spry at seventy as he ever was in his life. He's worn out three wives and no woman in her senses would go down there alone. You wouldn't be able even to get back in the saddle by the time he'd finished with you, if he ever did finish. Think of something else.'

There was always, by the end, however, the same thing about which to think. She heard his panting breaths like an animal's, using her once again. There was after all no choice about what to do. She shouldn't have let him bring her up here. She knew he was changing her, causing her to give ways to instincts and desires she had never before admitted: he was in fact debauching her, and they both knew it. Lucy looked at herself naked one day in the glass after her bath and fancied her own long eyes grown sleepy with lust, her lips fuller than before with much kissing; she seemed to have put on a quantity of creamy flesh in only a few days here. Her mind whirled; what was she by now?

Wint soon told her, his hand as usual caressing her inner thigh. She was amazed at his energy, his resilience; after all he wasn't as young as herself. He left her presently and Lucy combed out her hair thoughtfully, still naked: she was getting used to it. She wouldn't have stayed naked as long in Boston, even at Clonough. She wouldn't have lain across Wint's knees in front of the stove, again naked on the hide rug there, in afternoons, exhausted with his lovemaking, not minding by now if Reck came in. She was a different person now, perhaps a whore. It wasn't Wint particularly, it was perhaps all men and what they could do.

She once saw Day of Reckoning come in when she was alone, with logs which he put in the stove as usual. She surveyed his bent buttocks in the sky-blue trousers. What would it be like to have a black man as lover? He was alone up here, without a woman. He seemed to have nobody but himself. She'd asked him about it once already, while Wint was round at the stables. Reck had smiled gently.

'Missy, I need no one. I have my God.' He had begun to sing a soft hymn then; now, he turned round. Lucy saw herself stretch out a hand and the treacle-dark eyes dilate a little, less in desire than fear; their whites showed for moments. At the same time Wint, coming back unheard, walked in. He jerked his head and the negro vanished silently. Wint came to Lucy, laid her face down across the bed and smacked her hard on the bottom twice or three times. 'Cut that out,' he said. He then made forcible love, twisting her round viciously for it;

110

tears were running down her cheeks with the pain and insult. 'You asked for that,' said Wint. 'In a minute, you'll find yourself come. It makes all of that work faster.' He bit her ear gently. 'Did you suppose,' she heard him murmur, 'that I'd let a full man bathe you, see you without clothes day after day? I had Reck dressed when I took him into my service. Cassidy and I did it between us. Reck's a neutered tomcat. I'm a stray. Is that better now, eh? I've often made you so's you can't stand or walk, Lucy, my girl; now you can't sit either.' He chuckled, thumbing her upper arms harder than usual.

It was true; but the pain had transformed itself by now into a mysterious golden flooding through all her veins, pervading her whole body: an orgasm came almost like the one under the trees at Lost Pond had been. It was the sixth day. What was it that had happened in the Bible on the sixth day? *Male and female created he them*. That must have been it, because even God had rested on the seventh. She wondered what Mehitabel must be thinking, if she could see them now from heaven. Perhaps she herself could soon rest, like God. That wasn't a proper thought, not like one Isobel O'Hara would have approved. Lady O'Hara seemed a long way away. Lucy remembered Clonough and began once more to cry, wanting suddenly to go out in the garden there and lay her face against the wet

111

leaves of the philadelphus. As it was, she'd never be received at Clonough again if they knew about all this. It would soon be time to get away. Wint laughed, and kissed her open mouth.

*   *   *

'Sometimes you're like a nun, Lucy,' he said to her. 'Shall I tell you a little story?' He did so, his hands by now caressing her thighs. 'These are like ivory velvet,' he said. 'I brought a real nun up here once, all the way from Cincinnati. She'd got permission to visit her sick aunt. The aunt got a whole lot better soon; that visit did her a power of good. I guess that nun is a Mother Superior by now.' He laughed, and bit again into Lucy's flesh. Lucy shut her eyes and felt him enter her as usual. The story might be true or might be a lie. He was ruthless enough for it to have happened, and yet, in his boasting, like the little boy he partly was, telling stories to impress. One couldn't dislike him. For the first time she thought of prim genteel Gertrude, whom Wint said he was about to marry. Gertrude would certainly learn one or two things. Lucy wondered if he would bring her up here, but didn't ask; a response had come again, and she savoured it in silence, biting her lips.

'That's my nun,' said Wint, patting her approvingly. 'That's my good little mare.

112

Come, little mare; trot, trot.'

*   *   *

On the seventh day, he handed her the jointure agreement and got her to read and sign it. It was handsome; Lucy had no complaints. She saw Wint regarding her keenly, a business man again, no longer her insatiable lover.

'The New York offer is still open, if you care to consider it. I shall be married by then; you understand that already.'

'I don't want to consider it.' She shut her mind to the thought of kept ease, jewels, carriages; she could buy all that for herself without him now she had the money; there was enough. As always, Wint read her thoughts, and his eyes narrowed.

'There's one thing you won't be able to buy, or not as a rule, Lucy,' he said. 'I've left you so's you will never be able to do without a man in your bed for long. It'll take you in the middle of the night, or at some tea-party. Think again; you won't be able to marry, unless it's some useless character who doesn't want children. At that rate, he won't be as good in bed as I am: bound not to be. Think of it again.' She stared at him coldly. If he could drive a bargain, so could she.

'I have fulfiled my part of the contract with you and you have given me what we agreed.

113

From now on we are strangers, except for civility in public: I am your daughter-in-law, Mr Wint. I wish you success in your marriage.'

'Then go your own way, little bitch, and take your tail with you: it'll miss what I've been putting up it,' Wint replied equably. 'I've given you a receipt for living: use it your own way.' He took Lucy by the shoulders then and pressed his mouth down on hers in a last demanding kiss. She was almost fainting; she felt her lips open involuntarily to receive his tongue, the way it had so often happened. He mustn't be allowed his way with her, as the romances put it, any more; once more would mean many times. She wrenched herself away and went out to the waiting carriage. The baggage was already inside and Lucy did not look back. She signalled to the man to drive off, knowing that Wint, the part of her life she was leaving, stood at the door of the clapboard house, staring after her. He didn't like to be outwitted in business. She must think of it that way.

*   *   *

She heard of his remarriage as soon as Jeremy and she reached England; Jerry pointed it out to her in the morning paper. 'He's netted himself a fairly young one,' her brother said. Gertrude Pryde Coxon was twenty-eight years old and came, it stated, from one of the oldest

Boston families. There was no doubt that Luther K. aimed high. Mayflower blood might yet populate Quinty, if everyone made haste. Lucy, recovered fully on the voyage, was already enjoying her money. She had never had much before; at Clonough they had always, as Hubert used to put it, scraped hell for sixpence anyhow. After an understandable burst of buying new, fashionable clothes Lucy found she had the ability to spend wisely. She even toyed, in a little while, with the stock market, having a predictory sense of what people would want to buy and what they wouldn't, before they knew for themselves. Mehitabel would have approved. So did Papa, who touched Lucy for a loan quite shortly. Lucy knew she would never see the money again; Papa had a soul above such things. Likewise, she bought gifts for the children at Aylors, and won their hearts less by that than by talking to them as if they were already grown up. Little Maria was much like Lucy herself had been at that age, except that the wide eyes in the child's face were a light, predictable, rather shallow blue. Young Lucius was a plain, pale, grave little boy who did not resemble either of his parents, in looks or nature. He liked to read already from a flannel book, and would seldom willingly join his elder sister in her games and happy unsupervised dancing about. Jerry was pleased enough with his pretty daughter, bored with his son; he

115

would toss young Maria up in his arms to the sound of her giggling, while Lucius stared somewhat primly at the ground. Lucy went once and took the little boy's hand. He had been drawing.

'What is it a picture of?' she asked him.

'It is a house with chimneys.'

That was far on for his age; children took some time as a rule to draw chimneys on a house; Lucy herself remembered struggling to put in the criss-crosses of the windows, then giving up. That had been when she was at Clonough already. Clonough, Clonough! But she could not go there or to Fermisons quite yet, till she had paid the arranged visit with Jerry to Scotland, to visit Robert Napier the famous old shipbuilder.

*   *   *

On the long train journey, Lucy sat opposite her twin in the compartment and thought, firstly as everyone always did, how extremely handsome Jerry was; it was like sitting in a train with Apollo, perhaps grown a little heavier than he used to be, but still without rival. Secondly, it occurred to Jeremy's sister that he and she had enjoyed more of one another's sole company over the past few weeks than they had ever been able to do before in their lives: on the ship, the handsome couple, brother and sister, like as two peas, had been sought after, a little too much so for comfort on close shipboard, and had protected one another's privacy as far as was feasible. Nevertheless Lucy had had time to find out that Jeremy Meggett was on the whole a little too pleased with himself. It was natural; being so handsome, he had always been spoilt, even no doubt by the school matron. He was talking expressively now, his shapely hands waving, about the suggested consignment of carbon-treated steel that was to be negotiated between Quinty and the Clydeside works on this visit.

'One hundred and seventy-five thousand, our price; he wouldn't get a keener.' Jeremy went on talking, and Lucy knew a sudden flash of discomfort. One hundred and fifty thousand had been the figure. Luther K. had boasted about it once when they were in bed; her mind remembered such things. She spoke carefully, flecked eyes fixed on her brother's face.

'Jerry, don't cheat Luther Wint; he trusts you. If he finds that you are dishonest, remember these Coxons may oust you altogether; the brother is in business of some kind already in Boston.' She remembered meeting the Coxon brother briefly and hadn't liked him; he had come once to escort his sister away from a sewing afternoon at Mehitabel's. They mustn't get a foot into Jeremy's place and young Luther's if it could be helped: it was foolish of Jerry to risk it.

Like most men, Jeremy Meggett resented

being found out; his comely face reddened and he began to bluster. 'How the devil do you—' he began, then realised he had given himself away and grinned, a trifle foolishly.

'You're a sharp one, Lucy. How did you know the figure? Wint, of course, allows me to bargain up or down; it's possible the old fellow in Scotland will have rival estimates of his own. Leave it to me; don't speak up while we're at Shandon, there's a good girl, I handle my own business.' He hadn't given her time to answer about how she knew, which was as well. She realised that Jerry very seldom listened to anyone; no doubt Sabine liked being mastered in all ways.

*   *   *

The glittering prospect of the silver Gareloch met them from the deck of Robert Napier's paddle-steamer, which had met them by arrangement at the Glasgow dock. Lucy held on to her hat's brim in the wind on deck and surveyed the loch and, presently, the rising single square tower of Shandon, the old millionaire's palace beside the long hill-girt loch; the house itself was secretly laughed at for being top-heavy and grandiose. The surrounding walls contained marble statues in regularly placed niches, posturing to make it perhaps clear that they were classical figures and not mediaeval saints, Robert Napier's brother being a well-known Church of Scotland minister.

Robert Napier and his wife Isabella greeted them together at the house door after the carriage had delivered them through the grounds from nearby Rhu pier. Napier himself was a dignified old man with silver hair and side-whiskers, and small wise eyes the colour of gentians, set obliquely so that they sloped outwards. He bowed over Lucy's hand in courtly fashion; there was no trace of the rough manners of a blacksmith, but his blood was Highland and by now, he moved by custom among great folk. His wife was still beautiful, with high cheekbones and fine silver hair dressed simply; they were first cousins, but Isabella Napier's delicately modelled face was individual and not a mere echo of her husband's, as happens so often with couples mutually devoted after long marriage. They went inside all four to the warm house, where tea was served at once in the winter garden among the palms. 'You will want to rest before dinner,' Mrs Napier said to Lucy. The latter was not tired, but on the contrary exhilarated and diverted: there was the constant heavy sound of a ticking clock somewhere above them, predictable as doom. She asked about it, and was told it was hung in the tower and had been made in Birmingham. Later Lucy was taken up to see it, and its pendulum swinging the minutes as it had done now for nearly twenty years, when the great house had at last been completed and Napier's collection of old masters suitably housed in its long galleries. Lucy was taken round these by her hostess while the men talked privately in the office. Lucy, who had not greatly liked the house itself—it reminded her of a great ugly church with its darkly varnished interior arches—was amazed and transported at the beauty of the world-famous paintings, the Leonardos and Titians and the rest; she had never before seen great art. Isabella's own portrait hung on the stairs, less notably painted—it had been done proficiently enough by a Napier cousin—but showing her as she must have been in her younger days, the sunlight filtering on her bright hair as she sat at a spinning-wheel with fleece waiting carded on its distaff. 'I never did spin,' Mrs Napier told Lucy, smiling. 'I never had to. Robert was doing well already when he married me; he and my brother David, who was a great inventor, worked together for many years in the yards by the Clyde.' She paused at the head-and-shoulders portrait of a bearded man with fiery, brooding eyes. 'David never recovered from a dreadful explosion resulting from one of his inventions, a great ship's boiler in which many poor men lost their lives. He gave up his profession and went to London alone, and never returned to us.' She looked sad and Lucy hastened to cheer her.

'You have children?' she asked, knowing

nothing about the family. Isabella brightened. 'Why, they are married long since, with children of their own,' she said. 'The grandchildren play hide-and-seek among the palms downstairs when they come. Tomorrow you must come out and see the roses; Robert and I take great pride in them.'

The rose garden, the winter garden, the paddle-steamer, dinners given to visiting royalty; all these things had accrued to a former blacksmith with great talent, who had designed the first steamship to cross the Atlantic. At dinner, old Napier's brother Peter, the minister, came with his eldest daughter Kate and her husband Richard Robb Grant, and said grace before they ate the excellent local salmon: afterwards, Grant sang Mendelssohn's songs in a fine tenor voice to Isabella's accompaniment on the pianoforte. Still later Jeremy told Lucy that there had been two strange marriages of the minister Peter Napier's; he always managed to hear such gossip. He smiled in satisfaction about the matter of Robert and the estimates, as they sat again together in the train back to London. 'In fact, the old boy beat me down to a thousand and twenty-five,' he told Lucy. 'Trust a Scot to do sharp business. He says he was born with a hammer in his hand. That must have been uncomfortable for his mother, whoever she was.' He laughed, a little too loudly.

His mother was a douce old lady in a white

mutch, drawn long ago in pastels beside her grey-haired husband, and they themselves came of an ironworking family and so did their parents, Lucy thought; Isabella had shown her those portraits also, placed in twin frames on an escritoire downstairs. Perhaps one day the Wints and Meggetts would form such a shipbuilding dynasty, depending partly on whether or not Luther K.'s marriage brought heirs; if not, there was, still, young Luther. She found her thoughts recede already from ugly Shandon with its matchless surroundings and irreplaceable works of art, and returned to the present situation. It was possible Jeremy was lying again about the price asked, and that he would in any case make himself a profit one way or the other. Well, she'd warned him already to treat Luther K. with honesty; if he wouldn't, he himself was the one who would suffer, and Sabine, and the boy. But Lucy said nothing; there were times when nothing but silence was wise, and she was perhaps by now learning wisdom.

*   *   *

She did not return to Aylors with Jeremy, but went straight to Ireland by boat from the Pool of London. Clonough! It would be like a drink of water after long drought to see it again, and Hubert, even though he was married now to Annis; and their little boy. She would see to her own nearby house of Fermisons also while she stayed with them: much needed to be done there. It must be made habitable, and become her home.

The results of the visit to Clonough, which had already been arranged, were however to prove dire.

CHAPTER SEVEN

It happened this way. On the Irish crossing, Lucy had gone prudently as usual to lie down. However the boat was crowded, and she gave up her place on the bench on deck to a swaying young woman in plain rough clothes, carrying a white-faced child. The young woman herself was so ill Lucy took the child from her and walked up and down the deck for some time with it in her arms. The feel of the small warm body moved her strangely. She had encountered several living children lately; the memory of tiny Hartley, wax in his coffin, and Mehitabel's tears had begun to fade, also her own unforgotten personal tragedy. However she would never hold a child of her own, and so held this one closely, trying to cheer the little creature by making the sounds women make to young children, clucking and cajoling; but it turned its head away, whimpering even after it was returned to its mother, in sight at

123

last of the port. 'I'm grateful to yourself for holding him, I'm sure,' said the girl pleasantly; she could not have been more than nineteen. 'We'll maybe feel better, both of us, once we're on land again.' She smiled wanly, and in a short time vanished out of Lucy's life.

Lucy forgot her; there at once was Hubert's cheerful hook-nosed face waiting by the horses. He had driven down with the carriage and would take her back; it had all been arranged by means of letters from Aylors. They kissed, as they had been used to do, in almost the same way; nothing had changed, after all. 'It's good to see you again, Lucy,' Hubert said shyly. His prominent brown eyes were wistful as a frog's, surveying her like some goddess. Perhaps the new dress helped. Lucy had put off mourning since coming back to England; she was tired of it, it had seemed to go on and on.

They talked like old friends on the journey, with Lucy perched up on the box the way it had always used to be. 'You'll like to see Alan,' Hubert said. 'He's grown a good bit. Annis dotes on him. She wouldn't leave him even to drive down today.'

He then forgot his wife and son and talked instead about horses, which he understood better. He had, Lucy decided, gained in confidence since fathering an heir. He told her Lady O'Hara and old Pat, who was still alive, had gone back to Liskey to live. 'Annis made them go. She said she would be mistress in her own house. It was time someone said it.' His voice regarding Annis was flat, not particularly interested; no doubt she made a good housekeeper and mother. They had grown, he added, a good crop over at Clonough farm last year; Cathy was a better manager than her husband Arthur, who was lazy. 'But you knew that; you remember him, great long lump of misery. He'd hang about our house more if Annis let him, but she says they only have the house on condition that Arthur does some work, so work he must. It's really poor Cathy who does most of it, as I've said.'

Lucy smiled. Hubert himself was disinclined for work and never did any; even Annis couldn't alter that. She watched his great chestnut-curly head intent above the reins. He hadn't changed; he was happy while driving or riding, horses had always been his passion. They talked about the hunt and its fortunes while the bays spanked along the rough approach to Clonough. Lucy felt tears rise at the remembered sight of the old trees. How long it seemed, though not in fact so very long in years, since she had left here, and how much had happened that it was best not to speak of! 'I feel,' she said aloud, 'as if I'm coming home.'

The ugly attractive face turned to regard her; Hubert Meggett looked at his cousin very kindly.

'It is your home for as long as you like to

125

stay on with us, Lucy. You know that.'

Lucy smiled as usual, thinking that perhaps Annis would not agree. 'I must look over Fermisons,' she told him. 'There are things to be done there. If I may stay till it's ready for me, that will be very pleasant.'

'Don't get Fermisons ready too soon,' said Hubert.

*   *   *

Annis was in the nursery with her son; she had not come down to greet Lucy and hardly heeded her arrival. She was a short thin young woman whose forehead bulged in an ugly way above permanently hostile gooseberry eyes. Lucy, having met her in early days, disliked her again at sight but tried not to show it; Annis was after all probably doing the same favour to herself. Alan, the heir, was delightful and surprisingly handsome, as someone, she remembered, had told Jeremy in a letter soon after his birth. He was rosy-cheeked, not in the least shy, and staggered about dragging a painted wooden horse on two wheels. He wheeled it towards Lucy and laughed up at her, showing several neat little milk-teeth. She picked him up and kissed him. 'I'm Aunt Lucy,' she said, which was as near as made no difference. Alan cuddled against her like a smiling cherub. Annis' voice came harshly.

'We do not allow strangers to kiss Alan,' she

126

said. Lucy put the child down gently. 'I'm not a stranger,' she said. 'Shortly I hope to be your neighbour, at Fermisons.' Annis made no reply, took her son's hand and led him away. She perhaps remembers that I was to marry Hubert and didn't, Lucy thought; or perhaps she's like that anyway. Some people were.

*   *   *

Lucy stayed at Clonough for a fortnight, never a long stay in Ireland. She rode over early to Fermisons, which proved to be in a disastrous state of repair; nothing had been done to it in her lifetime. Lucy gave orders for the mending of the roof first of all, then visited some of the tenants and saw the state of their cottages, which were worse than the house. She was angry with the steward, who like too many of them considered only himself. He was an ungracious fellow named Wandrell who obviously resented her return: well, she would show him that a woman could contrive well enough. 'These poor souls are to be given daily milk from the dairy, and eggs and butter, and bacon when it's ready,' she said. 'I will be over often, and will ask them if they get better food than their own potatoes from now on.'

'There'd be no money in it if you had your way,' the man replied insolently. 'We sell all that to England.' Lucy flushed.

'That is not your concern as long as you are

127

paid your wages. You will feed these people so that they can work for pay. Once they are working, the estate will prosper. Remember that, and that I am home again, and will move in here very soon; I expect to find everything as I want it: see that it is done, and I will have a close look at the rent-rolls as well.'

She would never, in earlier days, have heeded such matters; but in the years with Mehitabel she had heard some of the stories of Irish labourers who came over to the States looking for work, and the conditions they had left behind them. It took a good deal to make an Irishman leave home. Her tenants should stay if they wanted to.

*   *   *

Hubert drove her into Waterford to buy house-linen for Fermisons; Papa had long ago taken away what there was to Aylors. Lucy would go home with the linen, and remain. She was beginning to feel that she had outstayed her welcome at Clonough, not from anything Hubert said or did but because Annis resented the fact that little Alan had begun to run to Aunt Lucy oftener than to his mother. Lucy saw the pair stand for the last time at the great door of Clonough as they themselves drove off, Annis with her son's hand held firmly in her own lest Alan try to run after the departing carriage. He had cried when he was told Aunt

128

Lucy was going away. 'I'll come back to see you often,' she had promised, as she had promised the older children at Aylors. She blew kisses to Alan till they were out of sight. There was no need for sadness, after all; she would see him frequently, they would visit her and she them.

They drove out past the farm. Cathy's humped figure was bending over vegetables in the kitchen garden: she looked up and waved. Lucy had seen her once or twice, but as usual found she had very little to say; except for her known visits to the convent house near Enniscorthy to hear Mass, she was quiet and shy, bullied constantly by her idle useless husband Arthur Meggett-Clees. 'He's nowhere in sight,' grumbled Hubert now. 'He'd be at the house oftener, drinking our whiskey, if Annis hadn't put a stop to it. He's no manner of good.' Lucy remembered Cathy's ugly little face, with the hook-nose Hubert had also, and the brown eyes, in her case sad, gentle and submissive. She had, after all been married young to Arthur against the latter's will and his mother's: but old Lord Meggett had agreed to pay his debts if he married the hunchbacked second daughter, his cousin, who everyone knew was unlikely to give him children: and there had of course been none. Cathy loves Arthur as part of her duty, Lucy thought now. She herself considered Arthur Meggett-Clees unloveable, not only because of his colourless eyes and loose thin lips like a lawyer's, and his long limbs slumped constantly in other people's chairs, but because of his nature. He was sullenly aware that by his marriage he had been deprived of any hope of the Clonough inheritance, which was what the old lord had fully intended. It was cruel, no doubt, to Cathy—but as young Alan was very much alive, and there might be more children born to Hubert and Annis, there was small hope of the inheritance for Arthur Meggett-Clees in any case.

Other visitors during her stay had of course included Isobel, without her old husband Pat who by now mostly kept his bed. Isobel had recommended a pleasant young replacement steward to Lucy, who was determined to get rid of Wandrell as soon as possible. This new young man wanted to get married and would be glad of the job at Fermisons. Lucy had seen and approved him, and looked forward to telling Wandrell to work out his notice at once. She did not quail at the task: she felt equal to anything now.

They stopped at the shop which sold especially fine Irish linen, hand-sewn and with the silvery sheen and rare smooth quality that was becoming difficult to find elsewhere, even in London. Lucy chose sheets and pillow-cases to take home and use. Home! What care she would take in laying out this matchless linen in the shelved cupboard at the top of the stairs, smelling fresh as it did now the roof above was mended and she had had the cottage women clean it out both before and after the men had painted the shelves! They were glad to work for the lady of Fermisons, who fed them better than they had ever been fed in their lives and paid them for any such work. The latter necessity gave Lucy pleasure; the money was there. The way she had had to earn it, back at the Vermont clapboard house, was perhaps justified after all. She told herself that if she hadn't gone there with Luther K., he would have got at her somehow in the brownstone house in the end; and she would still have been poor, on a small jointure or even none, still in Boston.

'What are you thinking of, Lucy?' asked Hubert, hands on the reins.

'Of my life.'

'It'll be a happier one now you're home.' He knew, of course, about the baby and Sebastian; not about the rest. She saw him smile as they drove up the turn to Fermisons. 'You must come over to us often, and see Annis and the boy.' He wasn't very perceptive, she thought, dear good-natured Hubert. He helped her out with the hand-baggage before the men came running. Lucy kissed him goodbye. 'I won't wait,' Hubert said. 'I know you're busy with the linen, or soon will be.'

She waved him off, went into the echoing house, and unpacked her Waterford parcels. She told the women to air them and then to put sheets and pillow-cases on her own bed for tonight. How satisfying it would be to sleep under her very own roof; hers, not Papa's or Jerry's or the Wints'! Mama had wished this house to be left to her, Lucy, as her separate inheritance, and Lucius himself had been glad enough to agree; Aylors was enough expense, at the time. The last would of course go to Jerry, and at the present moment was naturally filled with Italian incunabula Caterina helped the maids to dust. One must soon ask for the children to be sent over from there on a long visit, unless Jerry took them after all back to the States.

After seeing the linen shaken out to air Lucy wandered through the house, reminding herself that among her baggage was lavender picked lately at Clonough; Annis hadn't grudged her that, and she'd plant the roots here at once. The essential things were mostly done now; the roof, the stables, the house-linen. Soon the place would be fit for guests. Lucy made her way into the L-shaped drawing-room which ended in the long garden Mama had used, one was told, to love; how little one knew of Mama except her name, Maria Flaherté! Papa had removed her only portrait to Aylors long ago. However here was Grandmama still, a young woman painted in a white high-waisted dress, her brown hair curled in a fashion prevalent at the time George IV had visited Ireland in 1821.

Grandmama Flaherté had been one of the few presented to the King, who had been in official mourning because of the death of the estranged wife he loathed, and he'd stayed mostly on his yacht in Dublin harbour. Such things she had been told long ago floated up now into Lucy's mind; and there was Grandmama's harp also, a tall ghost shrouded in holland among the covered neglected furniture. Its strings must be frayed long since and she herself couldn't play: nevertheless it was one of the matters that would be put right, brought like everything else out of its covers, and in some way used again.

The sensation of being watched disturbed Lucy and she spun round. Wandrell the steward was standing there, his eyes secretive. 'I thought I heard someone moving upstairs,' he said. His glance surveyed Lucy in a way she disliked. She took the chance to tell him that he might work out his notice. 'I have found someone else,' she told him briskly. The man scowled.

'I've worked here all these years on my own. It's a poor reward to lose my place as soon as the owner calls in.'

'It's the reward you deserve, as well you know. Work out your time, and I will give you some kind of reference. Mr Cawley will come to replace you next month.'

'That's not long enough to find a new place, and move out.'

'It will have to be long enough,' said Lucy firmly. She thought how much pleasanter the place would be without Wandrell. He had neglected the tenants and, without doubt, salted away some of the rent money over the years for himself; they mostly did. She must examine the books more carefully when she had time, before he left.

'Take yourself off,' she said now. 'I do not want you in the house unless I send for you.'

He turned and went, by the set of his shoulders bragging slightly in defiance. The filtered sunlight through the tall fan-shaped windows soon obscured his departing figure among motes of dust. She must have the windows cleaned, their glass again made sparkling. Fermisons should become once more the place it had been in her grandfather's time, full of laughter, hospitality, perhaps music played by someone or other on the harp. It was still a fashionable instrument. She might even have young Maria taught to play it.

*   *   *

Her days passed busily, having begun with the pleasant waking each morning in the old four-poster bed among the sweet new linen. At the week's end a letter was handed to her in Hubert's scrawled familiar writing. Alan was ill of a fever; they had had the doctor, who said it was measles. *You and I both had that as*

134

children, Hubert wrote. *Alan calls for you often. Come over and comfort him.*

She rode over at once on the new mare Molly she'd bought to take out to the hunt later on in the season. She remembered having measles herself, and how they had tied her hands in padded gloves so that she wouldn't scratch and spoil her complexion.

*   *   *

Alan lay tossing in his small cot bed, his cheeks flushed; the rash had not yet appeared. 'Don't worry,' said Lucy to Annis, who sat by the bed. 'It's better to get them over in childhood, the way we all did. He'll soon be better, and running about again.'

She bent to kiss the flushed cheek, regardless of his mother. However the little boy did not seem to know Aunt Lucy today; he was running a high temperature still and his hands and face were hot.

'I have not myself had measles,' said Annis primly, 'so I will probably catch them from Alan. However it does not matter.'

Riding home, Lucy was aware of a sudden sinking of the heart. Wasn't there something someone had told her, probably on Mehitabel's sewing-circle days, of the danger to young children whose mothers hadn't had measles? It wasn't yet fully understood, it happened so rarely. At the same time, Lucy

135

recalled the sick child she had carried about on the boat. Had he perhaps been sickening for that, and had she herself brought the infection to Clonough? She prayed not. She would send a servant daily to ask how little Alan was: it was all she could do.

She only had to send the servant once. Word came back that the child was dead.

*   *   *

Dead children everywhere: Hartley, her own baby, and now Alan, who had loved her. It was as though her touch, her very presence, brought death. Numbly, she had the mare Molly saddled and rode over at once. It had begun to rain and Lucy had put on her thick hunting-gear, with her hair bundled up into a net beneath the tall hat, and a veil tied over. The rain beat against her as she rode and by the time they galloped into Clonough yard, Lucy and the mare were soaked. There were several carriages in the yard. A groom came and Lucy handed him the mare to be rubbed down after being taken into the stables for shelter. Then she walked into the hall.

They were all there, the family and those who had come to condole. They were seated about the small coffin which still lay open. Inside lay Alan's body, its face showing no signs of any rash; perhaps that had been the danger, a rash should come out. Annis sat at

136

the head, stony-faced, and did not rise as Lucy entered. Beside her was Cathy, who, having like the peasants become a Catholic long ago, was telling her beads. Isabel O'Hara was of course present, seated starkly upright in her black hooded cloak, a thin presiding crow. Hubert, uncomfortable in his own formal blacks, made a move to welcome Lucy and lead her to the dead child. Annis rose at once. Her face was the colour of parchment and she had evidently shed no tears.

'You will not touch my son's body,' she said to Lucy. 'You killed him.' Her grating voice was clear and could be heard by everyone in the hall.

'Why, my—' Hubert made to put his arm round Lucy, then thought better of it; he loathed any kind of unpleasantness and would go out of his way to avoid it and be left in peace, as he had after all done when he allowed his half-sister to rearrange his own marriage. 'There's no need for all of that,' he finished weakly. Annis did not look towards him and he might as well have kept silent. They could hear the rain beating down outside.

'The children down at the cottages have caught it since you were here,' Annis continued pitilessly. 'Some of your own tenants' children at Fermisons will no doubt catch it also. A few of them will die. You brought it with you in some way; it wasn't here before. You killed my boy, and you will not

137

touch his body now or come near it, or stay in the house.' Her voice had risen to a harsh bird's cry, and Arthur Meggett-Clees, who was nearby, suddenly put a long sustaining arm about her shoulders. 'There, Annis,' he said. 'Hush, now.' His pale eyes stared at Lucy in hostile fashion. Nobody else spoke.

'As you do not want my company, I will leave,' replied Lucy quietly. 'I am sorry about all of it.' She turned to go, and Hubert gave an oath.

'By God, you can't ride back again in that rain,' he said. 'I'll drive you home. The mare can follow later.'

He guided Lucy out, her eyes still blurred with tears at not having been allowed to kiss the little dead child goodbye. Hubert jerked his head to the groom to harness the carriage-horses, saying Molly should be left in the stables and sent over when it had stopped raining. They set off. Hubert's mouth was still unwontedly grim: he seemed less in grief for the death of his son than anger at the behaviour of his wife.

'She's a hard woman,' he said. 'Try not to mind,' then in a quieter voice as they drove, 'She's a bitch. She hasn't let me near her since Alan was born. I've had to take housemaids or tavern women instead. When the boy died, Annis told me to my face it was a punishment for my sin. The thought of making another heir, if I'm let, is not pleasant.' He added

138

miserably that he supposed it would have to be done. On reaching Fermisons, he at first refused to come in, saying he must get back to the mourning women. 'Have some whiskey to warm you first,' said Lucy. The rain had stopped.

She herself took some with him, for she was shivering despite the drive; her soaked clothes clung to her and she longed to get them off. On the way back to the carriage she had said, to try and cheer Hubert, 'Look what I've done to improve the stables. You have to mind your head on the lintel; it was made in the days of the little Irish ponies we used to ride. Molly can't go in unless I dismount first. Otherwise, it's much better; come and see.'

He followed her, ducking his head, into the clean whitewashed stable with its grilles, its new hay mangers and fresh straw. Lucy took his hand to draw him inside. Suddenly, in the half-dark, he looked at her.

'My God, Lucy, I should have married you,' he said thickly. He began to sob suddenly like a child and laid his head against her shoulder. Lucy clasped him in her arms, to comfort him. 'Never mind,' she heard herself saying. 'There will be other sons, perhaps like Alan.' She knew no other child could ever be so, and that he knew it also.

She heard him give a great gasp, and then and in some manner, they were lying together in the straw; Lucy could not remember falling on her back. She let Hubert take her: it was the only natural and compassionate thing that could happen, Hubert's taking her now, in the stable straw. The familiar ugly head lay on her breast, as it should often have done if they had been married after all. Lucy heard herself murmuring to him still as though he were a child behaving as a man: and at the same time, knew that she should not have come back to Ireland, to bring nothing but trouble and death.

*   *   *

After a long time he rose, leaving her still lying there in the straw. 'Go now,' Lucy told him gently. 'I'll stay here for a while.' She wanted to be left alone, not yet to try to think or remember; only to sense, meantime, the clean smell of the straw where they had lain loving together, dry and warm after the incessant rain and the short cold drive. After a time it came to her that she hadn't heard the carriage drive off; Hubert must be still about. She recalled now, or thought she did, hearing a brief curse of his as he went out, having of course hit his head against the lintel. It was easily done, and like Hubert to forget to look out for it.

Lucy rose and shook out her skirts, brushing the loose ends of straw from them. When she went out she saw Hubert lying not far off on the ground, quite still, in the puddled yard. He was dead. She knew it even before she went and knelt down by him and took his head, his poor hurt ugly big head, in her lap. A slow trickle of blood came from the corner of his mouth because of her moving him at all. His heart wasn't beating any more.

*   *   *

Someone came. They must all have come, in the end, because Hubert's body was taken away as Sebastian's had been. Afterwards Lucy found herself lying on her bed, still in her soaked habit; they hadn't unlaced her. She was aware of pervasive cold again and got off the bed, starting to peel off her wet clothes and unlace her stays. The first thing to do, after all, was to get warm.

She found a dry chemise in the chest and put it on, and spread her riding-things over a chair to dry also. None of the women seemed to be about. Lucy turned to the door to call them, and saw Wandrell the steward standing there, as once before. She had no idea how long he had been watching: it was possible that he had seen her naked body. She reached for her riding-whip, kept in its slot in her belt, still on the chair with the rest of the clothes.

'Leave that,' he told her. 'I saw what happened. I saw everything.'

'Get out,' Lucy said. The man did not move. He said 'I saw you, with the straw still on your back, kneel down by himself later on, and him with straw on his coat. The pair of you were in there together, on the horses' straw, for long enough, and his lady left alone with her dead child at Clonough. You are a wanton, and I knew it from the beginning when you came here: you have no shame in you at all. I will tell the county all of it unless the next man in your bed is myself, this minute.'

He moved closer. 'You killed the heir, then lay with his father. Get on your back now; I'll show you I'm as good a man as he was, rest his soul. A man's what you need, the likes of you, and you will not rid yourself of me from here when all's said. Get on the bed; I'm your master.'

Lucy slashed out with the whip. 'Leave me,' she said. 'Be damned to you and say whatever you choose; tell anyone and everyone. Leave me—leave me—' At each saying of it she slashed out again and again, and saw, almost incredulously, his face break out in blood, a great weal rise by his mouth and another across his eye. She raised her knee and kicked out at him; he buckled then. He backed away, bent over in agony and cursing in an ugly fashion.

'I'll make the place too hot to hold you, Mistress Wint. You've signed your own doom this day. Not a house—arrgh—will receive you in these parts when I've done with my tale. Arrgh.' He clutched at his parts and staggered

142

out. Lucy went and put the hook on the door and the whip back in its holster. She found that she was trembling again violently, but with anger this time rather than cold. That was something, at any rate. After she was certain Wandrell had gone she put on a flannel wrapper and crept downstairs and poured herself more and more of the whiskey she had taken only today with poor dead Hubert. Already it seemed as if that also had happened in another life. Presently, drunk, she went back to bed and sobbed her soul out; for Alan, for Hubert, for lost Clonough, lost Fermisons, her home. There could be none now for her anywhere in Ireland. That man would do as he'd said, and nobody would doubt him; how else could Hubert have died in so foolish a way, hitting his head on a stable lintel? And she, a barren woman who brought only death, must move on, like the wanderer she had become; there was a curse upon her whatever she might do.

*   *   *

On the day of the double burial, Alan's and Hubert's, Lucy drove over, using the old carriage which sat always in Fermisons coach-house and which had hardly been used since her grandparents' time. The old dry girths made travel slow lest they snap their leather. At last the carriage stopped outside the gates of the church near Clonough, and Lucy knew the other mourners were already inside; the hearse waited ready, empty. When she made her own entry the place was full. The women averted their black skirts as she passed. No one acknowledged her. The two coffins, large and small, sat together on trestles at the end, near Clonough pew where Annis sat with bent head among the rest. Lucy herself had always sat there, and had gone too far now to turn back. It would not have occurred to her to sit anywhere but with the family. Cathy and Isobel, both in black, sat next Annis; Arthur Meggett-Clees was at the end beside the women. As Lucy was about to take her place, he rose.

'Lady Meggett has requested that you withdraw,' he said clearly, adding in a low voice 'Please go. You should not be here.'

The vicar had not yet arrived. Lucy made a little curtsey to the two coffins, went forward briefly and touched Hubert's in farewell; then turned and went out. As she walked to the door there was no sound from anywhere in the church except the hushing of her own skirts along the aisle. It should have been here that she walked down to marry Hubert, returning as now on his arm: the thought came to her clearly. She saw Wandrell's face, bruised but triumphant, at the back of the church. Perhaps he hadn't had to tell everyone; they would have spread it anyway, those he had told.

She went out and got again into the ancient

carriage and safely back home, and sat with her feet up in the drawing-room, again drinking whiskey. The great harp was still shrouded nearby, a persisting ghost. Nobody would ever string and play it now. She herself must go away, but not at once; it would seem like defeat, and she could not abandon the tenants till firm arrangements had been made for their welfare. It was probable that Lady O'Hara's recommended steward would no longer come.

*   *   *

She was right. Shortly a civil letter arrived with the postman's donkey from young Cawley, politely regretting that he could no longer take up the appointment offered him at Fermisons. He gave no reason. No doubt Isobel O'Hara had dictated the letter and had found Cawley a place elsewhere: good stewards were in demand. Wandrell had gone, and thankful as Lucy was at his departure there were things to be done which nobody meantime could see to except herself. She put on an old woollen gown from Boston days, tied a kerchief over her hair like a peasant, and went out to the dairy. Wryly, she wondered if Mehitabel Wint would approve of her now. Mehitabel would certainly have gone to milk her own cows, but would have been the last to have to do so for the reasons that had occurred lately and somewhat less lately.

145

The dairyman Timmy was milking his third cow as usual, and Lucy took on the fourth. She had been used, as a child at Clonough, to help with the milking sometimes as a treat. It was useful now to know exactly what to do. 'I'll take Jess, Timmy,' she called, and took down a scoured pail from the stack, dragging across a milking-stool with her free hand. The cow's flank was warm and smelled of rain, animal flesh, green fields and fresh grass and friendship. Lucy leaned her cheek against it, feeling the hard teat ease and pull under her fingers. The warm milk began to gush rhythmically into the pail and she felt triumph, the first for days. Timmy had said nothing at sight of her. No doubt he had heard as well; they would all have heard. They must get used to it, and so no doubt must she.

*   *   *

Timmy had four children and his wife was expecting another. Lucy asked him outright if any of them had caught measles. The man straightened from his pail and looked her in the eye, his thin face expressionless.

'Annie's sickening,' he said. 'The rest have had them, and so has the wife, and so have I. It's a thing that happens.' He looked at the ground, then up again, and said firmly 'Don't you trouble about what they say, Mrs Lucy. We all know you've been good to us. There was

146

more folk dying of starvation than measles before you came, with that Wandrell, him and his clattering tongue: never heed it, or any of them.' He added, without her questioning him, that Wandrell had gone off to Cork.

Lucy returned to the house a little comforted, and presently opened Wandrell's account-books. They were filled with a careful enough copperplate; so had young Cawley's letter been: they all learned it. She would manage well enough for herself meantime: as the months passed, matters would ease, though never again for her at Clonough. She would go in any case, with her head high, to church on Sunday as usual. That would be a beginning: they shouldn't keep her away.

*   *   *

The visit to church went off uneventfully, though still no one addressed Lucy. Some days later she heard carriage wheels drive up to the door of Fermisons: somebody had called. It proved to be Cathy, limping in by herself and carrying a small valise; the driver had already gone off. Lucy rose from her rent-book, aware of two things; that her own white fingers were stained with ink, also that Cathy had been crying. 'What is it?' she asked gently. Nobody had ever been allowed to know Cathy Meggett-Clees very well; she devoted her time to her house and her husband. Now—

'Oh, Lucy, please take me in for a time. Arthur—he—he is to get rid of me and marry Annis. He—they say ours was never a marriage. Annis has gone home to Meath meantime and he is at Clonough, and has sent already for the lawyers. He says he wants children to inherit, and I—' She broke down into ugly crying.

Lucy went and put her arms round the forlorn, hunched little figure. Cathy was more than usually to be pitied today, and one recalled hearing how the old lord, her father, would never willingly look at this crippled younger daughter when he had hoped for a second son: the servants had been instructed to stand in front of Cathy when her father passed by, or else hide her in their skirts.

'Cathy, were you happy with Arthur?' she asked. 'He was never good to you. Will it be so bad to be free?'

'He is my husband,' said Cathy obstinately. A flush spread over the pale hook-nosed face. Lucy led her to a chair. Cathy smelled of rough soap and housework; the man had used her as a servant, not a wife. Lucy began to stroke the roughened hair from which the hood had fallen back. Cathy wiped her eyes with her sleeve and began to speak almost calmly. 'Annis will stay at Meath till things are settled,' she said. 'It has been arranged between them since Hubert died.'

Lucy remembered the officious presence of Arthur Meggett-Clees himself at the end of the

148

church pew, telling her on Annis' behalf to leave Hubert's funeral and Alan's. 'I will tell you of it before you hear from others,' Cathy continued. 'Arthur says he can obtain an annulment of our marriage because he was forced into marrying me when under age, and against his will. Also I have become a Papist, as he calls it.' She smiled, her ravaged face breaking out into sudden secret radiance: then it grew stern. 'He says our marriage is nothing, and never has been,' said Cathy. 'That is not true.'

'Then he has consummated the marriage?' asked Lucy outright. No one had ever been certain. There was a pause; then Cathy, against Lucy's shoulder, nodded and hid her face in her hands. 'It happened twice,' she said in a low voice. 'He—Arthur—was drunk. He may not remember. Nobody can blame him, seeing the way I am; but I'm his wife.' She began to cry again, like a child: so many were like children. Lucy sat back, her mind coolly assessing the matter. It was impossible that Meggett-Clees wanted Annis, Hubert's widow, for anything but her money, which was essential to Clonough; that, and maybe after all children. 'Say nothing of it,' she advised Cathy, adding again 'Are you not best free of him, to lead your own life, enjoy your faith without constant reproach and unkindness? It could mean everything to you.'

'Husband and wife are one flesh,' said Cathy

obstinately. 'That is what Christ said and what the Church says also. Whoever parts them commits adultery.'

'Then you must undergo a medical examination to prove that you are a wife; the law will almost certainly ask that of you.' She did not know how she knew this. Cathy shrank away.

'No, no, I could never allow that—never, I—'

'Then if you will not allow it, they will make that a reason for annulling the marriage. Consider: you could stay here with me, and be of great help to me; I am quite alone. You have managed your own house well and you could manage mine. Think of it; by the end, or perhaps quite soon, I could leave you here, your own mistress, at Fermisons. I would come over now and again with my nephew and niece; whether we were here or not, you could always do as you chose.' She felt her mind running smoothly, coldly, having told her such things about the law and its cruelties as she had not known she knew. She felt the frail little body weaken and yield, and the stubborn mind would no doubt follow; she herself, the new cold person she had become, went on talking reasonably, clearly. 'The poor tenants at the cottages need someone to keep them fed and looked after,' she told Cathy. 'If some casual steward is left here alone again, he will cheat them once more to fill his own pocket; it

150

happens all the time. You could undertake all of that for me, and do it well; why not consider it?' A steward, however, would come, in any case, now Cathy was here, against whom no gossip had ever breathed a word; Isobel O'Hara at least would visit her sister. Lucy smiled. 'Why did you come to me, and not to Isobel?' she asked. Cathy's sad eyes lightened a little; she turned to the other.

'It is because of my faith,' she said. 'Sir Pat won't have a Papist staying in his house. It is one of the things in which Isobel lets him have his way; there aren't so many.' She smiled. 'I came here to you, Lucy. If you had turned me away, there would have been nowhere to go. I—I couldn't stay on alone at the farm, knowing what was happening at Clonough.'

She raised her head and stared across the room, perhaps seeing many things; the ghost of the old lord passing by, his eyes averted from her; the cruelties of her marriage; the future of Arthur and Annis, their unborn children's laughter she herself must never hear. 'I will stay,' she said, 'and I will pray for you, Lucy. I pray also for Arthur, each day and night of my life. He is my husband before God. One day we will meet one another again.'

Lucy rose. 'Let us send for tea,' she said, 'and take off your cloak. This is your home now; do as you will here.' She could not understand love of such a creature as Arthur Meggett-Clees. Annis was welcome to him,

151

and Cathy was welcome here instead.

*　　　*　　　*

It turned out as predicted. Cathy proved adept with the rent-books and with handling matters about the estate; the larger size of Fermisons after her farmhouse and vegetable-garden did not deter her; she was practical and full of determination, also an immense charity; the tenants came to love her and the servants obeyed her without question from the first. Lucy made her own quiet preparations to return to England, to Aylors and Jeremy's children. Young Lucius must soon have a tutor, the little Maria a governess and dancing-lessons; Jerry was too idle to see to any of that; perhaps he had been back to Boston again to see Sabine and young Luther, perhaps not. Neither he nor Sabine ever wrote. It was time she herself returned; but she did not want to leave Cathy alone until news had come about the annulment of the latter's marriage.

CHAPTER EIGHT

She had written off to Jeremy and to Papa, whom one supposed these days to be oftener at Aylors than formerly; his devotion to the little Maria by now largely stilled his

152

wanderings, and in a letter written some time before he had remarked once again how greatly she reminded him of Lucy's dead mother, Maria's namesake. However there was no reply from him on this occasion and Lucy took it that he had again wandered off abroad. That left Caterina to look after the children alone, and dutiful as she was in such ways, other company was needed for them. Lucy had selected her things to pack, waiting for no more word, when one day a horseman clattered up the drive at Fermisons. To her astonishment and delight, it was Jeremy himself. Lucy flew into his arms.

'Why, Jerry! Why did you not send word? I would have had dinner ready; as it is, Cathy is out at the cottages and I was to eat cold bacon by myself. Perhaps you have already eaten?' There was no doubt his breath smelled of wine. Jeremy Meggett smiled engagingly, the sun shining on his bright hair, and held her away from him, looking down at her.

'Lucy, you're as beautiful as ever,' he said slowly. 'No need to trouble about dinner; I ate it at Clonough.' He grinned, a thought shamefacedly. 'I've been staying there with Arthur for the past few days, truth to tell. We got to men's talk and one thing led to another, and he sent me up to Meath last week to visit Annis.' He grimaced. '*That* wasn't much of a treat; I'm happier to see you by far, but I've not been free to come over sooner.'

153

She hid her hurt that he had not come straight to her, had not even sent word of his presence in Ireland. 'How is Sabine?' she asked, turning away. Jeremy replied that he had been over lately to Boston, and had left Sabine still there with her father and stepmother and the small boy Luther. There would, he added, soon be a companion for the last.

'Again?' said Lucy. Her brother shrugged.

'You know the way it is; she's like a tigress. Births don't seem to give her any trouble, the way they—' He realised his tactlessness, and began quickly to speak of Luther K.'s second marriage, which so far had produced no results. 'Gertrude is determined to do her duty if she can, but the old man's not what he once was,' Jerry added, and winked. Lucy downed dislike for the whole situation; Sabine and the boy ought to be at home with her husband and the other children, not kept abroad in the hope of inheriting Quinty. One could not dislike Jerry, naturally, but he was inconsiderate; most men, after all, were.

'Did Sabine agree to be left?' she asked roundly, and Jeremy flushed a little.

'Truth to tell, I didn't say goodbye,' he said. 'There would have been a scene, and she'd have been upset in her present state: I left Gertrude to tell her I'd gone. It isn't for ever, after all; I'll be back and forth as usual. Old Napier wants to see me again in Scotland about the third steel consignment; Luther K. has entrusted me with all arrangements, naturally, though the Coxons don't like it and neither does Nat Passmore. Nat's only the office manager now; he hasn't got the persuasion needed for the Clydeside business, and he's the father of a growing family himself; I forget whether it's the second or the third arrival by this wife. The talk there was dull, at any rate; I was glad to come away.'

How thoughtlessly cruel you have grown, thought Lucy; but did not say it aloud.

She asked him about his two children left alone at Aylors; he had not seen either for some time. 'We'll both go over soon, and you must come with me,' he told her. 'It'll take your mind off things here.' He knew, of course, about her present situation; Arthur would certainly have told him, in course of their vaunted men's talk over the port. Lucy turned away. 'I will be glad to come with you,' she said. 'If I may, I'll stay at Aylors for a little. Cathy manages Fermisons very well.'

'That cripple,' said Jeremy contemptuously. 'One can't blame Arthur for the annulment; he'd endured the sight of her for years, and her comings and goings to the nuns.' He stretched his handsome limbs. 'Can't say he'll have much fun with Annis either, from what I saw in Meath,' he said. 'The house at Mackens was as cold as charity, no fires lit; and she's so damned ugly, and strait-laced as well. She's

155

preserving her reputation, of course, as a virtuous widow, for all she can't wait to get back to Clonough and her former position here. Arthur says he's heard from the lawyers that the annulment won't be too long delayed. He's impatient, naturally, to get his hands on the Fox-Strangways money again, to improve Clonough further. All in all, things have turned out for the best, I'd say.'

Lucy made a little motion of her hand to silence him; she had heard Cathy come quietly into the hall. The uneven footsteps came upstairs past the drawing-room; the dragging sound grew ever fainter then in the passages. Jerry grimaced.

'Can't endure cripples in the first place,' he said. 'Ought to have been a nun from the beginning herself, Arthur says. I must go back; we'll meet again.' He kissed her, and went off. Lucy watched him go with something less than her usual uncritical affection. He'd changed, she thought, grown hard and spoilt: no doubt the years of his marriage to Sabine, her adoration and constant scenes, had helped to make him so, and Luther K.'s dependence on him had added to his self-importance. Lucy thought of Sabine that night in her own solitary room upstairs, pressing her hands uselessly as she often did against her full breasts under the nightgown; they would never now feed a child, and Sabine was expecting her fourth. How strange life was! It was as well, perhaps, that Jeremy was lingering in Ireland; she herself couldn't, after all, leave Cathy till after news had finally come about the annulment.

*　　　*　　　*

When it came, Cathy and she were seated together in the downstairs parlour, sewing. The brief came by post and Cathy read it wordlessly and handed it to Lucy. Then she sat with the sewing put aside, turning her gold wedding ring on her finger. 'I will not part with this, whatever they say,' she remarked fiercely.

'Cathy, you are happy here. Forget the past, and go on as you are. You have made my house a welcoming place. I am going to go away for a little, to England, now that this news of yours has come, but I will return soon.' It was after all the waiting that had been so cruel; now, the other seemed to accept what had happened. They laid the brief aside. Cathy spoke aloud suddenly in her soft voice.

'Lucy, there is a thing I have been waiting to say to you, when you were about to go to England to visit the children; I know that you have been waiting here on my account. It is this; the poor nuns I visit for Mass have nowhere to go. The owner of their present house, where they went after fire destroyed their own convent seven years back, has died, and his son in England wants it for himself, to come over and hunt. Would you let them stay here, even for a little while? There are eleven of them. They would not waste the time. They would work. Let me show you what I have here.'

She plunged a hand in her reticule and brought out a piece of handmade Irish lace. It was so exquisite that Lucy held it out for some moments in awed silence. There was a repeated pattern of roses and shamrocks, crocheted in hundreds of tiny stitches with fine thread. 'They make a little money by selling that, and sewing delicate underwear for orders from Dublin and London,' Cathy said. 'They have no money at all except for what they make. They own nothing. Timmy the dairyman wants to emigrate, did he tell you? The nuns would milk the cows, smoke bacon and see to the tenants and the gardening. They can do anything in that way, and do it well.'

Lucy stared down at the immaculate lace. She was glad Cathy had some matter to occupy her mind other than the annulment. She herself had known, of course, that Timmy wanted to emigrate; he had told her some time ago, since the little girl Annie had died. It was for the children's sake rather than his own, he had said; there was work to be had in the States. He had refused Lucy's offer of help with the fare; he'd almost saved it up, he told her. No doubt others from the cottages would follow: she knew very well the nuns would come to stay.

'Do as you choose, Cathy,' she said gently. 'I told you that when you came.'

When the other had gone out, no doubt hurrying straight to her nuns, Lucy sat down at the rosewood writing-desk which had belonged to her mother, and wrote to Jeremy, still at Clonough. *I will be ready to come as soon as it may be done*, she wrote. *Cathy has enough to occupy her.*

She sent it off, and in passing looked at herself in the mirror. She had put on weight a very little, but otherwise seemed the same. When they were in London, she'd buy new clothes again, begin a new life. She knew very well that she had done with Fermisons, and with ostracism. It would hardly follow her across the Irish Channel; and there were after all the children.

*   *   *

The nuns moved into Fermisons, and quietly took charge of everything, the house and dairy, the laundry, the feeding of pigs from parings of vegetables grown in the garden. A sister dug that over as it had never been dug before; the long black oak table in what was now the refectory shone with beeswax polishing. The drawing-room was consecrated as a chapel and the Bishop came to dinner afterwards. The parish priest had already called to thank Lucy. The nuns were a silent order and said nothing,

159

but Cathy told Lucy they were praying for her.

'They are very grateful,' she said. Lucy noticed that Cathy herself was held in great respect among them, almost as though she, and not the old lady who had come with them, was the Superior. Cathy herself could not join the order, as she still considered herself Arthur's wife and so did the Church; but the world beyond moved on. Annis and Arthur were married up in Meath before Lucy left with Jeremy, who had been the groomsman there. The new couple returned quietly meantime to Clonough, and Lucy did not visit them. Jeremy, ready at last, and she herself departed together for Aylors before the year's end. Fermisons was in good hands and she would visit it again: her chief memory was of the great harp, re-strung already and shining in the new chapel beside the new altar. One of the nuns could play it at Masses and the other services they might have. It was a new beginning, though not the one Lucy had foreseen. She must be thankful.

CHAPTER NINE

Lucy and her brother drove up to Aylors on an afternoon in late autumn. Before they had even glimpsed the grey frontage of the house the tall thin stooping figure of the elder Lucius could be perceived, his head protected from the wind by a fur cap with earflaps he had acquired some years before in the Apennines. He was planting in the formal beds, but turned, peering short-sightedly, lacking the glasses he now by custom wore, at sound of the carriage.

'Papa,' cried Lucy, and tumbled out into his arms. Jeremy, more greatly accustomed than his sister to the sight of the old man, followed more calmly, reflecting that Lucy had after all lived most of her life at Clonough; to come home to Aylors was an event for her. He himself was used to it, regarded it as his home, the place he would in due course inherit; but there was hope also on the other side of the Atlantic. He watched indulgently while the old gentleman returned Lucy's kiss, then promptly began expatiating on the shrubs and plants he was digging in with such care. They were, he explained, descended directly from a garden in Pompeii before the eruption. 'They used to be confined in beds behind criss-crossed canes; the holes of these have been found in the ground after excavation. I will do the same thing here. It remains to be seen how they will react to the English winter, however,' Lucius Meggett added thoughtfully. It was evident that he was by far more interested in the plants than in the arrival of his son and daughter, and he soon turned back to the beds. Lucy did not re-enter the carriage, leaving it to trundle up to the main door with their baggage. She had picked up her skirts, brand new and of an olive green colour, and made her way past Papa's cherished beds towards the lawns and the sunken garden, hearing laughter there. It came from her nephew and niece, who were playing battledore back and forth over the old sundial. Lucy stood watching them, smiling and meantime unobserved.

Little Maria would certainly be a beauty; she resembled oneself at that age, with the tossing golden curls perhaps a little darker in colour than Lucy's own. Lucius was still grave and pale, handling his battledore awkwardly, and often missing the shuttle: it reminded her of Sebastian. Her nephew had the face of a scholar, though why was uncertain; he resembled no one in the family at all. She remarked on it to Jeremy, who had come up behind her.

Young Lucius' godlike father shrugged. Unless Sabine had been unfaithful at the beginning, which was as unlikely then as now, there had been no scholars whatever in the inheritance unless one counted Papa: however the latter was less interested in books than in the ancient world and all it contained, pillars, vases, statues, and now plants. Meantime the two children had heard voices, and hastened up out of the sunken garden, still holding their bats. They remembered beautiful Aunt Lucy, and of course saw their handsome father now and again. As for Mama, she was far away with

162

the little brother they had never met. They presented their cheeks politely to be kissed.

'We have interrupted your game,' said Lucy.

'It was our duty to stop,' replied her nephew. Maria giggled. Lucius was always saying things like that, having had them fed into his head by the vicar at church on Sundays. She put her head to one side, admiring Aunt Lucy's fashionable clothes, especially her hat, which had a curled green feather and matched her laughing, creamy-lidded eyes. Such things were beginning to interest young Maria, who had a brain fashioned mostly of feathers. Aunt Lucy took her in one hand and Lucius in the other and they all returned to the house together, as it was growing cold. Maria blew a kiss with her free hand to Grandpapa, who was still busy with his plants; he waved back to her, and presently came in for tea with earth still on his fingers. They all talked pleasantly together; it was not often that the family met in such strength. As for Grandmama Caterina, she did not come down from where she was everlastingly busied upstairs, dusting things or else saying her rosary. Italians did not drink tea.

*   *   *

The days passed amiably and everyone helped to water old Lucius' Pompeian discoverings.

'Don't overdo it,' said he to the children, 'it makes the roots weak.' Lucy suggested that he put straw round to protect the delicate imported plants from the coming winter; she had successfully grown an arbutus at Fermisons in this way. She shut her eyes for a moment remembering: Clonough, Fermisons, Ireland, lost forever, and nuns left in the garden digging potatoes. Well, it was for the best. She opened her eyes to find her father's gaze regarding her keenly, surprisingly the colour of grey steel beneath the heavy lids she herself had inherited; but her mouth came from her mother, and Maria Flaherté's smiling portrait looked down on them now from the wall.

'You can't teach an old dog new tricks, my dear,' said Papa gently about the plants. Lucy wondered how much else he knew about her: he evidently listened to more than one thought.

*   *   *

Some weeks later, a carriage bowled up; it was the last fine day they had to spend in the garden. Out of the carriage erupted a slender dark figure in furs. It was Sabine. She made straight for Jeremy and flung her arms about his neck.

'Jerry. Oh, thank God. I thought I would never see you again, it's been so long. They wouldn't let me come to you, my father and that new bitch. They kept me locked in a room until I hammered on the door day and night. Why should I have to stay on with them? They had to let me go in the end, I gave them no peace. Oh, Jerry, Jerry, say you're pleased to see me. Jerry, Jerry, Jerry.' She punctuated the words with kisses. Her maid had followed her out of the carriage quietly. Sabine had taken no notice of her children, who were staring as though she were a stranger, which she was.

Jeremy was frowning. He freed himself from Sabine's clinging grasp. 'Where is young Luther?' he asked coldly. 'You have surely not left him behind?'

'Why not? He's well looked after; my father dotes on him, and they haven't any yet of their own. I wanted to come back to you, only you. Why aren't you glad to see me? Why won't you kiss me? You went away without even saying goodbye.'

As always with Sabine, it was as if there was nobody else present. Jeremy glanced at his sister in faint despair. They could see for themselves, his glance said, what he'd endured; and now here was Sabine at Aylors, and another baby expected within the next few weeks; its presence was evident when the furs were removed. Lucy turned to the two staring children. 'Kiss your Mama,' she said tactfully. They obeyed with civility, and everyone went into the house.

165

*　　　*　　　*

Over the ensuing weeks Lucy became increasingly concerned about her niece Maria. The child was old enough to notice certain things, and to imitate; when Sabine made one of her frequent scenes Maria began to follow suit. It was useless to expect the nursery governess to cure matters; she was a stout personage who had been found earlier on and who, Lucy was privately convinced, indulged in the bottle when alone; she did not at any rate recognise one when met with in the narrow upstairs passages, and her eye had a glazed look almost constantly. Moreover, Maria knew nothing about anything except what pleased her. It was time to find someone else, and Lucy suggested writing to an agency. She had earlier murmured discreetly about a possible school for young ladies in the near future, but old Lucius would have none of it. He liked, he said, to see Maria's curls tossing in the sunshine whenever he came home. Her silliness did not seem apparent to him; he adored her unquestioningly because she resembled her grandmother. On being assured, however, that at the present rate of things she might well grow up into somebody no one of perception would ever marry, he capitulated. 'Old Polly Mitchell has been drunk for years,' he admitted. 'She used to be

166

in love with the groom here, and he went off to Northampton.'

He and Jeremy between them agreed to the sacking of Miss Mitchell provided Lucy undertook it herself to save them trouble: and meantime there was her visit to the London agency, which had replied with promptness. She went there, interviewed several candidates, and decided firmly on one, a small plain sandy-haired bespectacled creature named Jane Ker. It was an economical name and the governess herself was a Scot. However she agreed on the necessity of properly spoken English, also the use of the globes and a grounding in history, French and arithmetic. She had left her last post after eight years, when her employer, a widower, had died and the youngest children been sent off to school. Her age was twenty-seven. It seemed highly suitable. She would come to Aylors in ten days' time.

Lucy meantime had to persuade Maria, who had been used to easy-going old Polly Mitchell and her ways, that it was necessary to equip herself to go out into the world later on, enjoy a season, attend balls and parties, and become a presentable young lady. 'You didn't ever have to learn sums very much, Aunt Lucy,' Maria said resentfully; she had heard of Lucy's carefree youth in Ireland. Lucy shut her eyes and remembered the warm, lazy days at Clonough, sharing Hubert's tutor, understanding Latin first of all by way of words carved in mossy stone on an old grave. 'I learned Latin, a little,' she said, smiling. 'It is not necessary for a girl; but you will learn to draw and to dance, for we will send for a dancing-master once Miss Ker comes.'

Thus bribed, Maria awaited the arrival of Jane Ker off the post-coach, carrying her own sparse belongings in a wicker hamper. Lucy made her known to Maria and to young Lucius, who of course would share lessons meantime. The governess would take her meals with them in the schoolroom. Her bed was that formerly occupied by Miss Mitchell, in a small room of its own; it was no more than an iron bedstead such as servants used, but Miss Ker's plain little face flushed with sudden delight. 'It is a privilege to have a separate room,' she said, 'and one's privacy.' Her speech was precise, somewhat pedantic, and contained no trace whatever of a Scots accent.

'What did you have previously?' Lucy enquired. Jane Ker replied that it had been a mere cubicle, curtained off in a corner of the children's room. She surveyed the humble iron bedstead now as if it stood in kings' palaces.

*   *   *

Time passed, and Maria settled down and showed an improvement in her manners: it was not necessary to point out to Miss Ker that the mother was difficult. Polly Mitchell had departed meantime without regret from anyone, shedding a few bibulous tears, and was soon forgotten. One day old Lucius asked his granddaughter when the Battle of Hastings had been fought, and why. Maria answered correctly, and the old gentleman was delighted.

'Don't turn her into a bluestocking, however,' he warned Jane Ker. 'She's too pretty to need it.'

Miss Ker smiled primly behind her metal-rimmed spectacles, which depended from a black cord pinned to her sandy hair. The remark had not been entirely tactful. However if one's employers were pleased, that was the main point. She herself made so unobtrusive a presence in the house that no one downstairs noticed her, as Lucy had already noted. She was glad her choice was proving a success.

*   *   *

'Deaths never come singly.' Lucy could remember Isobel O'Hara's smug, predictable saying of it in Ireland long ago, before the thing had happened in her own personal experience; it was one of the remarks one remembered having heard. Now, it happened again; less closely than before, except for one only: and for that Lucy could not blame her own presence; not this time.

First of all she had been saddened to read in

169

the papers of Isabella Napier's sudden death at Shandon. The old man would be quite alone; Lucy wrote to him, thanking him once again for the remembered hospitality to herself there on that earlier visit with Jeremy, when she had seen the paintings. There was no acknowledgement except for a formal black-edged card; she had expected nothing more, and Jeremy, who had gone north for the funeral, told her that Robert Napier had ceased to take any interest in living after his wife's death. 'It shouldn't have surprised him; they were both old,' said Jeremy callously. However the death of the old millionaire himself soon followed, as if he had wished himself quit of a life he no longer either enjoyed or needed. Jeremy travelled up again for the second funeral, which was an immense affair, with lines of waiting workmen stretching along the roads between Clydeside and Rhu church, where the packed service of notables was held; it reminded Lucy, when she heard, of Mehitabel's obsequies long ago in Boston, with the workmen in tears, their caps in their hands, heads bowed in remembrance. Jeremy agreed that the whole thing had been impressive. 'He didn't take any interest in the business latterly,' he said. 'The sons have it now; there will be changes.' He smiled a little, and Lucy knew, not for the first time, that he had more in his mind than he would meantime tell anyone, even herself.

On return, Jeremy stayed infrequently at Aylors, making increasingly long visits to London, he said to see about the possible Admiralty contract for Quinty which had developed out of the Clydeside visits. Sabine however was convinced that he spent his time with women, and made jealous scenes whenever he returned home; so he returned the less often. Lucy, on the contrary, guessed that Sabine's incessant demands on her husband caused Jeremy to seek even more of the male company with which he had always felt at home, the sporting fraternity. When at Aylors, he would go out early to hunt, returning late; and if Papa was at home would drink port with him and talk till all hours. Old Lucius however departed abroad again shortly, this time once more to Ephesus. Lucy waved him off and turned back into the house; she no longer accompanied Jeremy to the hunt. It made Sabine envious, and there was the latest baby, a little girl, to whom Sabine had lately given birth and who was now upstairs in her cradle in the nursery. They had called her Horatia at Papa's suggestion, as she had been born on the anniversary of Trafalgar.

Jeremy had gone off two days after old Lucius, weary of women's company and demands. Lucy reflected that she and he saw little of one another alone nowadays. However he returned, and they sat together in amicable converse for once without Sabine, who was

171

upstairs having her long hair washed by her maid. The children were with Jane Ker, and the baby was quiet; she gave little trouble in any case, and there was a young country girl who acted as nurse.

Jeremy stretched out his long shapely legs in the chair in the way he had used to do, and held his glass of Scotch whisky up to the light with appreciation. 'There's nothing like this stuff,' he said. 'It beats your Irish whiskey hollow.' He had got into the whisky habit on Clydeside, and began to talk as usual about the latter. Lucy quietly decided that when she drank at all, she preferred the Irish, extra e or not; but she had discouraged the habit in herself since coming home. She folded her hands and watched Jeremy drink; he was putting on more weight than ever, perhaps resembling Bacchus by now rather than Apollo; but he still made women's heads turn wherever he went, always would, and knew it.

He winked now above the glass. 'Don't say a word to Sabine, but I've been up north again, since the last funeral,' he told Lucy. 'Old Napier's sons are interested in buying Quinty. If the old man in Boston would agree to sell, it'd be better from all points of view. It would save journeys back and forth across the Atlantic; the Napier contingent could make those for themselves. I could invest the money for young Luther profitably over here: I can get good advice in the City.' He frowned into the depleted whisky. 'I don't want him to grow up as an American,' he said. 'If he wants to enter the shipping business on this side when he's old enough, that can be arranged. It's time I went across myself to persuade old Luther K.'

'He may not agree,' said Lucy. 'There's his new marriage.' It was not so very new by now; and there had still been no sign of a child, to maintain the hoped-for dynasty. 'That bitch Gertrude, and her brother, may make difficulties, but what good has she been to anyone?' remarked Jerry. 'It remains to be seen; I keep a foot in both camps. Personal contact is important.' He poured himself more whisky.

'Don't speak of this to everyone,' Lucy warned him. 'Remember the Coxons may resent it, and they are with Luther K. all the time. You've just mentioned personal contact.' Jerry frowned more deeply, his elegant eyebrows drawing together below his still thick, tumbled hair.

'I want my son over here,' he said. 'It's all very well while old Luther is alive; but what if he dies suddenly, like Napier himself? The boy will be left with the Coxons, who have no particular reason to love him. Some time, you and I will go across to bring him back.'

She was prevented from replying by the sound of hushing skirts on the stairs: Sabine came down, lovely as ever, her dark hair soft, clean, dressed and scented. She went straight to Jeremy and kissed him on the mouth.

'Bad boy, you've been drinking whisky again,' she said. 'Why didn't you say you would be back early? I wanted to make myself look pretty for you, and you came before I was ready.'

She glanced at Lucy with a look that was scarcely friendly, and the latter rose at once and said she would go up to the baby. Jerry raised his glass in a secret toast between them; Sabine had her eyes fixed on his face and did not see the gesture.

Once staring down into Horatia's cradle, Lucy remembered her brother's talk about selling out Quinty to the Scots firm. It all sounded rather too easily achieved; Jerry no doubt overrated his own influence with Luther K. Wint. His suggestion that she herself go across to help bring home young Luther appealed to Lucy despite herself: she had no particular wish however to encounter the old lecher again, still less Gertrude Coxon Wint. Nevertheless it would be pleasant to be away from Sabine's scenes and the feeling that she herself was no longer welcome at Aylors. Lucy downed guilt in the matter; Sabine ought perhaps to come with them as well, and that left the children alone again; but there was always Jane Ker, who was reliable: and it might not be for long, whichever way things were in the end decided, both about young Luther and the business.

174

*   *   *

The prospect of the voyage was delayed by an unforeseen circumstance: the third death, that of old Lucius Meggett himself. He died happily, digging on an Ephesian site where, as he had lately written to Lucy, he had found the head of a Corinthian column which had almost certainly been part of the ancient library there. *I am intrigued also by evidence of a club for men, situated in the public lavatory in the main street,* he wrote. *Think of sitting in comfort in one's toga, discussing the news of the day each morning and evening with trusted friends, perched on the seats adjoining, while the street outside is being washed down with clean water! We ought to introduce such a custom in England.* The letter had arrived after news came of his death: he had already left instructions that his body was to be cremated and the ashes scattered over the low field of wild yellow mustard below Troy, where Achilles had long ago dragged the body of vanquished Hector round and round below the gaze of the latter's young widow and his father, King Priam. Perhaps, Lucy thought, her own father had expected to die near the place. A packet of little wild poppy seeds found by him above on the high rock among the timeless ruins was forwarded to Lucy, but did not grow. Caterina the widow showed no outward signs

175

of grief and went on as she had always done, occupied with her personal cooking and dusting and her prayers, which now included those for the soul of her dead husband.

CHAPTER TEN

Maria cried a little for poor dead Grandpapa, then forgot him. As for Jeremy, he was now the squire of Aylors. No doubt as a result of celebrating this event, Sabine found herself once more already returned to that state wherein ladies are said to like to be who love their lords. This time she was not very well, and suffered a great deal from morning sickness. For her sake, and also because he hoped for yet another son—young Lucius was disappointing to his father, preferring his books to his pony— Jeremy postponed the Boston voyage for rescuing young Luther meantime; the matter of the Quinty sale accordingly hung fire until old Luther K. should be persuaded personally. However in the end, the new squire of Aylors was further chagrined; the baby proved yet another girl, born prematurely. She was christened Maude, put in the nursery with her sister who was crawling about determinedly upstairs, and looked after by the same young country girl as before, who seemed trustworthy. Miss Ker would of course remain in charge of the older children. Sabine was still low, and to cheer her, also to leave Jeremy to his own devices for a time, Lucy nerved herself to write to Annis Meggett-Clees in Ireland; might she bring Sabine and the two older children over for them to see Clonough? *I myself will stay with the nuns at Fermisons*, Lucy finished tactfully: it would avoid awkwardness to make that matter clear at the outset.

Annis replied civilly, saying she would be glad to welcome Sabine, Lucius and Maria; the latter could play with her and Arthur's own baby daughter Eithne, now aged two. She made no mention of Lucy's accompanying them, and Lucy did not expect to be asked to stay at Clonough: it had however healed the breach a little to have Annis' letter at all. Also, there had been a particularly unpleasant scene lately at Aylors: she wanted to take Sabine away for everyone's sake meantime: she was sullen and miserable, and Jeremy would have nothing to do with her.

*   *   *

It had happened in this way. Jeremy had for some time been poring over the Clydeside blueprints and estimates. The latter were in an old clerk's cramped hand difficult to read, and Lucy suspected that her brother did not follow the conclusions adequately enough to a degree calculated to change the existing plans of

Luther K. Wint. With the best of intentions, and very tactfully, Lucy suggested that as the governess Miss Ker was a mathematician she might be able to help. Jeremy, who might well have stood on his dignity in such matters as a member of the superior sex, agreed with open relief. 'If anybody can make sense out of it all it's more than I can,' he admitted.

Miss Ker was allowed to pore over the crabbed estimates, and shortly made a written résumé of the whole thing which was clear even to Jeremy. He thanked her cordially in person. 'Perhaps you will help me again,' he said. 'There's a good deal of this damned stuff coming down.'

The little governess had flushed pink with pleasure, in the way she had done when she had first glimpsed her humble private bedroom. She replied politely that it was a matter of algebra, to which she always reduced everything of the kind to make it understandable.

Thereafter she was frequently consulted while the negotiations lasted, and after some kind of temporary agreement was reached Jeremy had already begun to drop in, idly entertained, at the children's lessons now the hunting season was over for the year. Lucy was occasionally present and had been so from the beginning; not only did she like to watch the children's progress, but Miss Ker's own wide erudition surprised and interested her: an

178

astonishing variety of knowledge was contained in the plain little head, and Jane Ker imparted it clearly and without fuss, making everything easy to understand and follow. She was in fact a born teacher. Lucius, who had been put down some time previously for Harrow, drank in all information gravely. He was particularly interested in history and would make, Lucy had decided, either an Oxford don or else a politician, depending on events. She hoped young Luther, far across the sea, was being equally well instructed. They had written lately from Boston that he had a tutor from nearby Harvard, and was progressing. This was not enough to know; Lucy's conscience nagged at her increasingly about that solitary child, left from the beginning without company of his own age. He ought to be here at Aylors with his brother and sisters, whether or not he was the Quinty heir or shares were bought and sold, or even if Gertrude produced a baby after all.

Sabine, the only unfailingly fertile member of the family, occasionally visited the Aylors schoolroom herself, but only because Jeremy was to be found there nowadays; otherwise she showed no interest in the lessons. Her jealousy in fact impelled her to interrupt now and again with stupid, uncalled-for remarks; once Jeremy turned his head and quelled her. 'You don't know the first thing about it,' he snapped. 'Keep quiet if you can't listen.'

It was the wrong thing to have said in the presence of Sabine's children and of her inferior in status. Soon after, on a day when Jeremy was not present, Sabine appeared again with a pair of embroidery scissors. Miss Ker was wearing her usual gown, which in fact was her only one, and on its unexciting surface was a narrow braid trimming. Sabine marched to the head of the schoolroom table.

'You shouldn't have any ornament on your dress,' she said clearly. 'Have it removed at once. Servants don't wear braid unless they're footmen. I was taught that at my finishing school.'

She accosted the young woman and began jabbing and snipping with the scissors, tearing at the stuff of the bodice itself as she ripped the braid off with vicious wrenching white fingers. Miss Ker dared to protest, even to resist a little. Lucy hurried over and tried to drag Sabine away, but too late. The children watched in silence, shocked and entranced. 'Please,' said Jane Ker, 'it is my only gown.' She was almost in tears behind the cord-anchored spectacles. 'I promise that I will remove the braid myself in my room if it is objected to. *Please*,' but Sabine went on snipping and tearing, more savagely by now. Lucy was still trying to pull her away. 'Sabine, stop that at once,' she said sharply. At that moment Jeremy himself appeared at the door, still in his riding-coat.

180

'What—' he said incredulously, then, seeing, strode over and slapped Sabine hard across the face. She dropped the scissors and burst into tears. The dishevelled governess fled. What followed was witnessed by nobody except Lucy and the children. Maria's eyes held understanding, even enjoyment; she was growing up too fast.

'This is enough,' said Jeremy. 'No one knows what I've put up with from the beginning; you are insatiable, jealous, you make constant scenes, and now this. You will pay for a new gown for that poor girl yourself and Lucy shall take her into town to buy it. Meantime I am moving into a room of my own and I will lock my door. That is my final word; scream the place down if you want.' He jerked his head towards Lucy, his face red with anger. 'See to the matter of the gown at once,' he said. 'Take Miss Ker to London in the carriage tomorrow. Buy whatever else she needs; she doesn't have much.' He cast a handful of sovereigns on the table, turned and went out. Sabine tried to run after him but he had already slammed the door, and she stayed weeping quietly. Lucy scooped up the money: it was unlikely, despite Jeremy's command, that they'd get any out of Sabine; she was like a madwoman nowadays. If Jeremy really wouldn't sleep with her any more, they would have to lock her door as well if the household was to have any peace. It was at this point that

Lucy had thought of the visit to Ireland.

*   *   *

Meantime, she and a subdued Miss Ker—'I am sorry to have caused so much trouble'— departed in the carriage next day for town. Jane Ker had meantime stitched up the tear in her bodice and had carefully removed the rest of the offending braid, which concession left her looking plainer than ever. 'It was not you who caused it,' Lucy assured her. 'It is at least a generation since governesses were discouraged from wearing braid, or from making themselves attractive in any way at all.' She stared unobtrusively at the young woman during the journey, trying to think of what might suit her best. It would be pleasant to buy a becoming gown that flattered the sandy hair, discounted the lack of eyelashes and somehow enhanced the flat, unenticing figure. Did governesses enter their profession because there was no hope otherwise, or did the fact of being one cause them to become as they tended to appear? One must be careful not to purchase anything to which a new employer would object, although it was unlikely Miss Ker would lose her present situation: on the contrary, Jerry had issued a fiat that in future she was to eat dinner downstairs with the family, and no longer as, till now, in the schoolroom. It would enliven the conversation,

182

certainly; Miss Ker was intelligent enough to be good company, given the opportunity: Lucy had already discovered as much.

In the end they purchased a gown which was of an unusual shade between old rose, which would have been too frivolous, and lilac, which meant half-mourning. It had set-in, narrow frills of its own material down the bodice and skirt. Poor Jane drew a breath at first sight of it. 'Oh, Mrs Wint, I wouldn't dare wear it, it's so pretty,' she ventured. Lucy laughed. 'Why shouldn't you wear a pretty dress?' she asked. 'It does no harm to anyone.'

When they returned, Sabine was nowhere to be seen; evidently a tray had been sent up to her room by order until she could learn to behave herself. There were, accordingly, four people downstairs at dinner; Caterina in her blacks, who never in any case said anything; Jeremy, shovelling in his food like any hungry man; Lucy herself, and the governess toying nervously with her fork and, very occasionally, saying something shyly when addressed. She was wearing the new dress, and had brushed her hair till it shone.

*   *   *

The Irish crossing took place without incident; Sabine was no doubt glad to get away from durance, and the change would do her good. Maria, excited, was wearing a new dark green

183

dress and hat and looked very pretty. On arrival, the Clonough carriage was waiting, evidently with instructions to drive Lucy first to Fermisons and leave her there. She kissed the other three goodbye, waved them off, and entered what had once been her home, with Cathy serene and smiling, but very thin now, in the hall; everything was subtly different, cared for, chilly and silent. Lucy spent a few days peacefully among the quiet nuns, watching their activities other than prayer; the gardening, the beekeeping—she'd never tried it—and the continuing prosperity of the pigs and cattle; the cottages were turned into a row of adjoining single cells and the tenants had gone, to Australia and America. Fermisons had, in other words, changed from a house to a convent; she herself knew she would never drive the order out even if Cathy were to die. This last seemed possible; Cathy seemed very frail, and spent her life in mortification which Lucy could never have endured, kneeling for hours on the marble floor of the converted chapel where the harp still stood; hardly eating, and never now touching meat. 'Take a little to strengthen you,' Lucy told her, but Cathy said she had her strength from God. It was clear that she would be happy to be rid of her life, and to meet God face to face, as she anticipated. Arthur and Clonough, the man and the place beloved, were never mentioned between the two women. Lucy hoped privately

184

that Sabine was causing no storms there. However all seemed to have gone well. Maria rode over by herself once or twice, at last to say that the carriage would call for Aunt Lucy on Tuesday, thereafter to return them all to the English packet. She chattered excitedly about Clonough. 'I can understand why you loved it so much,' she told Lucy, 'it's so beautiful. Lord Meggett showed me himself round the stables and the farm, and the piggery. It's a pity he has such an ugly wife. She never smiles. Eithne is ugly as well.'

Lucy remarked charitably that ugly children sometimes turned into beautiful women, or perhaps even clever ones. Reading between the lines, it sounded as if Annis now treated her second husband as she had treated poor Hubert; there had at any rate been no more children. 'Mama has behaved herself,' said Maria, taking her cue from matters at home. Lucy did not reply and instead took the girl out to see the beehives; a sister was tending them, and beside her was Cathy, her sleeves rolled up above the elbow, bees crawling unconcerned over the wasted flesh as Cathy bent her hunched spine over the frames.

'Weren't you afraid?' asked Maria curiously afterwards. 'You might have been stung all over.' It was strange to see the pair of them, the ugly dying cripple and the bright-haired girl, confronting one another beyond the now safely distant hives. Cathy gave her strangely

185

luminous smile; she had gained a serene contentment here over the years. 'Bees know when one is not afraid,' she replied quietly. 'They know a great many things.'

They left her standing at the great door, her hunched figure wrapped in its great felt cloak, and drove off in the departing carriage. Lucius and his mother sat opposite, saying nothing. Sabine continued wrapped in silence on the journey and had no doubt maintained it for most of the Clonough visit: it was as though she had no existence at all without Jeremy. Asked if she had enjoyed the visit, she replied that it had gone well enough.

'Why isn't Aunt Cathy a nun?' asked Maria. 'She lives with them.'

Lucy explained that as Cathy was a married woman and her husband was still alive, she could not join the order. 'Who is her husband?' Maria asked pertly. Lucy would have turned the question in some manner, but Sabine answered suddenly and bitterly. 'Her husband is married to another wife, whom you have just visited. Men have no constancy: remember that.'

'Some men are constant,' put in Lucy gently; she did not want young Maria to grow up in the expectation of being betrayed: and Jeremy had been a faithful enough husband, as things were.

*   *   *

186

They arrived home to find the two younger girls surprisingly grown, and Horatia prattling. Life seemed to settle down to its usual pattern at Aylors; Jeremy had been home, had left and then returned again, one supposed from Scotland. The governess, still in her subtly coloured gown with its narrow frills, resumed lessons with Lucius and Maria, who however was restless and inattentive since the Irish visit; too much had perhaps been made of her over there. Now that Papa was dead there was no reason not to send the girl off to school, which might cause her to settle more readily. Old Lucius would never as he had said have parted with Maria; he had liked to be able to send for her as soon as he came home, and ruffle her bright curls with his fingers.

*   *   *

Jeremy returned, but would still take nothing to do with Sabine. He continued to sleep in his separate room on the middle floor, situated near Lucy's own. One morning she had for some reason been out very early indeed to walk on the lawn, not having slept; she was often assailed by restlessness of the kind Luther K. had foreseen. As she was about to re-enter her room she saw Jeremy, still in his nightshirt, come quietly down the turn of the stairs from where the governess slept; there

187

was nobody else up there. The eyes of the brother and sister met. Later, with his shamefaced grin, Jerry referred to the matter when they were alone, with Sabine out of earshot.

'I'm not doing her any harm,' he said of Jane Ker. 'We got acquainted, as one might put it, while you were away. They have drab lives; it'll give her something to remember for a change. When it's finished she can have a reference and go on to the next place. She's discreet; I find her restful for a change.'

His heartlessness shocked Lucy, even though she knew how irresistible he must be to women. To Jane Ker, with her flat uninteresting little body and short sight, Jeremy's nocturnal visits must seem like a god's. Lucy wondered how long it had really been going on; outwardly the governess was the same, going about her duties adequately and attracting no notice. Lucy was aware that her own feelings sprang not from outraged propriety—she supposed she ought to feel this—but from her own frequently suppressed bodily urges, which had troubled her last night again so strongly that she could not sleep; it sometimes happened. What was it Luther K. had said on parting? *I've left you so's you'll never be able to do without a man in your bed for long.* Well, she had none, and perhaps never would again since the matter of Hubert and the lintel. Meantime, she could not mention the affair of Jane to Sabine—that would be a disaster—or to Caterina; yet it seemed improper to allow it to continue, mostly for young Maria's sake.

Not knowing what to do, Lucy waited and did nothing. Sabine herself precipitated what happened next: she was found howling, a few nights later, outside Jeremy's locked door in her nightgown, rattling at the handle, her hair loose about her, late at night after the household had gone to bed. By good fortune Jeremy was not with the governess. His wife hammered on the door and demanded to be let in.

'I'm your wife. I want you. It's been a long time. Don't shut me out. I love you, I love you, I love you. You can't keep me out of your life forever. Jerry, Jerry, let me in, let me in; you're not asleep. Let me come in to you, the way it used to be.'

He opened the door at last, angry that the house should have been alerted, that he had in fact been made to look a fool. The only thing to do was to keep Sabine quiet in the usual way. 'Oh, for God's sake come in, then, if you must,' he muttered impatiently, took her by the wrist and hauled her inside. There was the sound of passionate kissing, then silence, then the customary creaking of the bed. Lucy had gone back to her room, her own senses churning in her. If only she herself could go to a man's bed! Her life wasn't spent; neither was

189

she, by any means. She passed the night tossing restlessly, once again unable to sleep.

Next day the governess came to her red-eyed, and said she wanted to leave. 'I will work out my notice,' she said colourlessly. She had changed back into her old plain mended gown.

'Where will you go?' said Lucy, trying not to put too much compassion into her voice; it would be pointless and not helpful: they both knew in some way that the other knew what had happened. Jane Ker replied that there had been a post she had lately seen advertised for a mathematics mistress at a girls' school near Doncaster. If she could have a reference, she would apply; it might not be filled yet.

Lucy had a sudden inspiration. Maria should go to school in Doncaster, with Jane. Apart from this recent lapse—and who could have resisted Jeremy?—there could be no better person to keep an eye on the girl's manners and her education than Jane Ker. Lucius could go to Harrow, and they themselves, Jerry, Sabine and herself, could leave the little girls at Aylors with their nurse and all three travel in the autumn to Boston to retrieve young Luther, and perhaps finalise the vexed matter of Quinty itself. It was as though Providence had arranged it all.

*   *   *

The brownstone Boston house looked much

the same as they drove up at last, large, opulent and shouting down its comparatively pedestrian neighbours. Inside, however, Luther's second wife had made what Lucy privately thought were disastrous changes, no doubt in the prevailing fashion. Mehitabel's Shaker furniture, in old days so carefully polished, cherished and tended to maintain its rare light woods and dedicated craftsmanship, had disappeared: in its place stood ugly, prosperous mahogany and chenille whose looped curtains shut out most of the daylight. Gertrude Coxon Wint flourished in this rarefied atmosphere like an aspidistra, several of which she had in any case introduced here and there in brass pots as they were known to survive most things without attention. It would likewise be difficult to kill Gertrude. She had welcomed them doucely, being of no notable appearance until one looked into the lowered eyes. These were the colour of mud, small, determined and hard as pebbles. Mehitabel's successor was neat, deft and quick in her movements, and had a soft credulous way of speaking which disguised what were in fact steely purposes: these were not immediately manifest, but Lucy suspected them from the start. Gertrude's brother Wilbur Pryde Coxon was in the house, creeping about like an underpaid clerk; he had found some occupation at Quinty. At the beginning, he ogled Lucy openly in a way she resented, and

191

promptly made this clear; thereafter, Coxon took umbrage and hardly spoke.

Before late supper they had all gone upstairs to see young Luther, who was in bed. Lucy had the astonishing sensation of looking at old Luther K. as he must have been in youth. The boy had his grandfather's square plump jaw and thick mouth; his body, clad in its flannel nightshirt, was squat and his hands already an engineer's. The dark hair was shaved close on his head in the way of American schoolboys. He received them politely, as he had been taught; he knew his father, from visits, better than his mother, and gazed with interest at her and at beautiful Aunt Lucy, her golden hair shining in the lamplight, her half-shut hazel eyes laughing at him between their secret lids. Sabine's stayed sullen; she had kissed her son formally and then stood back. Lucy however stayed on to talk to the little boy after Jeremy, with his wife as his constant shadow, had gone back downstairs.

'What do you want to be when you grow up?' Lucy asked Luther Meggett. The real answer was not in much doubt; but young Luther meantime said he didn't know. 'I want to look round a bit,' he told her. The Harvard tutor was evidently progressive. Lucy talked to the boy a little about England and Aylors, and how he must come to visit them there; then rose and left, and on the way downstairs was waylaid by a servant.

'Mr Wint would like to see you, madam, alone tomorrow in his office at eleven o'clock, if it is convenient. He has matters to discuss.'

I dare say, Lucy thought; but she was armed now against what it might still be, even yet. Luther K.'s appearance, briefly witnessed on their arrival, had however shocked her; he had lost weight and his flesh sagged, and there were dark bags of ill-health under his eyes. He didn't look happy and it was probable that the new marriage was not the success for which he had hoped. Well, it wasn't her concern: and it was after all on the cards that he wanted to talk to her about young Luther. She nodded to the servant and sent word that it would be convenient, in the office tomorrow at eleven.

Regaining the downstairs parlour, it was to find a conference in progress over bourbon, with madeira for the ladies: Sabine and the Coxons seemed equally displeased that she should join them. Luther K. himself sat in his upholstered chair, his sagging face briefly intent over the estimates Jeremy had brought with him. The talk touched again on the Clydeside offer, by now hanging fire. The Coxons were not in favour of it. Nat Passmore, who had joined them for supper, sat passive and flat-cheeked as ever. His wife Elizabeth was about to give birth to their fifth child, and was not present. That dynasty was well established by now, at least: but Nat these days

193

would never account for anything much at Quinty, having, as Lucy told herself with some irony, not much enterprise except in one direction. Luther K. had at least been able to vary his interests. Jeremy, who had drunk too much bourbon already, was expatiating on the long-ago glimpsed glories of Robert Napier's palace of Shandon, with its old masters, its long Gothic galleries, and the great clock ticking forever in the square stone tower.

'Don't know what will happen to it,' he said. 'The sons don't want to live there. A pity when one remembers old Napier himself had the Duke of Edinburgh to dinner there, with a flotilla anchored out in the Gareloch.' Nobody, however, was impressed by this information, royal Affie's reputation being as well known on this side of the Atlantic as the other. Luther K. murmured about the laying of the Atlantic cable years ago when Robert Napier had started up steam together with Cunard and the *Greyhound*. 'That was a long time back. Things have moved on, but there's still steam and always will be, until men take to the air.' He raised his head, the dead eyes showing a spark of life as they rested again on Lucy.

'Maybe the sons will be less cautious than their father; after all he started life as a blacksmith and had to make his way,' he continued. 'If they offer a touch more, the goodwill of a business this side the ocean could mean more than a mere office in New York.

I'd like to think over what you've said, Jeremy.'

'It means parting with your own rights, Luther K.' put in Gertrude softly. 'Is that wise at present?'

'If you mean again you think you're in calf this time, I'll believe it when I see it bulge,' said her husband roundly. He looked round the company and defiantly lit his cigar. 'Dear, you aren't supposed to have those any more,' said his wife, drawing attention away from her own repeated failures, which she had decided privately by now must be Wint's. 'The doctor says—'

'Damn all doctors to hell. What I'm considering is the future of young Luther upstairs if the Quinty business sells. That boy is myself over again; he's more than a son to me.' He looked round the room; nobody said anything. 'As things are and look to remain, he'd inherit Quinty when I die, but where is he if these Scots take the whole thing over? I've trained him in any case to think of himself as the next boss of Quinty.'

'He says he wants to look round a bit,' remarked Lucy, wondering if she was doing harm; but it was not right that the boy should have his fate decided before he was old enough to assert himself. The aromatic smoke from the cigar rose in a still column. Gertrude Wint got up and fussily shook the chenille curtains.

'That tobacco gets into everything,' she complained. Jeremy began to talk again, his

195

voice slightly slurred. Sabine as usual said nothing, watching him and twisting her long white fingers restlessly. Lucy was aware of mounting tension in the room.

'Young Luther ought to be with us, his family, in England. The Napier firm would agree to a clause that he has a place in the business in time,' Jeremy said with firmness.

Luther K. thumped his fist on the chair's arm. 'No! The lot of you can come over here. There's plenty of room; Sabine can go on littering like a cat if she likes. It's time there was some young life in this house again. Stay, the lot of you, and send for your other children.' He glared round the room, a troll in his own kingdom. 'Let's all go up to Vermont for a little holiday,' he said. 'It gets too hot in town this time of year.'

'I guess the travellers are tired, and want to go to bed right after supper,' Gertrude put in. She had primmed her small narrow mouth at the remark about Sabine and cats. They went into supper, and afterwards she approached her husband inexorably with a glass filled with cloudy liquid. 'Your draught, Luther K.,' she said. Wint grimaced, and drank.

'Don't know whether she wants to finish me off or spry me up,' he said, and winked at Lucy. Gertrude and Coxon saw the gesture and their faces again grew prim. They don't like us, Jeremy or me, Lucy thought, and one can't blame them. The boy Luther, she was more

196

than ever convinced, ought to return with them. She'd try to persuade his grandfather accordingly tomorrow. For tonight, she'd lock her door; she didn't want Coxon stealing in, or for that matter Luther K. if he was let, which last was doubtful.

CHAPTER ELEVEN

'Why, Lucy, Lucy, come right in!'

Wint had advanced with both hands outstretched, to welcome her; his face broke up into smiles like a boy's: he drew out a chair. Seated in it, Lucy found herself staring up at a portrait on the wall which had used to hang in the dining-room; Mehitabel at the age of about thirty-five, still handsome, with Sebastian as a boy against her knee and the young Susan standing behind, and Sabine to one side, in a dress with a blue sash, her long hair spread. It had been carried out by a mediocre painter, but it reminded one of many things; Lucy felt tears rise to her eyes.

'I had it shifted,' Luther K. said. 'I had it shifted when this damned house had everything altered in it so's I've never liked it since. I thought they'd throw the painting out as well, maybe.'

He stubbed out his cigar among the rest on the dish. 'Mehitabel had a high opinion of you,

Lucy,' he said. 'She was fonder of you than of her own daughters: and she wasn't the only one. I had a letter from old Robert Napier in Scotland, following on your visit and Jeremy's. That old man was no fool. He wrote to me that Jeremy was persuasive, had charm and was useful to us, but that anyone could persuade him back again; all of that doesn't appeal to a Scot. Nevertheless he wrote that you were wise and discreet, as well as pleasant to look at. As you know, he was a connoisseur of paintings.'

She smiled on, wondering what it was all leading up to: and as usual, Wint guessed her thoughts at once. He seemed possessed by more energy today, more hope, more like his old self, as if the dilapidated body was fired afresh by some engine started up once more in its brain. 'The fact is, Lucy,' he went on, 'that what I said last night is only a part of it all. I want you to persuade Jeremy back here for good for the boy's sake, and Quinty's sake: and I want you here with him. Sabine won't hold him, here or anywhere: you will. I will tell you a thing about Sabine; you can see for yourself she's crazier by the year, and I know how it will end; not many remember this, but Mehitabel's mother died of melancholy madness, locked up in a house in the redwood country long ago. Old Maule had hell's delight with her. Luckily she didn't last. You know Sabine's in pod again? That seems to be one thing she's good at that the rest of us lack. She told Gertrude about it last night, and Gertrude told me.'

He turned aside and spat into the cuspidor. It must have happened on the ship, Lucy thought; well, that makes six children. She hoped for Jeremy's sake that this time, it would be a son. Wint had begun talking about his second marriage, not in flattering terms.

'Fact is, I can't warm that woman,' he said. 'Too religious, or says so; one way or the other, her tail's as cold as a fish. Ever since it happened I've remembered you, and wished you were there in her place. Maybe it could still be so: Sebastian's been dead a long time. The Bible says a man can't marry his deceased wife's sister, but it doesn't say a word I know of about not marrying his daughter-in-law.' He lit a fresh cigar, as if it were a business proposition and Gertrude herself did not exist. Lucy murmured something to this end. Wint leered, and drew on the cheroot.

'I'll tell you something else,' he said. 'Religious or not, that woman would misbehave with that creep of a brother of hers, maybe has done just that more than once, although I keep an eye. If a child was to be born at that rate, and looked like a Coxon and not a Wint, who would think anything of it? But they'd say plenty in Boston if I got the evidence and produced it in open court. I can do that anyhow, if you and Jeremy will come here on your terms, any terms at all. Money talks, as you should know by now. I'll get my

199

evidence, one way or another.'

She was so numb with shock that she was for once uncertain whether she was listening to the maunderings of a senile old man or the machinations of a wicked one: and she had always known Wint to be wicked in his own way. In her upbringing, even in course of Papa's extremely varied talk, incest had never been referred to; the thought of it made Lucy uncomfortable. Perhaps that was why Sabine had always been as jealous of herself as of any other woman. She and Jeremy—it was not to be thought of, but that time she'd seen him creep downstairs from the governess she'd envied Jane Ker her lover. A danger was developing now in her mind which must not be permitted to remain there. She rose from her chair.

'I will think matters over,' she said to placate Wint, only anxious to get away from the room and his presence. 'I will speak to Jeremy about what you have said; but the decision is after all his, and he loves life in England and there are the two little girls left there, and Lucius.'

'Bring the three over; nothing simpler,' replied Wint comfortably. 'We could all be one big happy family without those Coxons; and Gertrude wouldn't hold out against the threat of a scandal like I've suggested, not in Boston. Folks worry here a great deal about what other folks say. They wouldn't say anything about you, now, returning here with Jeremy; without him, it's a different matter. Think of yourself as a business woman, like Mehitabel. You could help run Quinty when I'm gone, and it would be young Luther's by then. I'd rather it turned out that way than the other. Do I have to say it all again? I once offered you a place with Jeremy in New York when I was marryin' Gertrude. Now, you can both come here. Otherwise, as I've said, the terms are yours: but we had our little pleasures that time in Vermont, you remember? We'll all go there again in a few days' time; think it over, even there. The wheels can start turning when you have Jeremy persuaded to come here and live, with you and all the children and poor Sabine. Think about it.'

She went out quickly, and there at the door found Coxon, standing with a letter for her in his hand. 'This has just come,' he said in his wheedling voice, his eyes meeting hers without expression. She was convinced that he had overheard what had been said and that it could be dangerous. Her heart beat faster as she opened the letter, then missed a beat. The letter was from Ireland, from the Superior at Fermisons. Cathy was dead: and all Luther K. had said left Lucy's mind as she read about the death and how quiet and happy it had been, and how they had buried Cathy in the garden with the Bishop present. *Her grave is a place of prayer*, the old Superior wrote. *As our benefactor I felt it my duty to write and inform you*. She signed herself Harriet Torke, evidently her name when in the world. Lucy was convinced she had heard it before and later remembered, when her thoughts had settled out of their late turmoil. Hetty Torke had been the fair oyster-seller over whom two of her own Meggett ancestors had fought a duel and begun the feud between the two branches of the family. No doubt this was a granddaughter, or some other kin. She wouldn't ask, and it didn't matter. There was too much else to think about. Should she try to persuade Jeremy, or not? It was true that she herself no longer felt welcome at Aylors, but if Sabine was going out of her mind, poor afflicted Sabine, in any case, things there might change in time. Perhaps it was best to leave matters at least until they were all up at the clapboard house, when she might have more chance to talk to Jeremy alone, on a Morgan pony. The more she thought of it, the more the prospect seemed feasible: after all Luther K. had said she might come on her own terms. She would ensure that these did not, this time, include his incessant embraces. The thought of them induced a strange trembling in her still. He was a wicked man: perhaps she herself was a wicked woman. Isobel O'Hara would have been in no doubt.

She mourned Cathy, remembering. It was as though a light had gone out: and yet Cathy herself was somewhere: one could still ask for her prayers, and Lucy prayed. The right decision was hard to make, alone.

In fact it proved difficult to talk to Jeremy alone at Vermont: Gertrude Wint constantly for some reason sought out his company, flattering him in her soft way, flirting with him whether or not Luther K. and even Sabine herself happened to be present; Luther merely gazed ahead with eyes like dead oysters, and Sabine maintained for once her sullen silences: she could after all hardly take scissors and attack her stepmother, particularly as Coxon was constantly with them, his colourless presence inevitable as a shadow. Lucy sensed the alliance between brother and sister although they were seldom seen to speak together, nor did Coxon himself again trouble her. As things were, she was left largely to the company of young Luther and rode out with him often on the ponies: once they went down together to the farm, old Cassidy being long dead. 'I milked the cows here last time, when I was up with grandfather,' the boy Luther remarked, his thick young jaw raised to survey the healthy cattle, grazing contentedly in the fenced-off field. Lucy told him she'd milked cows often herself, in Ireland, and Luther turned his small brown eyes on her in amazement.

'I can't picture you milking a cow, Aunt Lucy,' he said, 'you're so elegant.' He added that he thought he himself might like to be a farmer. It was evident old Luther hadn't forced the notion of Quinty on him, or at least not yet.

The weather was fine, and one day Gertrude suggested that they go up next morning to Lost Pond and take a picnic. Luther K. did not look at Lucy and she knew that he remembered their time together there long ago; so did she. This time, predictably, he did not come; he seldom ventured far now and it was assumed from the beginning that he would stay with Sabine, whose state made it inadvisable for her to ride the rough roads in the buggy. Young Luther rode his own pony beside it, while old Day of Reckoning drove; inside, Gertrude sat close beside Jeremy, Coxon beside Lucy in silence. They passed Camel's Rump without comment: presently the trees closed in as before.

Luncheon was promising, eaten by the river on the way; wild turkey, champagne, and pecan cake, with hardboiled eggs and salt and a bucket of ice wrapped in a linen cloth to hold the wine. 'We'll be back for dinner,' Jeremy had promised Sabine, who as they left had clung to him, whimpering. 'Don't stay away too long,' she had begged. 'Promise you'll be back before dark.' But Jeremy seldom troubled to keep his promises, and Sabine had stood by old Luther's sagging form at the house door and watched them depart with brooding slate-grey eyes. Now, the sky had already darkened; the trees seemed to have pressed forward and to be narrowing the remote trail. 'They grow fast,' remarked young Luther. 'Grandfather says that bog will be dry in years and years, but none of us will be here by then.' He knew the bog well; Luther K. had shown him, it was evident, the countryside on their visits together and had made far more of a companion of the boy than he had ever done of his son Sebastian.

They left Reck seated by himself in the buggy at last and themselves took the overgrown way to the pond. It proved still to possess its green, deadly beauty: the air was warm and undisturbed above the flat lily-leaves. Somewhere, a frog croaked as of old, but it was later in the season now. Lucy remembered the small red eft that had run over her hand, and for whatever reason shivered. It was probable that Luther K. himself had seen this place already for the last time, and knew it.

Gertrude turned to her stepson, who was staring into the water for half-grown tadpoles. 'Luther, dear, run back to the buggy and fetch my wrap,' she said sweetly. Luther turned his head, unwilling to leave. 'It's not cold,' he replied. Jeremy then spoke up, anxious to be seen to assert his authority as a father and to impress Gertrude, who seemed to fancy him like all the rest: one never knew. 'Do as you're told,' he said to Luther, and the boy shrugged resentfully and turned back into the trees. He hadn't seen any tadpoles. No doubt they were frogs already; it happened quickly up here.

He vanished, and Gertrude took Jeremy's arm as before and led him towards where the bog laurel grew, rich with its amazing pink blossom. 'Isn't it pretty?' she said. 'Fetch me some. I can't wait to touch those flowers. They'll last to put in water when we all get home.'

She smiled up at his stalwart height. Jerry smiled, and gallantly waded out to where the bog laurel could be seen, thick and undisturbed among the lighter pervading green brush. Lucy remembered what she had heard long ago and gave a little cry of warning. *The bog isn't dangerous except in the brush. There, you can sink suddenly.* She didn't have time even to say it. She saw Jeremy go down even as his arm was outstretched to pluck the fatal pink flowers. He sank as fast as if he had been in water, calling out and briefly struggling, while the mud sucked him down.

She herself cried out then, at the same moment knowing that it had all been planned, even to the sending out of the way of young Luther; but there was no time to think. She began to run forward, ready to fling herself down at the bog's edge and pull at the still visible, struggling man's head and arms; the more he floundered the worse it got. Jeremy went down, ever down, his face plastered greenish black with mud; the deadly ooze suppressed even his gaspings. He had let out one final scream. Gertrude Wint stood in Lucy's way and thrust at her to go back towards the wood. 'Run,' she said. 'Run fast and fetch Reck. We'll do what we can here.'

Lucy ran when she knew already she should have stayed. Coxon was over near the place, flinging himself down the way she herself should have done, making pretence—Lucy knew both then and later that it was pretence—to pull at the drowning man when he was in fact thrusting him ever further down. There was no chance at all for Jeremy. Lucy found herself running and shouting 'Reck! Reck! Luther! Come quickly, your father's in the bog,' but her voice sounded thin and foolish among the trunks of the unheeding trees. She met young Luther returning with the unwanted wrap over his arm. He dropped it and they both ran back, Lucy's breaths pounding with the beats of her terrified heart; behind, she heard Reck follow. When they reached the place, it was to find Gertrude standing with mud on her skirts, Coxon still prone where he had formerly been. There was no sign of Jeremy and the laurels and brush were broken and flat, the only proof that a man had sunk among them.

'We did what we could,' Gertrude said sadly. 'He's gone, Lucy. It's very deep in there. They won't get him out now, not in time.'

You knew it was deep, but you made him go, Lucy heard herself thinking. She kept silence,

207

for a reason of which she was already aware. It would be easy for a man and a determined woman to overpower her also and, between them, young Luther, drown all three of them in the bog in the end, and say later they had gone out together after flowers. But here was Reck in time; good Reck, his eyes popping, knowing already that the big handsome man was gone, smothered forever in the ooze. He would know perhaps already that it was strange. With a little help they could have saved him, but they'd let him go down instead. It was best to say nothing.

Lucy knew also that it was best to say nothing. She watched Reck and Coxon scramble up at last, mud-soaked and stinking with the ancient vegetable essence of the bog. Around them all the life it contained had briefly quivered with alarm: the damsel-flies had fled, the lilies were smashed, the frogs no longer clamorous. It was a silent requiem for Jeremy Meggett, the handsome interloper who fathered heirs and had trafficked inconveniently with rival contracts in Scotland. Lucy saw all of it coldly; and knew also that the person who would have to break the news to Sabine would be herself, and that it would drive Sabine mad at last, like her grandmother in the redwood country long ago.

*   *   *

Afterwards the shock receded and matters became even clearer in Lucy's brain, even during the silent drive back to fetch help to sink ropes and hooks and try to retrieve Jeremy's body. None of them spoke because there was nothing to say. Young Luther's face riding beside them was white, but he had after all scarcely known his father. Coxon had put Gertrude's retrieved wrap round her shoulders and she shivered becomingly in the evening air. The thing was done that they had come to do; it was perhaps the beginning. Now, she herself, Lucy Meggett Wint, must prevent the end; and the first thing to be done was to see old Luther K. somehow alone, without his wife. She would arrange it. It was possible that the Coxons didn't suspect that she knew: that was vital. She kept silence meantime, unable to trust her voice.

*   *   *

When they reached the clapboard house again it was almost dark. Lucy went straight up to Sabine's room. Sabine was lying on her bed with the lamp ready lit on a side table. She looked at Lucy, standing alone by the door.

'Where's my husband?' she asked, and sat up. 'Where's Jerry?' I've waited all day.'

Lucy stood very still. 'Sabine, it's bad news,' she said gently. 'You must be brave, for the sake of the baby.'

209

'There's always a baby. Why hasn't Jerry come upstairs to me? Where is he?'

'Something has happened, Sabine. Let me tell you now, as kindly as I can; try to understand that it's over, that nothing can go wrong any more, because you won't see Jeremy again.'

'He's gone off with that Gertrude. I knew it. I knew what would happen when you all drove away together. She's been making up to him ever since we came. He shouldn't have gone with her, the scheming bad woman.'

'Sabine, Jeremy has not gone off with any woman. There has been an accident. He is dead.' There was no other way of saying it, after all; she heard the words drop like three stones. Sabine said 'I don't believe you. You're lying to me. You've always been jealous because I'm his wife. You know where he is and you won't tell me.' She began to pound at the bedclothes with her fists. 'Jeremy, Jerry. My husband. Where is he? Tell me where he is and I'll go to him before morning. They shan't part us ever again. Jerry, oh, Jerry.' She swung her legs out of the bed and stood up before Lucy, a lock of dark hair falling untidily into her eyes. She raised a hand and thrust the hair back. 'What has happened?' she asked suddenly. Her mouth had begun to tremble.

'You are bound to hear it in the end. He sank in the mud at Lost Pond. They are going up there now to fetch the body, if they can possibly reach it.' Men had driven up already from the farm in a cart with ropes, implements, spades to dig away the mud, wearing great boots to trample the lilies and bog laurel flowers that hid secret, ugly death. Jeremy dead, choked with mud. Perhaps his head would rise up again before them like a green-black ghost.

Sabine did a thing then Lucy had heard of, but had never witnessed before and had not, she supposed later, believed could really happen. Sabine began to tear her own hair. She tugged at the roots and brought away dark silken tufts, her face a contorted mask of Greek tragedy. She was silent and shed no tears. She had never lost her figure with childbearing and was still slender, beautiful, more than half crazed; Jerry had known it, perhaps from the first, but had always succumbed to her beauty. Now it would never happen again. What was to become of Sabine?

Presently she said, like a child 'When will they let me see him?'

When they have washed off the mud in the river, if they find the body at all, thought Lucy grimly. Day of Reckoning had driven back with them to point out the exact way they should go to the place where it had sunk.

*　　　*　　　*

They had found the body, retrieved and

211

washed it, and brought it home at last in the dawn. Whilst it lay stiffly in the downstairs room they were busy making a coffin ready down at the farm; all of Cassidy's sons could saw wood. Old Cassidy, like a Rhode Island cockerel, had worn out his wives to some purpose. Such remembered scraps floated up into Lucy's mind; she felt like a wrung rag today. While she lay on her own bed, Reck came to her, eyes still rolling and showing the whites in the way they had when he was frightened.

'What is it, Reck?' she asked. 'You helped them find him.'

'Missy.' Reck shuffled his bare feet. 'Don't tell no one. Don't get me in trouble. If anyone asks, I don't know nothin'. I'm tellin' you 'cos you've been good to me always; it's this. A tall man don't drown in Lost Pond Bog. It ain't deep enough, not when there's folks about. If no one came he'd maybe cover his mouth, maybe his nose, in the end, but not that quick: he'd have time to save himself, and holler out loud. If a man dies in Lost Pond, someone held him down in the mud. Don't say I said it, don't tell Mr Wint nor no one. I'm goin' to the woods to sing a hymn and get it out of my soul.'

'Don't be afraid, Reck,' Lucy told him. 'It wasn't your fault. You came as fast as you could, and did your best to save my brother.' She remembered the small amount of mud almost primly sullying Gertrude's skirts. It had

212

all turned out as arranged, without doubt: but she herself had made other arrangements. She handed a note already written to Reck. 'Give that to Mr Wint when he is by himself, as soon as you can,' she told him. He nodded, and went off. Later she heard him singing in the woods, a mournful hymn whose words Lucy could not define.

She had been by then into the death-chamber and had looked down on Jeremy's dead face. Deaths never came singly, Isobel had said long ago; who would be next? There was a fragment of mud, still damp, inside one nostril; they hadn't washed it away. Sabine hadn't noticed. She was here beside the corpse, having kissed and kissed the dead face: by now, she was kissing Jeremy's feet. In the end, they would have to come and take her away.

Luther K. himself sent for Lucy before the evening, and dismissed Gertrude who hung about. 'I want to talk to Lucy alone,' he said, 'about Sabine. You clear off.'

He had received the note. They began to talk together in low voices, his face unseen, the light from the newly lit wood stove flaring behind his head. It had begun to grow colder in the evenings, and he was already old.

*　　　*　　　*

'I knew he was murdered as soon as I heard about the bog,' said Luther K. 'A tall man
213

doesn't drown there.' That was what Reck had said earlier, and Luther K. himself earlier still. Lucy kept her counsel about that; she wouldn't involve Reck, he'd cured his own soul with his hymn. She went on listening to the old man seated by the fire; it was strange, and yet not so strange after all, to think that he had once been her lover. There had always been an affinity of spirit between them. It made too many words unnecessary now.

'He's dead,' said Wint, 'but the boy's alive. What you have to do now is get away with young Luther to Boston, then to England: put him to school there. I deserve to lose him for having been a fool, yesterday: I should have foreseen this. She came to me last night full of smug triumph and I couldn't bear to touch her, pretended I was past it.' He smiled, with something of the old lechery in his eyes. 'I'm not, but the doctors tell me I've got six months to live. That maybe means a year. Fact is, I haven't led my life the way it ought to have been led from the beginning. Maybe that's why Mehitabel's two other babies died.'

He reached into his coat and handed Lucy an envelope. 'I got that ready for you earlier, before I had your note,' he said. 'We often think of things together: we met out of the right time and situation, you and I. If I'd been a younger man, or you an older woman, who knows? That time, up at the bog wood, I like to remember best. Don't think of that place as only bringing death.'

Lucy took the envelope, and felt his fingers smooth her sleeve. 'Take the first boat you can,' he told her. 'In there is the signed agreement with the Napiers. I hadn't made up my mind whether to humour Jeremy or not, but now I owe it to him, and to you, and young Luther. Use the money—I've signed up the necessary clause—to buy shares for him; it's possible they may want him to join them later, but it's up to him what he does with his life. He tells me he may want to farm. He could have farmed here, but not with the Coxons around; not that there's any reason for them to do further harm to him once this goes through. See to it as soon as you can. Before you leave, see Passmore as well, about Sabine. You can't be expected to be responsible for her the way she will be from now on. Nat has a doctor friend who took in Elizabeth for a while between the births. He runs a place called Five Elms, just out of Boston. Sabine will be as happy there as anywhere, and later on, when the child's ready to leave her, you can maybe take it with the rest. Meantime, it's safe from the Coxons, and so is she.'

'And you?' Lucy said. His squat fingers left her arm and gripped her hand. Lucy returned the pressure of his grasp.

'I'll take what's coming to me: after all I've asked for it,' said Luther K. Wint. 'If there's a son born to Gertrude, it won't be mine, not

215

now. I tell you, she seems to me like one of those Greek women who tore a man to pieces. I don't know their name for sure. I never had that kind of an education.'

He was smiling, his wrecked face suddenly that of a mischievous schoolboy again. Lucy bent and kissed him on the mouth, aware of the smell of age and illness that came from him, knowing compassion rather than the distaste she would once have felt. She went swiftly back to her room, sat down and wrote one more letter; to Jane Ker in England, with the news of Jeremy's death before she should see it in the papers, and asking her to break it to her pupil, Maria. Then Lucy collected her things and packed them herself. She and young Luther would be ready to start in the morning, and she would leave it to his grandfather to put forward whatever explanation was needed as to why they would not even wait for Jeremy's funeral. Luther K. Wint would think of some plausible reason. He always had done. Lucy smiled, undressed quickly and turned out the lamp.

CHAPTER TWELVE

Lucy was at Aylors alone, again in black, for Jeremy, seated at what had been his writing-desk and sorting through his papers. As might have been expected after the departure of Jane

Ker, these were again chaotic; Jerry had achieved what he had by good fellowship and personal charm, but had neither answered letters promptly nor paid bills. Lucy had settled the latter and to help with the resulting expenses, had arranged to sell off most of the hunters her brother had kept; there was a letter written some time ago from Captain Clifton-Turner, of whom she had heard often enough but had never met, enquiring about the purchase of a certain bay. The bay was still in the stables, and Lucy had written to the address to ask if he remained interested before the rest were sent for sale at Newmarket. No reply had come and no doubt Clifton-Turner was by now suited elsewhere.

More importantly, Lucy had settled matters with the Napiers, sold Quinty rights, invested the money for young Luther, and written accordingly to old Luther K. All of it had taken time and without noticing, summer and autumn in England had gone by. Soon it would be the Christmas holidays, but she herself did not feel that there would be a cheerful enough festive season for the children at Aylors. In any case Lucius, who seemed to be developing a religious turn of mind, was going to spend Christmas with a vicar he knew of who ministered to the poor in Whitechapel, handing out comforts, food and clothes. As for young Luther, whom she had sent meantime to Jeremy's old school pending admission to

Harrow, he had struck up a friendship with two brothers of his own age in Wiltshire and had been invited to spend the holidays with them. That left the two little girls upstairs with their nursery governess, Caterina, and herself: also Maria, now at Jane's school in Doncaster.

Lucy did not think Maria should come home. Jane Ker, who took an interest in her and had as Lucy asked broken the news of Jeremy's death, had written lately that the girl still suffered from attacks of hysterical crying; it might be due to her age. For whatever reason—there had been no particularly close tie with Jeremy, such as the girl had had with her grandfather old Lucius, so quickly forgotten—Lucy had thought of a way for her to spend Christmas, together with Jane who herself had no family and nowhere to go except to stay on at the empty school. She herself had written, this time, to Arthur and Annis both, asking if Maria and her former governess might come over to them for Christmas, Arthur having been so kind to Maria on the last visit; it would cheer the girl greatly after her father's death. Lucy had felt a wry irony grow in her as she wrote, also sadness; to address a letter to Lord and Lady Meggett, which should have been Hubert's title and her own at Clonough, still brought feelings of unrelieved grief and resentment. However a pleasant enough reply had come, again written by Annis; they would be pleased

218

to see Maria and her governess. Little Eithne remembered Maria very well. She, Annis, had not been well lately, but was now somewhat better in spite of the winter's damp. The two visitors would be made welcome.

Jane Ker had replied thankfully; she had already written, but in a dignified and formal manner, regarding Jeremy's death: that door was closed forever. Jane had in fact grown so prim that Maria, a little later, stated in her thoughtless way that of course Miss Ker could never have had a love affair in all her life: teachers didn't. Well, one kept silent as to that. Lucy bent her head once more to the letters, shutting her mind to the thought of the comfort of Clonough at Christmas, forever denied to herself. She would be alone here instead, with Caterina and the younger children. She had been able to tell Horatia and Maude lately that they had a baby sister, born in Boston at Five Elms. Sabine was said to be devoted to the child. That was perhaps some consolation. Elizabeth Passmore had written about it and had said the place itself was comfortable and sunny, with fresh flowers in vases everywhere and, from Sabine's room, a view on to the garden. Perhaps Sabine would find peace.

The letters done, Lucy took them to put on the tray in the hall and wrapped her heavy cloak about her to go out into the cold garden. There was little to be seen there and most of

219

the Pompeian plants were either dead of recent frost or else below ground till the spring; but it was a walk, in the fresh air, and she had occupied herself with writing all morning: letters of condolence were still coming in, mostly from Jeremy's friends who had been abroad and had only just heard of his death. He had had many friends. She thought of his body, lying cold and alone in the grave far away in Vermont; they had not brought the coffin down to the vault in Boston. Lucy shivered, and thought of all the dead there had been. Had she herself ceased now to carry death with her wherever she might go? The next, no doubt, would be old Luther K.'s own, but that was expected, even by himself. He had written lately to say that he approved of everything she had done, including the buying of certain shares for young Luther. 'You have always pleased me,' he had ended. That was something to remember.

*   *   *

She walked up and down the frost-rimmed paths, seeing the sundial where long ago Maria and young Lucius had played battledore together. The shadows were lengthening about it already and Lucy peered at it to tell the time. It was four o'clock: and there was someone else in the garden. She sensed the presence before she turned and saw it, a man's; a slim

220

broad-shouldered figure, walking towards her with confident graceful strides. He came to where Lucy was, and held out his hand.

'Mrs Wint?' he said. 'I'm Jack Clifton-Turner, Jeremy's friend. I've come about the bay hunter. Perhaps it has gone. I've been in Ireland, you see, and only received your letter yesterday.' He added, in charming apology 'I told them at the house that I'd come straight out to you here.'

He fell silent, smiling. Lucy stared at him, and knew at once that they should have met long ago. Why hadn't it happened? He was as handsome as Jerry, but differently, as a man differs from an angel: perhaps a fallen angel. Jack Clifton-Turner had eyes of a twinkling worldly blue, surveying her boldly. His hair curled slightly and was a glossy light-brown colour, and he had a carefully maintained, but unobtrusive, cavalry moustache and handsome features. His clothes were superbly tailored, somehow giving the impression—she knew even then that it was deliberate—of a former army officer who is in civilian dress because he prefers it for comfort meantime, although he knows quite well he would look even better in officer's uniform. He had a bright high colour, like a schoolboy, and little ears set close against his skull. His teeth were perfect, showing a very little when he smiled, as he was smiling at Lucy now; at her, the despoiled and barren widow, a woman who could no longer

221

be of use to any man except for fleeting pleasure. Yet she knew at once that pleasure would be of extreme importance to Jack Clifton-Turner; that he pursued it like a butterfly, or perhaps a golden damsel-fly. She found herself blushing. They had both forgotten about the bay hunter. He continued to look at her intently.

'Jerry used to speak about you a great deal,' he told her, and did not dwell on Jerry's death; nothing unpleasant would ever stay uppermost in Clifton-Turner's mind. 'He didn't tell me,' he added now, 'that you were so beautiful.'

*   *   *

They inspected the hunter before tea, as that was after all what Clifton-Turner had come for. 'I haven't been able to take him out,' said Lucy, indicating her mourning. Jack Clifton-Turner ran a hand absently over the bay's satin neck: his hands, Lucy noticed, were not as one would have expected, but squat, with stubby fingers. This lack of perfection endeared him to her more than ever. He inspected the points of the bay, agreed that it had already eaten its head off, then said, with his own head turned away from Lucy, 'You've had enough mourning. Old Arthur told me about a good deal when I stayed at Clonough.'

So he knew; Arthur would no doubt have told him other things. They walked together back to the house and Lucy noted that he was about the same height as she was herself, not tall for a man. He was still talking about Clonough. 'He and that ugly wife go to bed early,' he told Lucy engagingly. 'It can't be too exciting when they get there. She has prayers said every morning, with the poor servants all lined up, even the bootblack and the potato peeler.'

She asked him if he had encountered Jane and Maria, but he had left before their arrival. He started to talk knowledgeably about the architecture of Clonough, the beauty of the portico, saying how like it was to Lyon, Lord Cloncurry's house further north. 'I'm fond of houses, inside as well as out,' he told her. 'I like interesting furniture and pictures, a bit later than the things your father brought home, and a bit earlier than dearest Albert.' He made a wicked little *moue*. 'I don't like aspidistras and I don't like chenille. Things must have been a lot pleasanter to live with in the Regency, including dear old Prinny, who isn't appreciated these days as he deserves. He knew what was what, at any rate.'

He rattled on, and they sat together in the drawing-room while Lucy poured tea at last from the silver George III pot the visitor approved; then let the tea grow cold while he talked on, and she listened; about them stood the familiar striped sofa and chairs, the faded curtains, the portrait of Lucy's mother and a later one of Sabine in a yellow dress, with Lucius aged two. Sabine's grey-eyed loveliness made no impression on Jack Clifton-Turner, who must have been here often and knew about the scenes she made: he continued to regard Lucy instead, as if she were a precious piece of porcelain, Regency period. Before leaving, he proposed to her.

'I haven't any money, Lucy darling: I'm a fortune hunter. I suppose I should have waited till the third visit, but I'm not a proper sort of person,' he said, still with the disarming twinkle and the smile. He was, on the contrary, Lucy thought, very proper indeed; a man who knew his world and the right people and made no pretence. She felt tears rise to her eyes; if only it could have come true!

'I can't marry anyone,' she told Jack. 'I can't have more children. I had a baby in the States, born dead. Jeremy may have told you.' To her amazement, she heard him laugh with relief.

'I loathe babies,' he said. 'Children would be the last thing I'd want. Think of it; nurses, nappies, noise, nuisance, everyone brought down after dinner and then sent upstairs again before they misbehave. It would be so much simpler if there were none. Darling Lucy, do say yes. Think how happy we can be as ourselves, the way we are now, sitting here. I knew I loved you the moment I saw you. You felt it too; you know you did. Say yes.'

He had clasped her hands in his warm dry

stubby ones. She said yes, hardly knowing what she did, knowing only that she could not in nature say no to him in anything. It did not occur to her that all prudence had fled, that she knew nothing of Jack except that he had been Jeremy's friend and that he hunted, and knew about pictures and furniture, and said he loved her, was a fortune-hunter as well, and didn't want children. It was surely enough for happiness.

*   *   *

The news of Lucy's second marriage, occurring quietly a few days later by special license, created little stir except among those ladies who preferred Jack Clifton-Turner as he already was. It was in fact a long time since anyone in England had seen or heard much of Lucy; there might have been some tattle at the Irish hunt, years back. Arthur was among the first to write from Clonough, a stiff little letter wishing her happy, enclosed in a dutiful one from Maria and a genuinely pleased one from Jane. They were enjoying their Irish visit. Maria, Arthur had mentioned, was an enchanting child and made a companion for his much younger little daughter Eithne. The old Superior wrote from Fermisons also, having heard, to wish Lucy and Jack happiness. She added that everything went on there in the same way, the vegetables had been particularly good this year, Sister Felicity the bursar had been ill, but it was thought that certain prayers by Cathy's grave had cured her. The community were continuing to pray for Cathy's soul and for Lucy as their benefactress, and would now do so for Captain Clifton-Turner as well.

Lucy closed the letters, smiling. Prayers were one thing; the bliss that bore her up like a soap-bubble now was quite separate, fragile, of this world, and utterly delightful. Not since the early days at Clonough when Papa had sent her a pair of scarlet stockings from Italy had she felt so light and carefree. Jack was wonderful in all ways; she loved him increasingly with each hour. She realised that never before, not even with Hubert, had she experienced this contentment, fun and laughter, agreeable company day and night, her every wish foreseen and catered for. There was lovemaking when they felt like it, delicious and knowledgeable in the way only Jack could contrive such things, still as though she were porcelain, perhaps a little too much so as she was, after all, flesh; but everything to him was rococo, breakable, to be cherished, caressed on its surfaces only: deeper one need not go, she herself had been deeper long ago, had plunged in fact to the depths, and up again to the heights; now, she was a china shepherdess, and happy. During the day Jack seemed always active, rearranging the furniture, re-hanging all the pictures his own way, and of course he must have his way in everything. Presently he decided that the furniture was all wrong with the new curtains they had had made and would have to go, or at any rate most of it: so they went to buy more in London salerooms Jack knew of, and had it sent home. The children upstairs in the nursery were not neglected by Lucy, but she left them mostly in the care of the new young governess, capable enough but not of the calibre of Jane; still, they should go to school to Jane later. Jack would at such times busy himself downstairs; having acquired a matchless Tudor oak refectory table somewhat like the one at Fermisons, it would of course be necessary to give dinner-parties, and he knew everybody to ask. Some of the guests Lucy had in fact met briefly in old days at Aylors on visits, but knew nobody well. She enjoyed meeting them; they were carefree, evidently rich people, and she herself by now had been dressed to kill by Jack, which meant no more mourning. 'You've had enough of all that, darling; there comes a time to stop,' he had said, and took Lucy round the leading couturiers, choosing her hats and gowns himself. Black, he admitted, suited her lovely fair hair, but there had been too much black for too long: so there must be only one hat of black velvet, with white ostrich plumes and a broad brim, to wear with a striped gown of faille whose draperies flattered the figure, skirts not quite as long as they'd been last year, and neat little half-boots which showed beneath the frilled hem, flattering a pretty ankle. Lucy must of course have her portrait painted in the gown, or perhaps some other; the painter, Toby Tothill, a friend of Jack's, came down and stayed at Aylors for a fortnight. The two men hunted, Lucy by then again as well, and ate and drank and talked together well into the night, or rather they talked and Lucy listened, feeling by now a little like a dressed-up china doll with eyes that opened and closed. At the sittings themselves Jack would of course be present, wandering between easel and sitter, saying things as usual which made everybody laugh; he was the best of company, it was understandable how greatly hostesses missed him; how lucky she herself was! 'Toby can't get on with his work,' Lucy protested one day, after Jack had set them off laughing for the fourth or fifth time and the light was fading. She herself was of course not to be allowed to see the canvas till it was finished.

'Oh, Sparrow's a card,' the young painter remarked absently, busy again with his long-handled brushes. Lucy wondered about the nickname, but did not enquire further; and at one point when they were briefly alone, asked Toby how he and Jack had met. In the army, she was told; but the life hadn't suited either of them. 'It's pleasanter here by far,' added the artist politely. He stayed for a further three weeks, and the portrait, when it was at last shown to Lucy, disappointed her a little; she looked stiff, more than ever like a doll, perhaps, but one mustn't say so.

Also, Toby's fingers were promptly itching for his bill: he stood with eyes like a briefly successful gambler's while Lucy wrote him a cheque. She began to realise that she had for some time been writing rather more cheques than usual; bills poured in, and she was taken aback by Jack's amusement when she paid, as always, by return.

'Darling Lucy, tradesmen expect to have to wait for months for their money; the name gets them other custom.' He indicated, in fact, that to pay before one had received several polite reminders was in doubtful taste; the best people didn't do it and never had.

At that moment, word came by way of the Boston lawyers of the death of Luther K. Wint. Lucy wasn't even certain that he had known of her marriage: there had been no word. The contents of his will were shortly made known to her, but contained little that was unexpected; his main bequests were to the grandchildren, and there was enough money to keep poor Sabine in comfort for life at Five Elms. Lucy herself would continue to receive her handsome jointure, which was paid regularly into her bank. She wrote with polite condolences to Gertrude; after all one could hardly do less. There was never any answer. Passmore was the executor; now and again Lucy heard from him in the way of business, also in course of information about the baby girl who was still with Sabine and who had been called Clara. She herself must not forget that child in her own delicious happiness.

*   *   *

Jack had been peevish at the contents of the will. 'Might have left you a lump sum, darling,' he said. Lucy laughed at him. 'You'd have put all of it on a horse,' she pointed out. He laughed likewise, ordered white peacocks for the garden at Aylors, then suddenly tired of it all, said the birds were noisy and messy, the country bored him, and suggested a little rented place in town. There would be Goodwood, balls, receptions; Lucy herself must be presented at Court; he knew exactly the person, a viscountess fallen on hard times. One paid her, naturally; one always paid, in the end. The little rented place was found, in Half Moon Street; an enchanting address, but with cramped rooms and vast expenses. One drove daily in the Park, where everyone was to be met with doing the same thing; one danced nightly in the great town houses, dressed up next day for the races, lost money on sure winners, kept a smiling face and grew used to it all. By now, it was evident that whenever Jack

230

backed a horse it lost, and it was not his own money that disappeared but Lucy's. She still found it impossible to be angry with him. He had made her ecstatically happy; she owed him something for that; and they hadn't, after all, asked each other enough questions at the time.

*   *   *

The first Saturday to Monday, which nobody ever called a weekend, was held after Lucy's Court presentation, at a famous house in Wiltshire. There Lucy met the faces she was beginning by now to be accustomed to see, the women, like herself, in one changing toilette after another as morning made its predictable, and cumbrous, way towards night. The right clothes for breakfast were worn for an enormous meal taken from dishes kept hot beneath great silver covers; scrambled eggs and bacon, kidneys and kedgeree, cold ham, buttered toast, smoked fish, enough to sustain an ordinary human being for the day and making it difficult to keep one's stay-laces tied as they had been, helped by Jack, before one came down. After that, one joined the gentlemen for a picnic lunch following their shoot, to which the ladies of the party did not as a rule go, but changed again into tweeds and a stiff hat suitably perched on the hair, boasting perhaps a few plain feathers. Later, on return after counting the slaughtered bag, there was tea, for which one changed once more, this time into a drifting tea-gown: and the further and most elaborate change of all took place for dinner, when one's appearance was no doubt carefully scrutinised and either pronounced to be divine or else not quite up to scratch. Jack of course always saw to it that Lucy was in the former category. This was easy, as she was still happy. In fact, she never did look other than elegant and beautiful, even later on.

*   *   *

As Jack put it, Lucy always looked top-notch. He himself would apply the finishing touches after her maid had done the rest; a rose pinned carefully in the hair, another perhaps at the laced bodice; a drapery subtly altered, the addition of a gauze scarf over her white shoulders, outrageous and intriguing alterations to the brims of hats: the meticulous use of a painted Italian fan. He became increasingly interested in foreign fashions, particularly those of Velasquez' fair-haired infantas; once there was a fancy dress ball at a house built entirely at the whim of the owner, one of the new set of moneyed personages cultivated by the Prince of Wales and who would not formerly have been admissible to the ranks of polite society. Now, their daughters were being married eagerly into it.

This, and the influx of American heiress brides, gave Lucy a hold by her knowledge of Boston, which was strange, exclusive and almost English country to most who came. It was known that she had been married to a rich man's son there, and now of course to dear Jack. The high nasal whines of the imported ladies hushed and modified themselves in face of Lucy's soft accents, which in fact were mainly those of Ireland.

For the ball, Jack dressed Lucy as a Spanish infanta. He had adapted a crinoline frame found long ago in the attic at Aylors, knowing it would come in useful in such ways; and had had it sewn under a silvery gown whose broad folds lent themselves to the antique deception and moved rhythmically to the tiny, nippy steps Jack assured Lucy had come straight from the Court of Louis XIV and had been adopted thereafter by the great ladies of Spain. She tittupped accordingly, feeling the frame of the farthingale swing and obey stiffly as it must have done in past ages, and was glad it did not have to be worn after tonight. Her hair Jack had combed loose with a long lock arranged over one shoulder, hanging richly by itself and unadorned; the other side was pinned up with a small scarlet bunch of ribbons he had himself put together, then smoothed the remaining hair over Lucy's forehead. 'You don't have to try to look as prawn-eyed as the infantas, darling,' he told her. 'They seemed so lifeless.

Remember Tum-tum will be there tonight, and I particularly want him to notice you. Hold the handkerchief with panache, there's a darling, against the skirt. That's exactly right.' The handkerchief itself, large, delicate, and trimmed with broad lace, he had acquired somehow for the occasion; he took infinite trouble over such things. There was also a dyed red ostrich feather fan. Lucy descended the stairs of the whimsical house in amused anticipation, playing her part as instructed. She had of course already been presented to Tum-tum and his beautiful deaf Danish princess at St James's. That seemed a long time ago; a recollection flitted through Lucy's mind of the height of the immense white plumes she had worn for that occasion, and how the band confining them had chafed her forehead, but it was not *de rigueur* to be seen to ease it. Lucy had got through the occasion creditably and the viscountess had been duly recompensed.

Tum-tum was watching Lucy now, interest in his pale-blue Guelph eyes which stared icily from beneath hooded lids and made him appear frequently bored, to the alarm of hostesses. He was not bored at present, and during the Lancers, that easier version of the old quadrilles which everybody enjoyed provided they knew it, stood watching, his eyes still on Sparrow Clifton-Turner's enchanting infanta, already presented to him at Court. His interest was noted, as that of royalty always is;

during the evening he addressed a few gracious words to Lucy, and she answered in a friendly and natural way. A.E.—he was known in this fashion in his letters, the reference to family obesity being kept entirely in verbal whispers—thereafter addressed his nobly-born hostess absently, and far from biting her lip in annoyance she had the tact to listen and ally herself with the shortly forthcoming request. The end of it all was that Jack came to Lucy when she was lying on her bed, unlaced and exhausted after the dancing; she had enjoyed that, her natural bent having been encouraged long ago at Clonough. Jack sat on the bed's edge, seized her hands and kissed them.

'Darling, you did very, very well; you were a credit to me, exactly what I'd hoped. Now, you will be nice to old Tum-Tum, won't you? He's taken a fancy to you, and that means a great deal in the way of further invitations; I'm dying, as you know, to go to Sandringham to shoot.' He talked on, using his squat hands expressively, and a growing horror took Lucy: she had of course known that hostesses at these house-parties arranged the bedrooms to suit certain mutual arrangements, but those had always been for other people, not Jack and herself; granted, they slept separately in great houses of this kind, and he didn't always come to her; she had assumed that that was because the events of the day had left him tired out, like herself. Now, suspicion took her; had Jack visited other rooms, as he evidently expected A.E. to visit hers now? She began to cry out and protest. Clifton-Turner frowned a little.

'Now, darling, don't be stupid and old-fashioned. Everybody does it. It's an honour sought by every sensible woman, but most of them don't have the looks, or else are feather-brained, which bores him. You interested him tonight, I can tell you; everybody noticed it. He'll sulk, in any case, if you won't be nice to him, and when he gets like that he doesn't forgive for a long time; look at the Randolph Churchills, they're not received anywhere meantime. Lucy, don't let me down after all the trouble I've taken; do it just to please me.' He began to kiss her bare arm, beginning at the wrist, working upwards along the soft flesh. 'He doesn't take long, they tell me,' Jack said. 'It'll be over in twenty minutes. He's not a bad sort. You know what to do, for my sake; you love me, don't you? You do love me?'

As usual, she could deny him nothing. She left her door unlocked; after it was dark, Tum-tum entered, in a Jaeger dressing-gown. Lucy smiled on, and welcomed him wordlessly, the light from someone else's bedroom faintly outlining her shining hair. It wasn't, when it happened shortly, any worse than being with Luther K. Wint at the beginning; the same sensation of a heavy stomach pressing down on one, a lust quickly sated: he mightn't, she decided, come back. His breath smelt of more

236

cigars, his sparse hair of lavender-water. Afterwards he kissed her appreciatively here and there, then went. They hadn't said much. Lucy thought it should perhaps have been made a little less easy for A.E.; too ready a conquest was no doubt taken somewhat for granted. However Jack was pleased. He soon obtained his invitation, solo, to Sandringham.

*   *   *

That was the beginning of it. By the end, matters had become intolerable.

CHAPTER THIRTEEN

Lucy lay alone on her bed at Fermisons, dry-eyed, drained of feeling, her heart a stone.

It hadn't been horses lately, or not so much: it had been baccarat, which Jack had taken to playing in the company of A.E. and the rest. He had lost more in the course of a few nights than anyone would have believed possible: far, far more than she herself received in quarterly installments under the generous terms of Luther K.'s will. It was no longer possible to impress the Bank; she and Jack had been living dangerously for a long time. 'Aylors is not your own, Mrs Clifton-Turner,' the manager had pointed out politely, and it was true: Aylors wasn't, it belonged to young Lucius. She had in fact no official security, except the allowance, long overdrawn.

She had thought matters over carefully in such time as there was; the debt of honour had of course to be paid at once. She had finally gone to Goodwood races with the express intention of waylaying A.E., and had done so, dressed to kill in a pale blue gown and hat Jack himself had chosen last year and which Lucy had refurbished, perhaps mistakenly, with black ostrich feathers. It made her feel like a horse at somebody's funeral, plumes nodding lugubriously; but it was too late to change. Tum-tum didn't seem to mind; he had taken her arm and walked up and down with her, no doubt to reassure such persons present as were becoming doubtful about the Clifton-Turners' continued social standing one way and another. That had been kind of him; but as far as such a sum of money went, the Prince could be of no direct help and Lucy hadn't expected it. She had hoped, however, that he might perhaps be induced to speak to his financier friend Ernest Cassel, who they said was ripe for a knighthood, having millions to lend which he had acquired by his own astonishing expertise in such matters; he was not yet middle-aged. He was said to have helped A.E. himself over several unmentionable patches. However it was not, as Jack would have said, evidently on the cards. 'It is hardly the moment,' the Prince said in a low voice. 'He is mourning his young wife; they were only married four years.' The guttural voice went on to mention another name Lucy might try; that of a Mr Bischoffsheim, to be found by appointment at an address in the City.

It was somewhat of a come-down from Park Lane, and the suggestion would not, as Lucy suspected from the beginning, have been made had she herself not been known to be somewhat pliable. However one had to take what offered, and the end, or rather the beginning, had been a veiled visit to Fenchurch Street in a cab, by arrangement. Other arrangements had then been made with Mr Bischoffsheim himself, cent per cent over six months, and the repayment meantime in cash.

* * *

Mr Bischoffsheim had one house in Hammersmith and a second in the country, but he did not take Lucy to either of them; his wife lived in the latter and his sons in the former. The sons were doing well in the banking business, his two daughters were suitably married, and Mr Bischoffsheim himself saw no reason why life should continue to be humdrum and had developed a connoisseur's eye, touch and palate. He took Lucy down to Bournemouth for the first of the little visits, small holidays as he called them, and they

239

stayed at the Bath Hotel. As usual, he registered there as Mr and Mrs Parks. As the establishment was respectable enough to be about to add Royal to its title, and as they knew his real name perfectly well and were moreover aware that the lady with him this time could not possibly be Mrs Parks yet again, meals were sent up, by request of the management, to their shared room. Lucy was relieved; she didn't want to meet anybody. The double bed was luxurious, and she lay in it and stared at the twin screens with gilded lattices and rose-coloured satin panels behind one of which Mr Bischoffsheim was at the present moment urinating into an elegant Second Empire chamber-pot. Presently he emerged wearing one of the new condoms. These had in fact been available since the year of Waterloo to those properly instructed in such matters, but Lucy happened never to have seen one before and it intrigued her briefly. Otherwise she shut her eyes, unable to endure the sight of Mr Bischoffsheim as nature had evidently made him; in its way, it was much like looking at Luther K. before she grew fond of him, but this client was almost completely hairless. Lucy submitted to what followed, sensing the gentle undulations of the bed in proper course. Hotels selected by Mr Bischoffsheim apparently did not have beds that creaked. She didn't bother to tell him that the condom had been unnecessary.

He himself was savouring to the full certain agreeable sensations without their drawbacks. Ah, such breasts! His plump smooth hands caressed them knowledgeably: and at the end, or near it, he sank his teeth, still his own and boasting several expensive gold fillings, in Lucy's provocatively bee-stung underlip. As a result, the latter remained tender for some days. In its way it was like poor Jerry's wedding night.

Otherwise, things were relatively pleasant and the food superb. The spa was only just beginning to be discovered by those of moderate means, and had till now been the province of millionaires who had built their villas high up above the town among the scented pines. On the second or third day Mr Bischoffsheim hired a carriage and drove Lucy up to see these and then down again past the famous chines to the sea. While there, he spoke, saying that he was very pleased with her; would she consider a more permanent arrangement?

Lucy shook her head, and he persisted for some time, his eyeglass, which he no doubt wore to enhance his somewhat unadorned appearance even when to be beheld in city clothes, gleaming importantly in the sun; it was a fine day. 'It is necessary to be prudent, my child, and to think of one's old age,' he told her. 'This husband of yours, pffff.' He then went on to offer Lucy a little flat in town, an

241

allowance, a French maid and other delights. When she still refused, he told her to think it over. In his own fashion he was like Mr Collins, Lucy thought, having at one point been permitted to read Jane Austen long ago at Clonough: or like Nat Passmore. As though the remembrance of Clonough had itself raised ghosts, an appaling thing happened on the following morning, as they were emerging from their room after breakfast to walk in the Lower Gardens until luncheon, it being safely off season. Two people came at the same moment out of a further door, the last Lucy would have expected or wanted to see; Isobel O'Hara, in widow's weeds, and on her arm no other than Annis, thin, frail and evidently in the last stages of some wasting illness. Both gazed with freezing incredulity at the stout form of Mr Bischoffsheim as it followed Lucy unquestioningly out of their shared bedroom door; then the two women turned their backs and retreated once more into their own room, shutting themselves firmly inside.

'What is it, my dear child?' enquired Mr Bischoffsheim, who in the meantime was becoming very fond of Lucy; he must continue to prolong matters somehow, it gave him intense pleasure to possess this opulent and beautiful woman; what a fool the husband was, and how useful the recommendations of A.E.! Lucy murmured that they had been two old friends once, lived mostly in Ireland and were obviously here for their health. He patted her hand.

'You do not have to mind such women,' he told her. 'They have had no little adventures such as ours, and never will. You, on the other hand, are beautiful and desirable. Remember it, and that it has been a pleasure in any case to do this small favour for old Sparrow. Tell him to keep away from the tables in future, although I like it very much when he loses.'

He smiled complacently, and Lucy endured the smile and the situation. The money would be paid, and Jack wouldn't have to go to prison and suffer permanent social disgrace; but she herself was now the mistress of a fat German financier and had no reputation left even among the people who surreptitiously did the same thing. Also, the name Sparrow hurt her: lecherous as a sparrow, that was it. She hadn't previously realised, no doubt hadn't been allowed to understand, what Jack's nickname among the best people meant. It hadn't been used openly at the late elegant house-parties. There had been fewer of those recently as far as she herself was concerned.

*   *   *

The matter of the Pompeian vase followed. Lucy had spoken firmly to Jack about the repayment of his baccarat debt and that there must be no further losses on any such scale. He had promised faithfully, had kissed her ardently, then made love perhaps rather more in butterfly fashion than damsel-fly: after Mr Bischoffsheim's embraces Lucy was beginning to discriminate somewhat. Nor had Jack asked about Bournemouth, Ramsgate, Scarborough, Tunbridge Wells or even, on one occasion, Derbyshire and the Cheddar Gorge. Sleekly cherished like one of Solomon's concubines as she had been on those occasions, Mr Bischoffsheim had nevertheless exacted full value for cash; but the cash had, when all was said, been forthcoming. Likewise she, Lucy, did not pry as to Jack's own comings and goings when he was neither at the Half Moon Street flat nor down at Aylors. She had liked to think that for them both to come and go, freely and separately, meant mutual trust. Now, it was more like some unspoken commercial enterprise. However things seemed to be on an even keel again between them, there was no debt to speak of, and Jack did not ask Lucy for money for a long time. It seemed too good to be true. The dream was finally shattered by, of all people, Caterina.

Lucy had gone down to Buckinghamshire to be with her two nephews, Lucius and Luther, both home for the school holidays and both still virtual strangers to one another, different in nature, upbringing and outlook. This might be a good thing; Lucius was inclined to undervalue his inheritance, while Luther was instantly aware of the existence of hard facts of all kinds. It was he who was present when Caterina erupted into the room with a volley of Italian, of which Lucy still, culpably, understood only a word here and there. The word *vaso* kept recurring, then *vaso di Città*; then *doario, doario*, in a harsh despairing wail. Finally Caterina seized Lucy by the hand and dragged her upstairs to where old Lucius' antique treasures had been stored, muttering *sposo mio, il mio sposo morto*, still in distress. She thrust a finger towards one carefully dusted object and empty space after another; her days had been spent in dedication, dusting fragments of all kinds, stone, alabaster, marble, mosaic. *'Il vaso del mio sposo, il mio doario, non è lá!'*

'I think she means that a vase is missing,' ventured Luther, who had followed silently in his prosaic fashion. He sketched the shape of a vase now with his square hands. Caterina nodded violently. *'Sí, sí. Non è lá.'* She glared at the assembled company; the two little girls had crept upstairs, hearing the commotion, and were staring round-eyed. *'Non è lá,'* repeated Caterina. *'sposo suo—,'* she pointed accusingly at Lucy—*'la prendere surreptizioso, furtivo, è ladrocino. E il mio doario, perduto, furtivamente, è malvagio.'* Still with the finger pointed at her, Lucy suddenly understood. The Pompeian vase, Caterina's dowry, she herself hardly remembered, having seen it only once in Papa's lifetime without, at that time, having been greatly impressed; it had seemed dusty and old, and she had been sorry for Caterina, who was obviously of less importance than the vase, which had dancing figures on it clad only in vine leaves. Nevertheless there were those who would pay large sums for such objects; she had always known it, also that the vase was part of Lucius' heritage and she herself had no right to remove it, or for that matter anything else at Aylors. Jack's jettisoning of certain furniture had been an impertinence which Lucius did not however seem to resent; the young man was not concerned with worldly matters. But Jack—

Lucy tightened her lips. At the end of the stay, back again in Half Moon Street, she confronted her husband. He tried to laugh the matter off, but she knew he was lying; his eyes slid round in the way they had done when he confessed to her about the baccarat debt. This time, she was deeply angry.

'To whom did you sell it?' she said. 'It must be bought back without fail.'

'My darling, don't be idiotic: it would use up all your money again, and you said—'

'What I said was said to you when I trusted you. I have become a whore for your sake on different occasions to two men: it will not happen again. I will buy the vase back for Lucius; tell me to whom you sold it. If you do

246

not, I will advertise in the papers that you have done so without the owner's consent and that it is to be bought back at any price.' That was foolish, as she knew, but anger made her reckless. Clifton-Turner laughed with a sudden hard shallow sound.

'You'll have to pay through your pretty nose, my dear. If you must know, Cassel bought it for his collection. He admires such things. I doubt if Lucius even notices them. Why not forget it, there's a darling? Let me kiss you. Let me—'

'No. You will not touch me again. You are a common thief.'

'Damn it, Lucy, that's a bit much. I only—'

'You married me for my money; you admitted as much at the time. Now you have spent it, or as much of it as you can get your hands on. There will be no more made available to you; married women now can defend themselves in such ways. I will inform my Bank that you are to have no further credit. As for Aylors, I will instruct the servants that you are not to have entry to the house. I do not know what else you may sell or already have sold. I only know that I have done with you, and am leaving you.'

'Lucy—' His face was haggard. 'Truly, I love you. I—I know I'm a weak sort of a fellow, but, believe me, when we married it was for love, on both sides, wasn't it, my pet? Try to understand, to—'

247

'I understand only too well; had I been a poor woman I doubt if you would have loved me quite as much.' That was perhaps untrue; there had certainly been love between them; but she was bitter, and said more than she intended. She walked then into her room, locked her door, and sat down and wrote him a note. She heard him go out, and the outer door slam. Well, he would return at some point or other, and find her gone.

Jack,

I am going away for a little while; please do not try to follow me. Perhaps we have loved, but by now we are destroying one another; I do not like what I have had to become for your sake. If I stay with you, something else of the kind will occur sooner or later. I have to be alone for a little while, to think. I will send you word when I have decided what to do.

Your wife,
Lucy.

She knew where she would go, of course, after retrieving the vase: the only place in the world now where there was peace, and a welcome for her; Fermisons. She had been here ten days, and already longed for Jack with more than a physical ache; in a way, and beyond reason, she would always love him.

*   *   *

Outside the window now there was silence; it was almost dawn. Presently the bell would sound for Prime and there would be the silent movements of the nuns about the passages, and across from the cottages which were long since cells, each with their single occupant. The house was adapted to conventual life; it would never be a home to her again, but for a little while here, there was quietness, away from the world, to cleanse oneself, if not to forget. It was best not to think of past or future; one must live for the day. Perhaps Tum-Tum's wife, the beautiful deaf Alexandra of Denmark, had learned that lesson while, secluded no doubt from the full extent of her husband's infidelities, she must surely be aware of some; but that smooth perfect oval of a face would reveal nothing, any more than a mask would ever do. Was she, Lucy, revealing what her own life had become by her very appearance? She got up, lit a candle and peered at herself in the glass. She had stoutened lately, put on an amount of creamy opulent flesh at jaw and bosom; her arms were plump. Thumbed flesh, well fed, well fucked, as Luther K. would have put it; he'd never minced words: but this wasn't the place to think of it. *You'll never be able to do without a man in your bed for long.* It was true; hearing the muffled bell to prayers Lucy felt no envy. She could never be a nun.

249

The bell had stopped, and Lucy lay on in the narrow bed; presently a lay sister would bring in her breakfast. It was sparse, but it was time she lost weight; a pot of strong tea, a slice of home-made Irish soda bread and an egg, always boiled too hard; but one didn't complain. Lucy closed her eyes and found, floating up again in her awareness, a memory of the restored Pompeian vase. Its return had been pleasanter than she had anticipated; the courtesy of Ernest Cassel had been punctilious, whether or not by private request of A.E.; Lucy rather thought not. She had been driven to the Mayfair house and shown into the great financier's study, where already, on his broad leather-topped desk, there reposed the vase. Lucy examined it idly and found that the figures were not dancers, as in her youth she had innocently supposed, but satyrs pursuing nymphs and, in the end, catching them. It would be as well to keep the vase from the contemplation of the young girls at Aylors, particularly Maria, who was being brought up largely still by Jane Ker, a strict guardian with a particular and natural love for Jeremy's daughter. It was for the girl's own sake that this had been tacitly arranged; she, Lucy, might give a slightly rakish interpretation by now to any attempt to bring Maria out with a view to favourable marriage. In due course, she should be presented by some paid and titled stranger, as Lucy herself had been on marrying Jack.

She had sighed, remembering, and turned to the door as Cassel himself came in. He was even younger than Lucy had expected, in fact about her own age; it was astonishing to think of all he had already achieved, here and abroad with foreign banks and loans. He could have glittered now with honours and orders received from Turkey, Sweden and Japan, but wore a plain mourning frock-coat. He bowed over her hand and bade her be seated. Lucy found herself staring at the portrait of his dead young wife, hung ahead on the wall.

'I am grateful to you for allowing me to buy this back,' she told him. 'It was my stepmother's dowry, as I said when I wrote to you, and she was much distressed when it disappeared. It will in any case be the property of my nephew, not mine.' She spoke confidently; whatever else the association with Mr Bischoffsheim had achieved, it had left her, Lucy, with, as they would have put it, a little change over. However the young Jew smiled.

'There will be no need to buy it,' he told her. 'It is my great pleasure, having looked at it, and at yourself, to have it crated and returned to Aylors without delay; you may inform your stepmother accordingly.'

She gasped; the vase had had a certain value. 'That is more than kind of you, and I can

251

hardly accept it,' she told him. Cassel shrugged. 'I can buy more vases,' he said. He went to the window and looked out at the Park trees, heavy with leaf at this season. 'When I was a boy in Cologne,' he continued, 'Jews were not permitted to buy or live in corner houses, as they were the most commodious in the street. There are consolations here, as you can see.'

She reflected how A.E. had altered the status of English society by allowing financiers and those connected openly with trade to enter his circle and marry into it: the stuffy exclusiveness of former days had gone for ever. Lucy rose, and held out her hand.

'I wish you had known my father, who discovered many things beside the vase,' she said. 'He died digging at Ephesus, as he would have wished. His ashes are scattered below Troy.'

'I have friends in those places, by way of the Bank of Turkey,' replied Cassel solemnly. Before Lucy left he took her arm and showed her his growing collection of pictures and works of art; she was reminded of old Robert Napier at Shandon, who had beguiled his own latter years with such acquisitions: but this man was not old. Cassel pointed out two paintings he had bought from the Shandon collection, which was scattered now except for a nucleus kept stored in Scotland. 'They have nowhere to show it meantime,' he said. 'The house at Shandon itself is now a hotel. Perhaps one day a gallery will be built somewhere to contain such things and show them to everyone.'

A.E. had already opened an exhibition for the public at Bethnal Green, and it was said thousands of working people had tramped through to see the wonders they had never imagined before. Society was changing, opening, widening. She left the man who had founded the Bank of Turkey, had the gratitude of kings and emperors, loved beauty, and was lonely. There had been one small daughter of the brief marriage; Lucy had not seen that child.

*   *   *

Another child had been met with by her here at Fermisons, only the previous day, by Cathy's grave. The nuns took a few pupils now to eke out their income; the result could not yet be called a school, but carriages called in the mornings and returned in the afternoons. This particular child was standing by herself, not joining in the skipping-rope game played by a few of the others during their mid-morning break in the garden. She was small and ugly, with a protruding forehead. Her lips were moving in prayer. 'Are you Eithne?' Lucy asked her. The girl turned her head and it could be seen that although she closely resembled her mother Annis, her expression was different, without narrowness or bridling dislike. 'How did you know my name?' she asked politely. She wore a plain dress and rough shoes: her brown hair was quite straight.

'I am Maria's Aunt Lucy. You know Maria; she comes to Clonough for holidays.' Jane and Maria had been oftener over there of late years than at Aylors; it was better for the girl's sake, at her age. Eithne smiled, showing projecting irregular teeth; she was in all ways very plain.

'Maria's pretty,' she said without envy, adding 'Papa is very fond of her. I am praying today for my mother, who is dying. Perhaps the saint will help her.'

Lucy thought how strange, and yet how right, it was that Arthur's daughter by Annis should stand here by the grave of his rejected wife. It was true that Cathy might well be a saint; the nuns believed she would soon be beatified. 'I come here every day,' said Eithne.

'Perhaps your mother will get better with the prayers.'

'No, she is certainly dying,' said the girl without expression. 'It is consumption; she has had it for a long time. She went with Aunt Isobel to Bournemouth to try to get well, but did not. We all die.' She spoke like a wise old woman. 'Mama had a little son once,' Eithne continued. 'She says she has never loved anyone since. They will meet one another in heaven.' It was all of it spoken in an unemotional, practical voice. Lucy remembered little Alan and how she herself had caused his death, but said nothing of it. 'But your Papa loves you,' she said persuasively: surely even Arthur Meggett-Clees could not be entirely heartless. Eithne shook her head decisively.

'Papa wanted a son, and I have disappointed him. I mean to become a nun here, if the order will accept me.' She still spoke resolutely; the fact of the loveless home evidently did not deter or trouble her. Lucy bent and kissed her: she seemed a dear little girl.

'It is time for you to go in now with the others, Eithne,' she said. 'Perhaps I will see you again tomorrow.'

But Eithne was not there next day, or the next. On the third day Lucy went to the Bursar, a fairly young woman who took most responsibilities since old Mother Sophia had become bedridden. Her name was Sister Felicity, despite which Lucy did not altogether like her; she lacked frankness and looked in nunlike fashion at the floor throughout. She had greeted Lucy courteously enough, but without warmth, having come to the convent shortly after its original transfer to Fermisons. Speech was permitted to the nuns at such interviews and for teaching the children, but was always sparse.

'I believe that I may be embarrassing you by my presence here,' Lucy told her. 'One of your pupils has not returned. I talked with her three

255

days ago, in the garden.' There was no need to mention Eithne by name; her absence would have been noted.

'Lady Meggett died early this morning,' said the nun coldly.

*   *   *

So Annis was dead, as had been expected for a long time; but the child had been kept at home for two days before that. There was no doubt but that her own encounter had been mentioned and that further meetings had been considered unsuitable. Lucy packed her things, said goodbye to the sisters and to Fermisons; she could no longer feel welcome there. She had herself driven to Rosslare and took the packet for England. The Half Moon Street flat had been given up; there was nowhere to go now but to Aylors. At least they would not refuse her shelter there for as long as she needed it: and the hurt of her parting with Jack had receded a little.

CHAPTER FOURTEEN

She had a few months' respite at Aylors, where the silence held no reproach. She spent much of her time teaching little Maude to ride her pony without being afraid of him; Horatia was

256

bolder and had natural hands. The young governess, Miss Whitfield, would soon leave for a new post when the two little girls were transferred shortly to the care of Jane Ker, now headmistress of her Doncaster school. Maria was almost ready to leave and for the sake of having all of the children together for once except for poor Clara in Boston, Lucy invited Jane to come and to bring the eldest niece down with her for Christmas. The boys would be at home: Lucius had begun at Oxford that autumn and already stated that he intended to be a clergyman. Luther, on the other hand, announced that he was going to Australia when he left school. So much for dons, politicians and Quinty: it was useless to try to make plans for anybody. There was still no word from Jack: and the boxes from Half Moon Street remained upstairs, unpacked because Lucy could not yet bear to open them. It was better, still, to live from day to day.

She was able, for the first time, to give them all a cheerful family Christmas, with a turkey and plum pudding set on fire in the dark and crackers and a tree with wrapped shining gifts, which the little girls opened excitedly. Lucius had read the lesson at morning service in church, his long pale grave face suited to the occasion, his voice correct and clear. Lucy asked herself if anyone had ever known Lucius very well, or if the fact of his broken and uncertain childhood had made him withdraw

257

early into himself. Perhaps when he met a woman to love he would give up the idea, which at present he cautiously expressed, of remaining celibate. That would put the onus of providing heirs on Luther, by then no doubt far away. Meantime, they all sat down to dine, drink healths in lemonade and open their presents. Lucy's one from Luther was a ship in a bottle he had made and inserted himself. She liked it best of any; the boy's square hands had inherited the precise engineering skills of old Luther K. and Mehitabel. Whether in Australia or anywhere else, young Luther would always do well at whatever he undertook. Lucy was pleased with him.

*   *   *

Her respite ended a few days later. It had become intensely cold, and as the sky was still heavy with snow while none had yet fallen, it was hoped that the ice on Halton pond would bear. The party from Aylors set out, and as they did so thin flurries of flakes began to drift, obscuring the distance. No one minded; Jane Ker sat with little Maude beside her in the closed dog-cart, while Maria, very pretty in a deep furred hood and matching muff, seated herself opposite in the shadows among the piled skates. Lucy rode beside Horatia, who of course scorned the cart and wanted to be equal with her brothers. Lucy reflected that Horatia

258

would benefit from Jane's school; otherwise she was in danger of becoming a tomboy, and, alone among Jeremy and Sabine's daughters, not handsome enough to offset it. Maria, on the other hand, with the good manners instilled into her by Jane, no longer giggled foolishly with every word, and even listened sometimes. Although she would never be very intelligent, she was a joy to look at even now, beneath the spread tarpaulin hood the groom had erected above the cart before their starting off, so that Maria's furs would not be draggled and everyone's clothes soaked. Jane loved Maria dearly as Jeremy's daughter, almost as her own, having been left with her for so long: but a society chaperone must be found soon.

Lucy stared ahead into the snow. Yesterday she had at last made herself unpack the boxes from Half Moon Street. She had come first on Jack's folded brocade dressing-gown and his army dress coat, and a pair of soiled white gloves he had worn last time they danced together at a ball. She had laid the flimsy things briefly against her cheek; it brought him nearer. Where was he now? It was best not to think of it. She knew he had friends, and perhaps for a change there had been winnings at Newmarket, or even at baccarat. Had Jack been in straits or in public disgrace, she would have seen it in the papers.

They reached the pond, and the young people buckled on their skates and went out

259

on the cautiously tested ice. Luther, taught abroad, no doubt in Vermont, was already an expert skater; he demonstrated figures of eight and then of three to the enthralled Maude, then seized Maude herself by the hand and guided the child round with him. Horatia could skate already; she went off competently by herself. Lucius progressed conventionally, less well than his brother. How different they all were! Lucy sat beside Jane Ker, who was watching myopically from beneath the cart's tarpaulin hood. The snow had stopped meantime, but there was more still to fall. It was very cold. 'Perhaps we should walk about,' Lucy suggested.

'Someone is coming,' said Jane Ker. 'It is Garfield, I think.' Her short-sighted eyes peered behind their glasses. Garfield was one of the Aylors servants who worked mostly in the garden. He approached now, pulled his forelock, and handed Lucy a letter.

'Came by special messenger, ma'am,' he said. 'I rode straight out: hope I did right.'

'You were quite right,' Lucy said. She tore open the envelope, which bore a crest; it was already too dark to see details clearly. She peered over the paper, as Jane had lately done ahead: but the writing was precise enough to see. Lucy's heart stopped. It was from the Prince of Wales. There was only one reason nowadays why Tum-Tum should write to her.

My dear Lucy,
    My son has just told me this news or I
would have sent word at once. Poor Jack is
very ill indeed with fever at the enclosed
address. Eddy confesses that he has been there
now some time. I know you will want to go to
him without delay.

He signed himself her devoted friend, A.E.
Lucy stared at the address. It was in Shadwell,
a district she had barely heard of. Prince
Albert Victor, heir to the throne, was a young
man whose propensities led him, young as he
was, already into such places. If Jack had fallen
into his constant company, it was bad news;
and in any case she must go at once. She
turned to Jane, and on an impulse showed her
the letter.

'I will ride back,' she said. 'You stay here
and bring them home when they are ready.'

But Jane said 'You cannot go alone.' She
signalled to Lucius, who was skimming towards
them on the ice by himself. He came up to the
edge and stumbled in the way skaters on land
do, hastening in ungainly fashion towards the
two women. Jane was crisp and practical,
suddenly in command of the situation. Lucy
had already gone to mount her horse.

'Wait, Aunt Lucy,' said the young man who
so seldom spoke. 'We will all three drive back
together at once. Luther will look after the
rest; leave the horses for them. Come.'

They started in the cart at once, its wheels only slightly clogged at first by snow. Lucy sat with the letter in her hand, then put it in her reticule. Only Jane had seen it; but Jane would ensure that Lucius fully understood the contents.

*   *   *

A nightmare journey followed, through the thickening snow. Lucy realised for the first time how she herself had, despite all that had befallen her, been physically sheltered all her life; warmed, fed, driven everywhere in comfort, her every need met, even on board ship or driving up to remote Vermont. Now, there was only growing darkness, redeemed by the carriage-lamps casting their yellow blur on the constantly falling snow; the cold lessened with it as they journeyed towards London. Presently, as the city enveloped them, there came river fog, hurrying figures and crowded buildings alike enveloped in thick, impenetrable grey-green, slowing everything. Lucy shivered in her warm travelling-cloak and tried not to feel sick at the delay: opposite, Jane Ker and young Lucius sat silently, the latter staring out of the window beyond which could be seen, now and again out of the opaque night, the houseless poor, hurrying forever across streets to huddle for warmth in available doorways; half-naked, barefoot, ragged, skeleton-thin. This was the other world Prince Eddy knew by night; Collars-and-Cuffs, they called him, because of his long thin neck and long wrists sticking out of his braided uniform coat. Collars-and-Cuffs, and her own husband Sparrow, making their way together among soot-blackened buildings in what could hardly be called streets; a jumble of tall hovels without room between. The river was somewhere, running unseen in the fog. Lucius spoke then.

'There will be heavy traffic along as far as London Bridge. It would save time, I think, to go by the steam ferry from World's End.'

World's End. She had no more memory of it later than the name; a block of buildings, a glimpse through the fog of grey water and mud with a few figures stooping there; mudlarks, out even on such a night as this, hoping to find something worth coppers or even silver in the sludge; they lived so, were never at any time dry, and had short lives accordingly; she'd heard of them. She'd heard of several things, but never before of Pickle Herring Street, the place where Jack had chosen to come and die. He must be dying; A.E. wouldn't have written otherwise.

Lucy made herself stare at the ferry, remembering afterwards that it had been named *Pearl*. *Pearl* lumbered and hooted her way across the crowded water sooner or later in some manner: perhaps Lucius had been right, there would be a press of carriages on the roads, not able to pass. The boats couldn't see their way either, three deep with the wherries anchored at the water's edge on each side; it made too narrow a channel through which to pass safely. There had been an accident lately in which two ships had collided in the Thames; the *Princess Alice*. One remembered reading about it in the papers. Almost everyone on board had been drowned. She herself didn't greatly care if she drowned or not, if she died or not; except that she wanted first to reach Jack while he still lived, to tell him she loved him.

The journey by water seemed interminable, and pervasively cold. There were few other passengers; anyone who could afford the sixpenny fare was no doubt in an ale-house instead, getting warm. She glanced at Jane, wordless and patient as always, her nose red with the cold; it was good of her to have come. Lucius also was a rock on which to lean; one hadn't expected it. Lucy hoped, a little wildly, that Luther had seen the girls safe home from the pond. For all the speed they themselves were making along the river now, she could have waited, and made sure they were all of them safe. But Jack . . .

*   *   *

They alighted at last stiffly on the stones of the

wharf, and Lucy would not stop for warm ale or tea. Lucius asked the way and was told where to go; again, she was thankful for his helpful presence. They turned right at the river's edge and presently found the street behind, and the house itself, which had a peeling door. Lucius knocked, and a woman opened. She didn't look like a prostitute, as far as Lucy knew. She was thin, perhaps forty-five, and lacked teeth so that her mouth was sucked in like an old woman's. She wore a drab apron. In the pallid light from a culza lamp in the inner passage she looked Lucy up and down.

'What does your sort want?' It wasn't said aloud; but Lucy asked calmly for Captain Clifton-Turner. Perhaps they wouldn't know his name; but the woman knew.

'You his wife?' she said. 'Might have come sooner. He's in a bad way, I can tell you. It's the clap. Daresay you don't know what that is. All the gentlemen gets it, some worse than others. He's bad, more than most are, because it didn't ever come out.'

Like measles, Lucy found herself thinking wildly: it's better if there's a rash. She followed the woman up the rickety stairs, smelling cabbage-water, urine and what was probably patchouli. Sparrow had ended here, in such a place. She should have kept him with her, in spite of everything.

A door creaked open on the left: inside was what must once have been a four-poster in

265

some noble house; it leaned sideways now crazily, shored up with driftwood from the Thames. On it lay what had once been Jack Clifton-Turner. He was bright with fever, tossing and raving; the stubble had grown on his chin and the ragged moustache drooped sadly. Lucy knelt down by the bed and took his hand. It was dry and hot, far too hot. She could see new lines of dissipation on his face.

'It's Lucy, Jack,' she said clearly; the others had stayed outside beyond the inner door. 'It's Lucy, my darling. I've come to take you home.'

'Can't move him now,' said the woman behind her. 'He's too far gone. I've looked after him, and some others here, and I know. It takes some of 'em like this and it's the best way. Others go crazy, or lose a nose, later. He's better gone. He was a sweet bugger. He come here often, him and Collars-and-Cuffs. We all know who *he* is.' The pitiless murmuring voice went on; Lucy paid no heed, chafing Jack's hand always. At last, she felt the returned pressure; he knew she was there.

'Lucy.' It was a sick man's muttering, trying to regain consciousness. 'Lucy . . . can't make love any more. No good. I was never any good.' The head suddenly turned towards her, eyes bright with fever. 'That vase,' said Jack in a clear voice. 'You got it back?'

'Don't think of that any more, darling. Yes, I got it safely. You shall see it again at Aylors. You're coming back with us.' Even as she said

266

it she knew that that last was impossible; a journey such as they had made tonight was out of the question for a dying man. 'Remember I love you,' she said. 'Remember I love you always.'

She said it often during the many hours it took him to die. She could not remember eating, drinking or relieving herself. Jack talked on almost till the end, but with increasing vagueness and no longer sensibly; Lucy would try to forget some of the things she heard then. At last, the hand which still held hers grew rigid, then limp as the blue eyes at last glazed over. 'I love you,' Lucy still heard herself saying; perhaps he could still hear; they said the hearing went last of all. Where had she heard that? The night outside was cold: Jack's spirit had gone out somewhere into it.

'Can you get a coffin?' she heard the woman ask. 'Can't keep him here; there's others waiting. I've lost business over this, these last few days, but I was fond of him, poor old Sparrow, Gawd rest his soul.'

Her hand went out, wordlessly, immediately, for money. Lucius came forward and counted out coins into her palm. Lucy bent over her dead husband and closed his eyes. She could still feel nothing. She heard Lucius make arrangements about a coffin and the other things. Then Lucius led her away.

'We won't go back on the boat,' he said. 'We must get you to a hotel for the night, Aunt

Lucy. Miss Ker and I will go back, and will return tomorrow with what is needed.' He was practical, this young man of God. She was glad he had come with them.

*   *   *

In the hotel—it had had a sign, glimpsed beside hung lamps in the fog, of a swan above a bridge with painted houses—Lucy felt the grief come in waves, assailing her as soon as the others had gone and she was alone in her upstairs room. She would stay in it till they came for her tomorrow; Lucius and Luther, and the girls would stay at home looked after again by Jane. She knew it all as though it had been her chief concern, but for once others than herself would deal with everything; for once, all she had to do now was mourn, mourn Jack, her lost and errant love, a dead man lying in a four-poster in Pickle Herring Street. Pickle Herring Street, a Shadwell brothel. It was so like Jack to end there. Lucy began to laugh; and shocked, heard the sound of her own laughter, still echoing helplessly against the curtained walls. It wasn't a bad inn, though shabby. Lucius had said all the others would be full; they'd been fortunate to obtain this room.

Lucy unlaced herself and climbed wearily into bed. She was still very cold and for a time lay shivering, trying to think of Jack as he had been in the days of their early, happy time together as lovers. That was what she must remember; not what had come later, the vase, Mr Bischoffsheim, debts, baccarat, quarrels. She began to laugh and cry again, and realised that what she needed was whiskey; good Irish whiskey, and at once. She sat up, leaned over and pulled the bell to summon the night waiter from downstairs. He came, and Lucy ordered the whiskey and a stone hot water bottle, like the one they'd brought her long ago on the ship the night Sebastian died.

*   *   *

The man who appeared with the hot bottle and whiskey was different from the one to whom Lucy had given the order. It was impossible to help noticing it as his presence filled the room. He was a tall broad creature of about forty, muscular, almost beefy, like a boxer; for some reason she could not define he reminded her of Hubert, although his hair was closely shaven on his bullet of a head. His eyes, brown, small and shrewd but not unkindly, assessed Lucy as he tucked the hot bottle under the lower sheet. His mouth was narrow and his nose a strong triangle.

'It was lucky I had the whiskey,' he said. 'It isn't often asked for.' He spoke with an Irish accent Lucy was glad to hear. She drank the stuff thankfully, downing it almost at once; its glow dispelled the chill she had felt and the bottle began to warm her feet. Evidently this was the manager, or at any rate someone who provided Irish whiskey. She asked him about it, handing back the tumbler.

'No, I'm working out my notice here, Swan on the Hoop or not,' he said. 'I've been here five years, ever since I fell out with my wife. I left her in Kerry, with her old mother.' It was all stated without any change of expression, baldly as though he had been discussing the weather. Lucy changed the subject politely. 'Why do you call it the Swan on the Hoop?' she said. 'I saw the sign, and asked myself.' She had in fact done so, in spite of everything.

'Because there's another Swan, a worse one, I daresay, lower down. This used to serve London Bridge direct, but soon they'll pull it to pieces when they build the new one across from the Tower. The building creaks, and it's tired of towns I am.' He stared at her, turning the empty tumbler in his fingers; his hands and chestnut hair were like Hubert's. 'What is your name?' Lucy asked him suddenly.

'Torke. Bernard Torke. They call me Ben. I can turn my hand to most things. I'm going back to Ireland, to an estate there, as factor; that'll be in March.'

Ireland! She could never go there any more. She forgot the echoes the name Torke roused in her; hadn't there been the oyster-seller two brothers had fallen out over long ago? It didn't matter. She was dead. Everybody was dead.

The old Mother Superior had been called Torke as well. They were all dead, and she herself was drunk. She, Lucy, could never go back anywhere. She began to cry dolefully, the tears coursing down her face.

The man Torke looked at her. He had a kind heart, and this golden-haired lady, not too young but plump and well worth having, needed consolation: that was evident. He came closer, seeing Lucy's white arm flung across her face; the movement revealed her breasts beneath the chemise, and they were magnificent. Torke felt certain reprehensible stirrings in himself. It would suit both of them, no doubt, in the circumstances.

'What is it, now?' he said, and without waiting for an answer 'There, now. There now, my pretty. There now, my pretty. There now.'

There was no need to say much more; he was used to comforting women. Afterwards Lucy lay in a kind of wonder, remembering the pleasure his great virile body had given her, her response soaring at last like an arc, like it hadn't in fact done since that time long ago in Vermont, and never—she had to admit it— never quite with Jack.

Jack, dead today and by now no doubt in his provided coffin, leaving the four-poster free. She, his widow, had been unfaithful already. What sort of creature was she? Last time, the first with Luther K., there had been fog as well; drifting in at the joints of the ship's porthole,

271

pressing in outside now round the sign of the Swan on the Hoop. It was the fog's fault. She must on no account meet Torke again before tomorrow when the others came; she'd keep to her room. He could work out his notice by himself. Ireland. He was going back to Ireland, where she, Lucy Clifton-Turner, could never go any more.

She began to weep again, but differently, having been comforted. She tried to tell herself that the tears were for Jack, and at the prospect of yet another funeral. Then the whiskey came to her aid, and she slept.

*   *   *

They buried Jack two days later at Kensal Green. Numerous people came to the service and burial whom Lucy did not know and would not ordinarily have expected to have known. Sparrow had had a broad acquaintance among whores, bookmakers, and the racing fraternity as well as the smart set themselves, who turned out in fair numbers now he was dead. Lucy was thankful for her black veil and bowed and went on bowing behind it like a mandarin, Lucius on one side of her and Luther on the other. Jane had stayed at Aylors with the girls and Lucy watched almost coldly as the coffin was lowered into the grave; she had seen so many coffins lowered into graves, and by now Jack himself seemed like a stranger,

272

somebody once briefly known. One tied away memory in bundles with pink tape, like certain valued letters: and sometimes opened them again. She would be glad to go home meantime to Aylors. London had grown alien and strange.

*　　　*　　　*

On return to Buckinghamshire, Lucy observed a carriage already outside the door; no doubt someone had called to condole, and she herself was not yet prepared; there had been enough of that in London. A figure in black rose thinly at last from the drawing-room sofa beside Jane Ker, who had done her best to entertain the visitor till their return; Isobel O'Hara, as usual the last person in the world Lucy would have wanted to see at this or any moment. The girls, who had all three run down to welcome her on arrival, were sent upstairs again, even Maria. Jane Ker rose and went quietly out. Lucy stood coldly in her blacks, not seating herself; the two women in mourning confronted one another. Hubert's half-sister had changed little and had always in any case looked like a bird of ill omen; she still did so, although her hair had meantime turned iron grey beneath the hood.

She condoled stiffly on Jack's death. 'I saw it in the paper,' she said. 'I was on my way here in any case. I can feel for you; my dear husband Pat passed away seven years ago, in his sleep.'

There seemed nothing much to say to that; Isobel had always told Pat exactly what to do, as she did with everyone, and there it was. 'You say you were on your way here,' ventured Lucy. She herself would have had a colder reception, she knew well, at Clonough, where Isobel had stayed quite firmly for the last few years of Annis' lifetime, moving respectably out and back to her own abode immediately upon the latter's death. No doubt Isobel had expected Arthur to marry her at last, but it had evidently not happened.

'I was on my way with a suggestion which may please you.'

'You have not been at great pains to please me over the years: what is it?' There was no need to placate the woman now, and never had been; how she had ruined one's life! But for her, Lucy was thinking, I would be at Clonough, I, now, this moment, Hubert's happy wife; he wouldn't have died; our son might have lived; everything would have turned out differently.

'Your own conduct determined it; we will not dwell on that,' replied Lady O'Hara coldly. 'What I have come to say is this. Before she died, Annis Meggett knew and approved this suggestion I am about to make. We were of course close friends. It was not however then made evident that Eithne refuses to marry. She

274

has stated, quite firmly, even at her age, that she intends to become a nun with the order now at Fermisons. Her father was at first against it, but this plan I am about to outline gives him a certain hope, naturally, of heirs.' Her mouth grew prim; the begetting of heirs was seldom a mentionable subject, and Isobel prided herself on her gentility.

'If you are suggesting myself, it is useless on that head or any other,' said Lucy. 'I can have no more children, and would in any case not consider a proposal from Arthur Meggett-Clees; he treated poor Cathy abominably.'

'I was not proposing yourself, naturally, but your niece Maria,' replied Isobel with some sharpness. 'Her manners are considerably steadied under the care of that excellent headmistress, and Arthur himself is extremely fond of her.'

'Indeed? They must be almost like father and daughter. How old is Arthur now? I have never been certain.' The notion of young Maria as old Arthur's second selected brood-mare disgusted Lucy; he had tried now after all three times. There was no question of considering Lady O'Hara's proposal. She was about to say so clearly, when that redoubtable personage put in a further word.

'You used to love Clonough as a child, I remember. You would be welcome there again. Arthur says you could have your old room, at any time.' Isobel studied her own covered wedding ring, its presence evident beneath the fine kid glove. Every lady, Lucy thought wildly, wears fine kid gloves, fine kid boots or shoes; nothing less will do. One had been reared on such rules. Clonough ... again, to be made welcome there ...

'I think,' continued Isobel, 'that despite the discrepancy in ages, the marriage could be a most happy one. Maria loves Clonough and comes there for holidays whenever she can.'

'That is a little different.'

'Oh, I grant you, she will need guidance till she is somewhat older; you and I can give it together over there. If you will think of it, perhaps suggest it to Maria herself, accustom her to the idea of becoming Lady Meggett—'

Lucy closed her eyes for moments. You yourself, you bitch, she was thinking, have done well enough out of Clonough over the years; no doubt you expected at last to become its mistress lately, but Arthur wants his heir like Luther K. Aloud she said, hearing her own voice grown thin and cold like the other's, that as Maria was still very young it would be preferable for her to have a London season first, then make up her own mind one way or the other. 'But meantime she may meet young men to turn her head,' riposted Isobel promptly, her smile fixed and hard. There was little doubt that this might happen; Jane Ker's strictness had ensured that Maria met no young men, no men at all, the ecstasies Jane

276

herself had known with Jeremy thrust down long since within her boned headmistress's bodice, unremembered except, perhaps, in the middle of the night.

The inexorable voice went on. 'At the moment,' Isobel was saying, 'Maria would be happy and excited at the prospect of such a marriage. As I have said, she regards dear Arthur as a father, having after all scarcely been permitted to know her own. It is moreover not advisable to introduce her to such circles as I have heard are now enabled to enter London society. In Ireland, we are a little stricter in such ways still.' She smiled, showing primrose-coloured porcelain teeth. 'Arthur would prefer his bride to come to him still innocent and untouched by the world,' breathed Lady O'Hara.

And touch her himself in bed, the old goat, Lucy thought. Again she said that she must certainly consult Maria herself. 'I would never force her against her will,' she ended, a little more weakly then would have been the case at the beginning.

'Naturally not; but I think you will find that the prospect is not disagreeable to Maria,' stated the Gothic figure opposite. 'She would sooner be at Clonough than anywhere else in the world.'

As would I, thought Lucy: as would I. The old room. It looked out on to the garden where the philadelphus grew, the mock orange with

277

its creamy blossoms wet in the rain. Was it so wicked to consider this marriage for young Maria? In all ways except age it seemed most fortunate.

The parted, Lucy promised to consider it, and when Isobel had driven off went upstairs to her room at last, her mind whirling.

CHAPTER FIFTEEN

'Of course I should love to marry Uncle Arthur, and live at Clonough. I like it better than anywhere. Last time, the sow had nine piglets, and Uncle Arthur took me to see them in the farm buggy.'

'He's so kind,' Maria added, her dimples deepening. She had been the prettiest girl at school, and knew it. It would be fun to be married first of anyone. She—

'You can't call him Uncle Arthur once you are married, and he's a remote cousin anyway,' Lucy replied prudently. She asked, again, if Maria wouldn't like to have a season first, with dances to follow Queen Charlotte's Ball, and pretty dresses. 'I can have some for my trousseau in any case, can't I?' asked Maria shrewdly. 'Truly I don't want a season, Aunt Lucy. One of the girls at school has an elder sister who was presented last year, and she says the carriages took four hours to move before

278

they got where they were going, and everybody was frozen stiff in their ostrich feathers and couldn't say so.' The giggle came, reminding Lucy that her niece was still hardly more than a schoolgirl and that Jane would not in the nature of things have told her anything at all about marriage, because to know nothing was still the pre-requisite for the polite marriage market: and asked tactfully if when Maria saw the piglets she had seen any of them actually arrive. Maria said no, they'd been pulling at the sow's underneath in some way. Lucy then enlightened her briefly as to the facts of mating, saying it was to make babies and happened to most people.

'It didn't happen to Miss Ker,' said Maria inaccurately. 'You can tell from looking at her.' She appeared unconcerned by Lucy's revelations. She flaunted her own pert little breasts beneath the sprigged bodice, and fingered her earrings; she'd only just begun to wear them. The blue eyes turned vaguely on Lucy, who reflected that except for those, the girl was almost a replica of what she herself had been at that age; though even younger than the time when she'd pulled up her skirts that fateful day to show Hubert her Italian stockings. How much had come about since then!

'You were married twice, Aunt Lucy, and didn't have any babies,' said Maria. Lucy replied quietly that she had had one little baby, but that it had died.

'That's very sad. You can come and share all my babies. I hope I have a lot. I'd rather Uncle Arthur did what you said than anybody. He's so kind.' It had been interesting to hear about it from somebody who knew; at school, they'd contributed a vague general knowledge in the dormitory, but its sum didn't add up to half what Aunt Lucy had just talked about. It sounded rather fun. Meantime, Lucy promised to take Maria to town to buy the prettiest clothes she had ever had; and that made the whole thing well worth while.

*　　*　　*

Horatia and Maude were to be bridesmaids, but Arthur had refused to bring Eithne to make a third and wrote that his daughter would prefer to remain in the convent. Lucy was uncertain whether or not this was the exact truth, but perhaps Arthur felt shy of returning with his young daughter as well as his bride. He also requested that there be no guests at the wedding, which was of course to take place at Aylors; and this enabled Lucy to win a point of her own which had been troubling her. She had no wish to have Isobel O'Hara in the house on the wedding night, supervising it and drawing her stony conclusions. *Dear Arthur, I do agree that no guests should come, not even Isobel*, she wrote, and hoped that that settled

280

that.

*   *   *

It did so. Arthur arrived alone, as Lucius had agreed to be groomsman and Luther would give his pretty eldest sister away. Lucy was stunned at the change time had wrought; she hadn't realised how greatly Arthur had aged during the narrow and uncharitable years with Annis, though he had acquired dignity with the title. His hair was white, his lugubrious face a mass of wrinkles, and he boasted the same variety of primrose china teeth as Isobel O'Hara; no doubt they both went to the same Dublin dentist. Maria, however, was unperturbed; she ran instantly up to the tall shambling figure in its mourning blacks—it had no doubt been assumed that these would do in which to get married again—and kissed him fondly on his unattractive cheek. 'Dear Uncle Arthur, isn't it exciting?' she said innocently, forgetting everything Lucy had tried to teach her in the intervening weeks about remembering not on any account to say Uncle.

The clergyman arrived and Maude and Horatia came in behind the bride, slowly crossing the drawing-room which Lucy had already filled with early flowers, a few forward daffodils, and snowdrops which had carpeted the lawn where Maria herself as a child had

281

used to play battledore. Luther looked suitably grave and had shaved himself carefully for the first time: like his grandfather he would have to do it twice a day from now on. The tall thin figure in black and the small graceful golden-headed one in white made their vows, and Maria became Lady Meggett and seemed pleased about it. Afterwards they all drank wine and ate dinner and then the pair went upstairs to bed, the bride assisted thereto by her two sisters and Aunt Lucy.

'Tell us what it's like tomorrow,' muttered Horatia as they spread Maria's fair hair over the pillows. Horatia always knew more than other people. Maria looked appealing and beautiful and Lucy kissed her with tears in her own eyes. Had she been right in permitting this marriage? The sight of Arthur as he was now hadn't, however, been as much of a shock to Maria, evidently, as to herself; over the years, visiting Clonough as she had done, the child must have grown used to it. Lucy lay awake for a long time that night, wondering if she should reproach herself; she knew perfectly well that the bribe of the old room at Clonough had influenced her. However, if Maria had shown any unwillingness at all, she would not have insisted on such a marriage.

*　　　*　　　*

Arthur came down complacently late to

breakfast on the following morning; Maria's was duly sent up on a tray. Horatia wanted to take it, but Lucy forbade her. 'Let the maid do it,' she said. 'It's what she is employed for.' The truth was that she did not want Horatia to start asking her customary robust questions quite so soon: Maria might in any case be upset. Horatia muttered pertly 'Wonder if he kept his teeth in or not?' and went on with her breakfast, fortunately having spoken out of the bridegroom's hearing. Later Maria appeared, somewhat subdued and no longer giggling, her dimples stilled. It had happened, evidently. Lucy stared at the card with a flower picture Jane Ker had sent, quietly expressing the hope that Maria would be happy. Above it hung Lucy's own not altogether satisfactory portrait, in the striped dress Jack had chosen long ago. It stared back at her from the wall. Now that Maria was married, and the two younger girls put down in time for their finishing school, she herself would take the opportunity to cross seas once again and visit Sabine and little Clara in Boston. It was perhaps time that child was taken away from her mother: but one would see. Before that, of course, and as soon as possible, she herself would go to stay at Clonough. How she longed to see it again!

As if to further her wish, Maria had clung to her on parting later that morning and said 'You will come to Clonough soon, Aunt Lucy? Very, very soon? Promise.'

Lucy had promised, noting however that Arthur had not looked too pleased.

*   *   *

A fortnight later, having written, Lucy made the Irish crossing, which despite the tides was uneventful; no doubt she herself was becoming a better traveller as she grew older. At the port, however, she was angered to see, seated beside Arthur and Maria in the waiting carriage, a third figure; Isobel O'Hara. Worse, there was a more solid one in front holding the reins. It was no other than Torke, the man from the Swan and Hoop. Lucy's thoughts somersaulted, then adjusted themselves swiftly. Torke had indeed said that he was returning to an estate in Ireland, but hadn't of course said it was to Clonough: what would she herself have done if she had known? The vision of oyster-seller ancestry was quickly set aside; all that must be forgotten and nothing else of another kind permitted to recur. Lucy advanced, calmly smiling, her baggage on a barrow wheeled by a waiting shore porter; kissed Maria, nodded to Arthur and Isobel, got into the carriage, and from the beginning ignored Ben Torke. In whatever capacity he was here, he must be treated as a servant; that went without question. To do him justice he had shown no change of expression at sight of herself; it was possible, though not very

284

probable, that he did not even remember who she was: after all it had been a foggy night.

Arthur himself provided some enlightenment of the situation as they drove away, saying that Torke was his new factor, excellent with horses, good at everything, in fact a jewel who could take full responsibility for the farm and estate, anything at all. *I can turn my hand to anything.* 'He has already saved me a great deal of money,' Arthur remarked, adding placidly that an inefficient factor was worse than none. Lucy remembered Arthur's own chronic laziness in the days of his marriage to Cathy; he had left her to do most of the work about the farmhouse and garden. He had undoubtedly come up from those days. During his bleak marriage to Annis he had nevertheless developed a certain authority of his own. He went on discoursing now about Torke, who presumably could not hear. 'He came to me with excellent references, one of them from Isobel here.' Arthur nodded amiably towards Lady O'Hara. 'He seems honest enough; he tells me quite openly that he has a wife in Kerry, but that they do not get on. He sends her money regularly, which is commendable.'

Lucy agreed, then turned with relief to talk to Maria about Aylors, now left mostly in charge of Caterina as the young people had gone off in their separate directions. Maria listened wistfully, her blue eyes wide. She still

285

appeared subdued and on arrival at the house, Lucy found that her own ecstatic gazing at the famous portico after many years was spoilt because of the realisation that Lady O'Hara again lived here all the time, some remark or other on the way having made it clear that she was not merely a visitor. Asked about it later, Maria passively replied that Lady O'Hara always had been here when they had come to spend their holidays at Clonough, she and Miss Ker. She did not appear to resent the older woman's presence, or try to assert herself in any way as the great house's mistress: it was no doubt too much to expect of a very young bride, but Lucy determined to do what she could to ensure that Maria was not bullied into submission, as seemed only too likely to happen. She had changed already from the impulsive, affectionate creature she had formerly been and was by now acquiescent, almost sullen, and certainly not her happy former self.

That evening, after dinner, Lucy retired early to her own room; she was tired after the voyage. She went to the window and saw the garden, well enough tended, with the mock orange still in fine disorder below her window. In the distance, the man Torke appeared in his shirt-sleeves, wheeling a barrow full of dead leaves. Lucy withdrew hastily, trying instead to take comfort in the things in the room she remembered, which had been disturbed very little; there was even a wooden doll still here she had played with in childhood, and which had once belonged to Mama. That night, she lay in her own familiar bed and the sheets smelled as they had used to do of sweet Clonough lavender; no doubt the maids still dried the linen on the thick bushes of it which grew behind the house. Lucy slept.

On the following morning Isobel, not Maria, presided over the breakfast teapot. Lucy forbore to remark on it: she must not make things difficult for her niece, but at the first opportunity she would speak to Arthur about the matter, which perhaps a man would not have noticed. Her opportunity came that same afternoon, which chanced to be a Friday. Lucy wanted to be driven to Fermisons, as she had had the idea of a memorial window there to Jack, buried so far away; had she known of her own pending return, she would have had his body laid instead near Cathy's, but the window would perhaps atone. However she did not want to be left to herself in the carriage with Torke as driver, and in any case would have asked Maria to accompany her. Before the girl could answer, however, Arthur put in his veto. 'No, my dear, it is your afternoon with the household accounts,' he remarked pleasantly.

Maria said nothing, but set her lips. Lucy spoke up. 'It is a fine day, and we do not have too many of them here,' she said. 'Why not leave the accounts until it rains?' Her words sounded flippant, but she was already aware of the prevailing situation; Maria, except no doubt for being made full use of in bed, was treated as a schoolgirl and ordered by both Arthur and Isobel accordingly. It would not do. 'I will ride over, in that case,' she said coldly. Maria, who had turned away, stood still for instants. 'I'd like to ride to Fermisons with Aunt Lucy,' she said hesitantly. Her elderly husband smiled with closed lips and then spoke reprovingly.

'You heard what I said, my dear, and you know already that I do not permit you to ride. Go to your accounts. I am anxious for you to become proficient at them. Lady O'Hara is ready to instruct you; she is waiting as usual upstairs.'

Maria looked mulish, but went. Once she had gone out of the room Lucy spoke. 'You should perhaps remember that Maria, not Lady O'Hara, is the mistress of Clonough now,' she told the bridegroom roundly. Lord Meggett frowned a little. 'It is intended that Maria shall take her full position when she is ready for it,' he said. 'I shall require her in all ways meantime to accustom herself to the habits of my late dear wife, who was an excellent manager and most frugal housekeeper. Nobody is better informed than Isobel of the ways in which to achieve this; she and Annis were close friends for many years, and towards the end of Annis's life Isobel lived

288

here altogether and carried out all her wishes. It is a privilege to have her back with us.'

'I take it, then, that Maria is now a chaperone for Lady O'Hara. That seems a diverting situation.'

Arthur Meggett flushed a little; he had, in fact, little humour, which fact had enabled him to make his way through life to its present placid haven. 'Pray do not be ridiculous, my dear Cousin Lucy,' he said. 'You are made welcome here meantime as was promised, but do not presume on the fact; the house, when all's said, is mine.' His lips, which were of a plum-red colour these days and had always in any case been thin and rather loose, closed firmly over the teeth. Lucy felt rare anger assail her. 'You know very well that you promised me residence at Clonough at any time if I permitted you to marry Maria,' she told him. 'If you regard her merely as a means of making heirs, which seems to be the case, at least make her happy. She is more likely to conceive if you do so.'

She turned and left him, unable to trust herself not to say more; it was probable that she had already said too much. However she went to the stables, saddled her own mare, and rode over to Fermisons through the day's pale sunshine; it was strange to be riding from one home, evidently not a home after all, to a second which hardly ever had been, and would not, in the nature of things, be likely to become so again. However she saw the newly appointed Superior, old Mother Torke having died, behind her grille about the matter of the memorial window. She happened to be the former Bursar and, as Lucy had feared, was still, like Arthur, humourless. No doubt if one had been born without that faculty one never acquired it, and such persons were undoubtedly fortunate, going through life entirely pleased with themselves.

'There are of course two major saints named John,' said the Superior reflectively, 'St John the Baptist, and St John the Evangelist. The latter at the foot of the Cross, or else leaning on Our Lord's breast at the Last Supper, would make a magnificent window we would be proud to have.'

Lucy felt wild laughter rise within her; Jack hadn't exactly worn camel's hair or lived on locusts and wild honey, which Papa had however used to remark must have been a pleasant enough diet as fried locusts were a delicacy in the East to this day. She stated gravely that she thought the young Evangelist would perhaps be more suitable. John the Beloved Disciple, leaning on Christ's breast; or John standing at the foot of the Cross, or later taking down the body: she would leave it all to Toby Tothill, Jack's painter friend who had at least known what he used to look like.

Going out again, she encountered a young girl sweeping the stone passages with a broom.

It was Eithne, not yet a postulant; she said in a low voice that it would happen next year. 'We wanted you for a bridesmaid at Maria's wedding,' Lucy said, 'but you wouldn't come.' She added that Maria sent her love, which was not true; but it might cheer this solitary child whose parents had never loved her. The plain little face brightened. 'I didn't know,' Eithne said. 'Papa didn't tell me. He is not pleased with me because I am happier here.' Her glance dropped to the floor, veiling the amiable eyes so that she looked again like her mother., 'But you are still happy,' said Lucy gently. She was not surprised that Arthur had deceived them about the matter of Eithne's presence at the wedding; it was like his meanness; she liked him less and less. Maria must be diverted a little, made to enjoy her life and her youth while it lasted, though she would certainly be allowed to see nothing of this stepdaughter. Already a silent nun was standing at the end of the corridor, staring reproachfully at Eithne and the idle broom. The girl began to sweep again wordlessly; soon, perhaps as a postulant and certainly later as a novice, she would not be permitted to speak at all. Lucy kissed and left her, returning her thoughts to the projected memorial window. She told herself again that she would let Toby decide for himself which version to choose.

She wrote to him on again reaching

Clonough, and was pleased to receive a sketch in pencil almost by return of post. He had chosen the Deposition, with Jack recognisably as St John, herself with flowing hair as the sorrowing Magdalene. The irony was no doubt unintentional, but so wryly suitable that Lucy could not reject it. Toby wrote also that he knew a worker in glass who could have the approved design ready quite soon. Lucy replied to the effect that she was pleased with the sketch he had sent, and to work on that as it was. What did it matter if everybody recognised her as the Magdalene? It was no more than the county would have expected; and Jack himself would have been amused by the whole idea.

*   *   *

Meantime, she suggested to Arthur that Maria's two young sisters might come over to Clonough to cheer her with their company. They were to start at the London finishing school together in the autumn, and thereafter there would be less time for visiting than now: they would be occupied with practising of the Court curtsey and the formidable preparations necessary to try to find husbands of their own. To her astonishment, Arthur flatly refused to allow the girls to come. He would give no reason, merely firming his loose thin lips over his ill-fitting teeth in the way he unfortunately

292

had. 'You are unreasonable and unkind,' Lucy told him. 'You allow Maria no diversions at all. At least permit her to attend the Hunt Ball; we always used to go from Clonough.'

For some reason, perhaps because he wanted to prove himself more youthful at heart than was outwardly apparent, Arthur agreed, and Maria, dressed in her pretty white ball-gown, departed with him in the carriage on the date in question. Lucy did not accompany them, nor, thankfully, did Lady O'Hara: both older ladies had their mourning to consider, and dancing every dance was no longer for them. Lucy betook herself to her room and her whiskey; she had got into the habit of it again, it was a comfort. Drinking it, she noticed that a hook was missing in the curtains so that one of them hung loose. She sent for the maid, who said she didn't have a hook but that Mr Torke would; he knew about everything of that kind.

'Fetch him, then,' said Lucy recklessly; she had already seen Torke several times about the place, he should be used by now to her presence and she ought to be used to his. She considered going out of the room while he came in, but decided against it; there was no reason why the man should think she was afraid of facing him. She watched the ladders brought in, and Torke, with the hook; of course he had had one ready. A jewel, Arthur had said: that was something, at any rate. She hoped Arthur was enjoying his second spring at the Hunt Ball: perhaps the exercise would finish him off, autocratic bore that he was; it was impossible to understand why Cathy had loved him and Annis, with all her money, endured him as a husband at all. Lucy regretted increasingly having let him marry young Maria, but it could not be undone now. Maria herself looked enchanting tonight: one hoped she would have many young partners: everyone would in any case want to dance with the new Lady Meggett.

*   *   *

Torke mounted the ladder and adjusted and repaired the curtain, maintaining respectful silence as a servant should. At the end Lucy thanked him, then, unwilling to appear anything but at her ease, asked him lightly how he had come by his surname. 'It is an unusual one,' she said. The small calculating eyes in the heavy-featured face regarded her, carefully devoid of any expression.

'It is said to be taken from the name of a torque, which was a necklet made of gold worn by the High Kings of Tara,' he replied carefully. 'I had that from an aunt of mine who was a nun.'

Old Mother Hetty; Lucy did not mention her, or oyster-sellers either. His presence still reminded her of Hubert; no doubt there was a distant relationship. It had been raining lightly outside when Arthur and Maria set out for the Hunt Ball; this man's coat smelled agreeably of rain and of comfort. Perhaps it was the whiskey, but Lucy knew that she wanted him to stay and must however tell him to go; Maria's aunt must not be spoken of as having an affair with a servant.

Torke stood there like a monolith, evidently able to read her thoughts. He spoke gently.

'Do not trouble yourself about what happened before,' he told her. 'You were sad and I comforted you, that is all.'

He turned and went, leaving Lucy standing there with her hand on the back of a chair. His behaviour had of course been entirely correct. She tried to feel relief, staring ahead at the straightened curtain.

*   *   *

The rain continued all through the night and Lucy heard it, but not the couple returning at last, nor did she hear Isobel O'Hara come up to bed; no doubt she had waited for them. This in fact had happened, and at half-past two in the morning the dancers had returned, Maria flushed still and radiant in her by now somewhat limp white gown. Arthur himself seemed, Isobel had told herself, disgustingly spry, fondling his young wife's shoulders and never taking his eyes from her to look at oneself: he said said he hadn't been able to get hold of Maria for most of the evening, except for two country-dances. 'Her card was full at once,' he related proudly.

'I hope,' said Lady O'Hara, 'that you did not overtire yourself.' It was a depressing remark, and she herself was depressing, and knew it; that pert little Maria had all Arthur's attention now, and earlier today word had come that somebody was breaking the windows at Liskey. It would be better if she herself went home to see to things.

She lingered till the couple had gone upstairs, then crept up afterwards, as she often did, to listen at their bedroom door. The good oak doors of Clonough let little sound through, fitting well at the joints as they did, but listening with attention one could just hear, faintly, a man's grunting transports come: Arthur was getting full hold of Maria now. Isobel had constantly fostered the progress of the marriage, as she assured herself; but in the dark of the passage her long face looked suddenly blank and tragic. Truth came to Isobel O'Hara for moments alone in the darkness; long, long ago, she, with her sparse thin height and plainness, and Arthur with his long-legged shambling gait had made a pair at the Hunt Ball that year, and she'd hoped something more might come of it. It never had, because the old lord her father had told her young Hubert would never manage for

296

himself, though young Lucy might see to things later on, and so he'd married her, his eldest, to old Pat O'Hara and fobbed off Arthur, afterwards, with poor little Cathy, his debts having been paid, these mostly having arisen from fecklessness. Pat for his part had never been able to make the sounds Arthur was certainly making now. She'd mentioned that to nobody in her life but Annis, and Annis had said she envied her, that the act of marriage was itself disgusting and that she herself had constantly discouraged too-frequent attentions from both her husbands. Perhaps dear Annis ought to have been a nun. Her daughter, Eithne, was to be admitted as a postulant at Fermisons at the month's end, and they would all no doubt go, herself and Lucy and Arthur and Maria, and drink tea in the convent parlour and then drive home. Meantime, she would leave for Liskey in the morning. It wouldn't after all be agreeable to watch Arthur falling in love with his young third wife.

*   *   *

Lucy had already written to the residential home in Boston to ask how Sabine and the child Clara fared, and received an answer on the day it appeared that Isobel was leaving. She opened it at the empty breakfast-table, neither Arthur nor Maria having yet come down. It was unlike Arthur to sleep late; they

297

always went to bed early, he herding Maria upstairs without fail at eight o'clock prompt. Last night had of course been different. Lucy opened the envelope, thankful for Isobel's absence upstairs packing, and read the letter from the American doctor in charge: Sabine's condition was evidently no better and she remained fiercely devoted to the little girl, who suffered from constant changes of visiting governesses as her mother made things exceedingly difficult for them. Mrs Gertrude Wint had been approached but did not want to take Clara; it would be better if closer relatives could do so. The mother could be dealt with if this might be achieved gradually.

Lucy folded away the letter and thought hard over strong Irish tea. It would be an opportunity perhaps to take Lucius with her, in the Long Vacation, to see his mother: that might divert Sabine enough to let them take little Clara away once or twice, then permanently at last, home to Aylors. She went to her desk and wrote to Lucius, to the Boston doctor, and to Gertrude Wint, who still occupied the brownstone house with her brother. It was surprising Gertrude hadn't remarried, Luther K. having left her handsomely off. Perhaps Wilbur P. Coxon filled the bill.

Lucy put the letters on the tray, and went out to the garden. She also had looked forward to attending little Eithne's initial ceremony at

298

Fermisons, but might now have to miss it; however, she would go over there on return, to see Jack's memorial window installed. The thought gave her pleasure. Meantime, with Isobel safely gone, she wanted to explore the attics either today or tomorrow: there might be other things there that had belonged to Mama.

*   *   *

It was in fact a day or two before Lucy was able to go to the attics, as with the departure of Isobel she found that she herself was needed to help Maria a good deal in maintaining the efficient household standards laid down by the late Annis Meggett. Young Maria in fact left everything to her, escaping whenever she could. Lucy excused her niece, being herself glad enough to deal with all that was connected with Clonough; stores, errands, servants' pay on Fridays, their days off, the behaviour of the sluggish chambermaid, who came like Torke's wife from Kerry and took life as it was; the cleaning of the old silver, which Annis had always done herself; and the garden. It was what she had been intended to do from the beginning, and Lucy would have been happy had it not been for the presence of Arthur, who continued to cast a blight on everything at Clonough. In this way, she would be glad enough to set out for Boston: but Lucius had not yet answered, and Lucy hesitated to make final arrangements for the voyage before hearing from him.

One day, however, again, it was raining Irish rain. Lucy picked up her skirts and ascended the attic stairs. Arthur had gone to Wexford to see his lawyer, and the house was quiet; Maria was about somewhere, no doubt. The attics were extensive and ran the whole length of the long roof between its round towers; she remembered playing hide-and-seek there often as a child, with Hubert. Beyond, there was a further spiral staircase leading to an extra tower built on by some eccentric ancestor like Papa; it was asymmetrical and hardly showed from below, echoing the one at Aylors. Lucy forgot about it and meantime, examined with pleasure and interest the litter of assorted boxes, trunks and bric-a-brac left there by former generations, possibly even from before the family feud over the oyster-seller; there were crinoline frames, horsehair wigs, fans, petticoats, a curly-heeled satin shoe, other such things. Lucy moved about silently; and yet there was not quite silence, after all. From somewhere, if one listened, there came the sound of sighing; faint and unmistakeable, the soft, contented sounds of a woman's ecstasy.

Lucy stole up the spiral staircase. She had never before pried on anyone and disliked doing it now: no doubt it was one of the maids with a lover. That meant there would be a baby, a dismissal by Arthur, a fresh maidservant of assumed moral continence to be found and trained. It was no doubt meantime her business.

What she saw instead made her heart stop for instants. On the space of floor below the tower, at the top of the little staircase, lay Ben Torke, not alone. He saw her. Against his broad chest was closely held a fall of golden curls which could only be Maria's.

Lucy turned wordlessly and descended the stairs. She then went to her room and ordered a few things to be packed and the rest sent after her. To stay on at Clonough as things were would be intolerable. She was aware of no sensations except those of anger and betrayal. For the first time in her life, she would be glad to leave. The others could think whatever they liked.

*   *   *

As it happened Lucy did not take the first available packet boat. The rain, which had been worsening since the night of the Hunt Ball, had been whipped into a gale by the time they neared the coast. The packet, which was already in, rocked even in harbour, and after one look at the heaving sea Lucy decided to stay overnight at the inn and told the gardener, who had driven her over, to take her baggage out of the trap and straight inside. The inn itself was squalid and flea-ridden, but she would neither return to Clonough nor risk the outgoing tide till it grew calm. The man drove off and Lucy was left staring desolately out of the window, against which the rain still beat, bringing salt with it as usual so that the glass was dirty and clouded.

She spent the night in discomfort in a lumpy bed, not clean; when she reached Aylors a hot bath would be the first thing she needed. She was beginning to feel like one of the bottles sailors cast on the sea with a message inside, to be washed up here and there anyhow to anyone. She surveyed her situation grimly. It was in the course of nature, no doubt, that Maria had preferred the virile Torke to her dreary old spouse. One could not judge the girl; perhaps after all one could not judge Torke either. Lucy sent for whiskey and after it, decided that one could not judge anybody at all. The wind had died a little and perhaps by later in the day, she could sail.

A gaping girl in a stained apron came up presently to say there was a caller for her honour. Her honour went down, puzzled, to the inn parlour. To her cold anger it was Torke himself, standing with his round hat respectfully in his hand. What did he want? How had he dared follow her? The gardener must have told him she was still here at the inn.

Torke wasted no time, nor did his expression change; she wondered if it ever did so very much. 'It is bad news, if you like,' he

302

said now imperturbably. 'Maria found his lordship dead in bed this morning. She was wishful for you to be told so that you would maybe return for the funeral. The old bitch is back again, howling and caterwauling as though she and nobody else was the widow; I'll go on paying a boy to break her windows at Liskey, and that'll send her back fast enough, after it's all of it over and done with.'

Lucy opened her mouth and said firmly that she had had enough of funerals and was going on the packet. 'I have buried two husbands and a child, and my brother,' she said. 'You will manage very well without me, I don't doubt. You may convey my condolences to Maria if she wants them.' She stared at Torke defiantly; the kindly expression was coming into his eyes and Lucy almost dreaded it.

'There, now,' he said, almost as he had said it at the Swan and Hoop. 'You will not blame me for comforting her, the poor pretty thing. I found her crying in the summer-house, near the beginning it was. She would tell me about him after it always: he would bundle her up to bed early, and take his teeth out, and put them in a bowl and then get to it, but he didn't get all the way, or not as a rule, not at his age, you can picture it. The other night after the dancing was as far as he ever got, Maria said. She always came to me straight afterwards, as I say, and other times as well; whenever we could, because the old broomstick was forever about, and watched her. Now, we'll get *her* out again, after *he's* below ground; and there's another thing Maria bade me tell you.' He passed his tongue over his narrow mouth. 'She's in the family way,' Torke admitted. 'Whether it's his or mine God knows, and neither does Maria, truth to tell. She said to let you know, and to hope you'd come to her at the birth.'

Lucy had sat down. The inn parlour had a few customers at the far end, drinking; they hadn't heard, Torke had spoken low and discreetly. He remained, no doubt, in his way, a jewel. The Hunt Ball must perhaps have been too much for Arthur with everything else since. It was certainly her duty to go back now; but after all why? She resolved once again not to do so; they'd manage by themselves.

'Give Maria my love,' she said, 'and tell her I am going to America for a few weeks or longer, to fetch home her little sister Clara. After that I will be back in England, and if Maria can let me know the time, I will come to her then. Until that happens, look after her. She is very young.' It occurred to her that Torke had never, with the kind of honesty that somehow suited him, pretended to call Maria her ladyship.

'God go with you, and come back safe,' Ben Torke replied calmly. Lucy suddenly wondered about the unvisited wife in Kerry; he and Maria could never become more than lovers. It

304

was probably as well, all things considered. She let Torke escort her on to the swaying packet when it soon came in, handling her small baggage for her expertly. A jewel. She would almost have given him the stones by now to go on breaking Isobel O'Hara's windows. He must be one of the few who could manage that lady by subtlety, as he had no doubt lately managed herself.

The voyage was uneven, and Lucy felt queasy on landing and stayed another night at the Welsh inn on the further coast. That done, she travelled thankfully on to Aylors. There would be nobody there but Caterina, who was restful company except when voicing concern about her Pompeian vase. Any letter from young Lucius would no doubt be sent on from Ireland. She would wait till she heard.

*   *   *

On reaching Aylors she had them heat water, took her hot bath in her room, washed her hair, bundled up every article of clothing and told them to take it away, wash it and give it to the poor or else burn it, as it was probably full of fleas. She then stood naked, with her drying hair spread about her shoulders, and looked at herself pitilessly in the pier-glass. She was too fat. Her hair no longer had the shining lustre of former days, had dulled and would soon turn as white as Papa's. No wonder she had lost a lover to young Maria.

Lucy then went to bed and stayed there for two days. Presently she got up and had them lace her into an old pair of stays which were too tight, as were all her former clothes. She would go to town as usual and buy new ones, and they wouldn't all be black. It was true that at the time she had sworn to wear it for Jack for the rest of her days, but Jack would be the last one to expect her to go on looking as she did now. It was true that black was elegant, and made one look rather more slender, and she'd need one gown of that at any rate for the installing of Jack's memorial window at Fermisons, where no doubt they'd let her stay again now little Eithne was safely inside as a postulant, or perhaps by now a novice; at any rate nobody would take her away. She herself would visit Toby's studio in town to see how the window design was progressing, also the finishing school where Maude and Horatia were learning such matters as they needed to know before being launched on society. For all that, one would require to look one's best. Pale grey and lavender were after all half-mourning, and she would be able, now her finances were steady again, to suit her tastes as she would. It was astonishing how anger increased one's determination in all ways.

*　　　*　　　*

Madame, at the finishing school—she was half French, which was an asset—said that Maude was pretty, charming and biddable, and would no doubt attract offers in her first season. Horatia however would need more than one, without doubt. 'She is of independent mind, and that does not appeal to most gentlemen,' said the proprietress carefully. 'Do you know that, the other day, she expressed an interest in the workings of *automobiles*? That is not the kind of conversation in which a young lady should indulge, and I have assured her of it.' Horatia, produced, said she didn't really want a season. 'What would you like to do?' asked Lucy reasonably.

'Go to college, as women are beginning to be admitted, but they won't let them take degrees. Why not? Why should everyone have to get married? If I have to keep house for anybody I'll keep it for Lucius. He writes to me sometimes. He says he won't marry. He's going into Holy Orders.' Horatia made a face, which her aunt ignored. 'If Lucius sets eyes on some young woman he fancies, he may marry after all, and then you will be on the shelf,' she told her niece roundly. 'Enjoy the season, at any rate, while it's offered; at least you will make other young friends.' She was mildly certain that Horatia might have inherited a part at least of her grandmother Mehitabel's intelligence and interest in things mechanical; possibly one might cause the girl to meet some of the young Napiers from Clydeside, whose notions were no doubt similar; but not quite yet. Lucy went on then to the St John's Wood studio, having already visited the shops. Toby was there, and so was the completed window. Lucy gazed at it, seeing herself with loosened hair as the young Magdalene. Jack as the Beloved Disciple was not quite convincing; they'd had, naturally, to leave out his moustache. Lucy felt tears rise. 'It's very beautiful,' she told Toby, who was regarding her with consoling admiration; she was wearing one of the new draped skirts in pale lilac, and a small matching hat perched in front and trimmed with frills. Her earrings swung.

'Lucy, you haven't altered much,' he said. 'You never will.'

He then asked to be paid. Lucy wrote a cheque agreeably. It was possible that she might be still in the States when the window was installed, but at any rate she'd seen it, and would see it again. It was pleasant to be told she hadn't altered much, even if it was just before writing a cheque.

*   *   *

On return to Aylors, Lucius had already written. To Lucy's disappointment he said it was inconvenient to come with her to Boston; he had entered into an arrangement whereby he was to take responsibility meantime for a charitable centre in the East End of London, issuing food and clothing to the poor. No doubt Luther would accompany her instead.

On reflection, she decided Luther would make the livelier escort of the two in any case. It would almost, though not quite, be like travelling with his grandfather.

*　　*　　*

Boston had changed for the better. The business quarter, long ago destroyed by fire, had been rebuilt by means of stately stone offices: the site for the pending opera house was already cleared. The parks were green and trim, the riders out cantering sociably, the streets full of prosperous passing carriages. They stayed at an hotel. 'Why aren't we staying at Grandfather's house?' Luther asked; he was curious about everything and they had even visited a new gallery of modern paintings in New York, standing later looking down into an indoor pool in which goldfish swam and their two reflections could be seen, Luther's squat, Lucy's stout but fashionable.

She answered slowly now: he was old enough. 'Because Gertrude Wint and her brother almost certainly killed your father, that time at the bog. It will never be proved.'

'I thought so. Why?' The boy's face was white, but as usual Luther wanted the reason for everything. 'Because of trying to hold on to

309

the Quinty inheritance, which they didn't,' Lucy said. 'Your grandfather sold out to the company in Scotland and I invested the money for you; it's yours to do with as you like when you're of age.' She spoke with satisfaction; that, after all, she had achieved. Luther passed his tongue over his lips.

'I often wondered about that time at the bog, but I didn't say anything,' he replied thoughtfully.

'Well, let's say nothing now; it doesn't do any good, after all. Later I want to take you up to Vermont, to see your father's grave.' She recalled poor Sabine, said to have flung herself face down over it at last after the earth had been filled in over Jeremy: again, they had had to drag her away.

'We will go to visit Mama as well, and little Clara,' she said to him. Luther nodded, still in a state of shock at the statement of what they had after all both known: but he would keep silent concerning it. He was not a talkative boy.

They drove past the brownstone house, which had a shuttered empty look. Lucy wondered if Gertrude was away. They would not of course call, but she meant to do so on Nat Passmore and his family, perhaps even before visiting Sabine and Clara; it was as well to sound others besides the resident doctors. Next day, which was a Sunday, they drove over.

Nat was at home, unchanged amid his horde of well-behaved Louisa Alcott children. Lucy kissed him and Elizabeth, still a brown mouse, having like Leah left bearing; and was ushered into the parlour and given coffee. The Passmore household did not drink wine.

Nat said he was still employed by the Scottish company now at Quinty. 'You must visit us there before you go.' He went out, taking the older sons and daughters with him, to the long afternoon sermon at the Presbyterian church: Lucy and Elizabeth were left to talk together, with Luther playing in some embarrassment with the younger children. Elizabeth turned out to be full of innocent gossip.

'Gertrude and her brother Wilbur keep house together there, and are never seen,' she said, wide-eyed. 'They don't go out anywhere and folks don't call. Nat says Wilbur is sometimes down at the works, but not often these days. What do you suppose they do all day? The place looks shut up. Nat bought the clapboard house at Vermont from Gertrude five years ago or so: when there are holidays, we all go up there.'

'I wondered if Luther and I, and little Clara if she is let, could go up together to see Jeremy's grave.'

'Surely, Nat won't mind. Old Day of Reckoning is still there. Nat sold the Morgan farm, he wasn't interested.' Elizabeth rose and poured more coffee. 'Children, be careful with that ball; roll it, don't throw it in here, it's meant for the garden.' She settled back, smiling, to nibble one of her own home-baked almond biscuits. Lucy reflected on how differently her own life would have turned out if she'd married Nat, not that she ever would have done so. Security, respectability, housekeeping, rolling out biscuits, the neighbours calling to talk about the same things and nothing ever different. Given the choice again, Lucy knew fiercely that she would decide the same way. She'd known the heights and the depths, the differences between love and desire. Her life had been filled with things and events Elizabeth had never dreamed of and never would in all her days. The world was filled with women like Elizabeth Passmore; innocent, obedient, naïve, good listeners, good bearers, to be buried and forgotten in time. She herself—

'We hope to visit Sabine tomorrow,' she said aloud. Elizabeth launched forth into as much as she could comprehend about Sabine and little Clara, who had twice been allowed to visit them here by arrangement and play briefly with the children: but she hadn't seemed at ease, not being used to young company, and the home had sent word shortly that her mother was clamouring to have her sent back at once. 'It isn't good for her,' said Nat's wife, 'but I couldn't take on one more, and poor Sabine would have run quite mad. I haven't seen Sabine for years; nobody sees her at all.'

CHAPTER SIXTEEN

The residential home, Five Elms, was situated out of hearing of Boston's busy carriage-traffic and occasional passers-by; it stood in a discreet thoroughfare a little way back from the town, and outwardly presented no other appearance than that of one more prosperous grey private house, standing in its own well-tended grounds. The five pollarded elms stood predictably between house and railings. Beyond were parterres, kept full of tidy flowers, and a lawn on which a small dark-haired girl in a blue dress played with an orange ball, tossing it up and catching it again by herself. On an impulse Lucy turned away from the door on leaving the carriage, and went up to the child, who stared at her cautiously with wide grey eyes. Her hair had grown long, and flung about silkily as she moved with the ball.

'Are you Clara?' Lucy asked. 'I'm Aunt Lucy. This is your brother Luther. We have come from England to visit you and Mama.'

She bent and kissed the smooth childish cheek. Clara accepted the kiss but did not return it or volunteer any information. She led them passively into the house, across a floor of patterned marble tiles and upstairs. Luther followed wordlessly likewise, taking in all this as one more experience; he had spent most of the available time on their voyage down among the ship's engines questioning the crew. That this was his sister whom he had never seen before did not excite him; very little did. He regarded the prospect of seeing his mother again without curiosity; it was unlikely that she had changed.

Sabine's room was up two flights of stairs, looking by now away from the garden. Outside, on the landing, a large muscular female attendant was seated in a chair, engaged in some white knitting which she set down as the party approached, and rose.

'She'll see you now,' she told them; Lucy had sent prior word of her coming. They went in. Sabine was sitting in a chair, staring at the floor. She did not look up as they approached. Lucy kissed her, aware of a faint odour of enforced cleanliness; they kept Sabine clean, but it was not the same as looking after oneself. There was no other furniture in the room except a table, a bed and commode, and a second chair. Lucy introduced Luther, without response. Suddenly Sabine seized little Clara, covered her face with kisses and took her on her knee. 'I thought you'd gone,' she said fiercely, 'I thought they'd taken you away as well.'

Clara said nothing; she was probably used to it. Nobody would ever know what she thought about anything; she had already become withdrawn into herself. Lucy heard her own bright

314

meaningless talk, flung without answer against the white-painted walls; the home was progressive and the authorities believed in making the surroundings as light and as cheerful as possible. Other such places still kept to their brown varnish. Lucy regretted, without saying so, that Sabine could not look out daily any more at the flowerbeds; but no doubt it was a waste of some front room which others could use and enjoy the view. Sabine looked at nothing, even now, except the floor: she hugged the child to her, like a stuffed toy or a pillow. Lucy decided finally that it was time Clara was taken away; one must without doubt achieve it gradually. She had briefly thought over the possibility of having Sabine with them at Aylors, but the prospect of the voyage back with her in one's charge was itself daunting; here, Sabine was well looked after and as contented as she would ever be. Lucy wondered if she was always as silent; the silence was itself more terrible than screaming would have been. No doubt Sabine lived a good deal in her own mind.

'May we take Clara with us for a little drive to see Quinty?' she asked gently. 'We will bring her back safe, I promise you.'

'No,' said Sabine. 'They took my husband away. They shan't take her.'

'Jeremy's dead, Sabine dear. I'm his sister Lucy. Don't you remember Vermont, and the grave up there? Jeremy's with God. You'll see him again.' She felt herself mouthing what must seem like the platitudes this poor creature must have heard often enough from well-meaning clergymen who visited here; they had made no impression and neither, now, did she.

'Mama, do you remember me?' Luther asked. He stood there, stocky and reliable; he smiled at Clara. Sabine did not reply, or look at anyone. Luther asked Clara if she would like to come with them for a drive. Clara nodded, and wriggled off her mother's knee.

'I'll come back, Mama,' she said evenly to Sabine. 'I'll be back in an hour.' She was seldom elsewhere for longer; her longest expeditions had been those to the Passmore children, with whom she had found it difficult in fact to play. Clara played best by herself. Sometimes a governess came to give her lessons, but there wasn't one just now. She accepted what happened to her day after day, anything or else nothing.

'Come,' said Lucy. She took Clara firmly by the hand; there was no returning pressure, but neither was it drawn away. As they went out of the room Sabine began to scream and cry. The woman outside put down her white knitting and went in at once. They heard the screams subside presently to a whimper as they hurried downstairs. Lucy sent Luther and Clara back to the carriage while she herself went to see the resident doctor. He was a smooth-faced

316

man in rimless spectacles and a white coat. He answered her questions carefully.

'She will never be any better,' he said. 'She has these fixed delusions and they will be the same for the rest of her life. It is surely time the little girl was taken away, but hitherto there has been no one suitable and as you will have seen, we have difficulty with the mother when Clara is out of the room even for a little while. The break must be made, however. It isn't the right place for Clara or any child to grow up.' He added again that Mrs Gertrude Wint had refused to take the little girl, and Mrs Passmore of course had her hands full already. There was nobody else.

'We will gladly take her with us to England,' Lucy said. She had visions already of Clara's future; perhaps at Fermisons, at the convent school where Eithne would be among the nuns: it would be gentler than sending her to Jane Ker's. Once she was safely with them on board ship, they could make further plans together.

'We will take Clara driving today, and again every day till my sister-in-law is used to it,' she said. 'Then one day Clara won't come back. It's hard, but the only way.'

The doctor agreed that it was the only way. Lucy returned to the carriage to find Clara and Luther seated in companionable silence. Clara seemed a restful child. On the whole, Sabine's temperament seemed to have been passed on

317

to none of her children.

*   *   *

They went to Quinty, where Nat Passmore had invited them to call in on their recent visit to him at home. The great Bessemer chimneys still reared, but were cold now and silent; new methods had been found, Luther said. Luther already seemed to know something about everything. The half-naked workers were busy as before in rows in the sheds, wearing helmets nowadays, passing along the carbonised plates of steel in showers of sparks. Clara stared, entranced.

'Would you like Luther to show you round the yards?' Lucy asked; she herself would visit Nat meantime at his office.

'Yes, please,' replied Clara politely, and took her brother's hand. They went off. 'Mind the sparks,' called Lucy, and knew she needn't have said it; Luther would be careful. She herself went on up to the well-remembered office. It would surprise Nat to see her; she hadn't said which day they were coming over.

To her distaste it was not Nat who rose from behind the tall desk, but Wilbur Pryde Coxon. He had changed very little except to grow thinner and more pallid than ever, an unsuccessful tapeworm. He rose and moved, smiling, towards her. 'Well, Lucy,' he said,

318

and took her hand. 'Nat will be sorry. He's gone to Salem today on business. When that happens, I take over. I'm interested in the progress of things here; it keeps me young. We're none of us as young as we were, but you're a fine-looking woman still, Lucy, you know. Come and sit down and I'll have them bring coffee.'

There was something after all reptilian about him, something dry, scaly and revolting; even his tongue, flicking in and out of his pale lips, reminded Lucy of a snake or lizard. She felt him squeeze her upper arm in the immortal gesture of the sex-starved male, and backed away. 'I don't need coffee,' she said coldly. 'I will rejoin my niece and nephew. They are down at the sheds.'

'You can't go down there, you'll get your pretty dress dirty. Why not be friends? I guess we have a lot to forgive for ourselves, Gertrude and me, the way you persuaded old Luther K. to sell out to the Scots after all. They're good employers and know what they're doing, but we would sooner have kept Quinty as a family concern.'

His eyes never left her, sliding down from the fitted neckline of her gown; he fondled her arms and shoulders, tried to lift away her ostrich boa to make her seat herself. If incest goes on still in the brownstone house, Lucy was thinking, Gertrude keeps him on a short rein.

She freed herself from the questing hands

and replied calmly, 'I too have a certain amount to forgive. You and your sister murdered my brother between you, that time in Vermont. It will never be proved, but neither will it be forgotten. What else is on your conscience remains your own.'

She turned and left, feeling the boa slither off her shoulders, grasping its feathered softness firmly with one gloved hand. She made her way downstairs alone, with a brief memory of Coxon's mouth gaping briefly in betrayal; replaced the boa carefully, and went out into the busy yard. She would never see Coxon again, if she could help it. She called Luther and Clara to her and they went back together in the carriage, leaving Clara again meantime with her mother. The sooner they all voyaged back to England the better. Lucy reserved cabins for the crossing without delay: but it was the busy season and there were no berths yet for some weeks.

*   *   *

When Clara had been taken away from her mother for the last time they drove past the brownstone house on their way north; Nat and Elizabeth Passmore had said Lucy might certainly take the two young people for a few days' holiday together in Vermont before sailing the following week. It was a good way of keeping Clara from brooding on her mother, not that one could ever tell one way or the other about that. Lucy had found herself grow adamant about the child's parting from Sabine; it was necessary, Sabine's life was over and Clara's all before her. There had been no scene: it hadn't been stressed that this was the final parting before England. She made herself talk now, into the silence broken only by the clopping of hooves.

'You'll like to learn to ride a pony, Clara, won't you?' she asked. Clara said she would. Luther showed enthusiasm, talking more than usual.

'We can hire them from the farm. It's sold now but the new owners keep on the Morgans. I'd like to see those again.' He went on to talk to Clara, describing the farm, the trees, the horses and Camel's Hump, now respectably rechristened. Lucy had stopped listening meantime. As they passed the old Wint house, she saw the pale puffed shape of a woman's face standing at one of the windows; Gertrude, looking out. It was unladylike to be seen at a window and Gertrude wouldn't have done it if she had been aware; as it was, she didn't even see them pass, only kept staring out beyond. It was a lost face, the colour and blurred texture of a drowned woman's. No doubt the greenish gloom cast by the chenille curtains was partly responsible; that and the aspidistras. Corsets, aspidistras, chenille and widowhood in Boston: and memory of Lost Pond Bog and what had

321

happened there. It might have been her own lot, after all. As it was—

Memory flooded again over Lucy, also a certain charity. Old Luther K. had prided himself on marrying, on both occasions, ladylike young women of good family. Mehitabel had had a certain strength to pit against his: Gertrude had nothing but her pretensions, and old Luther had sworn to make short work of those: it was probable that he had left his widow with the appetites he had raised in Lucy herself, and knew it well enough. He'd suspected, too, before he died, that Gertrude and her brother might be trying to make a child together and pretend it was his. Gertrude wouldn't dare give birth to any child now; the town would talk. Incest, prudently and with a condom, no doubt continued in the brownstone house nobody now visited; the furtive attentions of Wilbur P. Coxon, duly curtailed, would take place carefully out of hearing and sight of the servants. It was one answer, no doubt. Lucy felt one of her urges rise, as they usually did by night, and closed her eyes for instants. At least Gertrude, drowning among aspidistras and memory, had someone: she herself had no one. Sebastian, old Luther himself, Hubert, Jack, all of them dead; A.E. and Mr Bischoffsheim didn't count, except that they had added to one's education, in a way. As for Jeremy, she wouldn't have thought of incest and neither would he; but after all he hadn't had to. As for Torke, he was probably in bed with Maria this minute. She must get Torke out of her mind: also Sabine. It was possible that Sabine would live to be very old.

*   *   *

'Yes,' said young Luther, 'it's fall.'

He stood with his back to the room, gazing out beyond the window of the clapboard house to where the trees had, suddenly and with their annual amazement, turned their colours overnight from dulled green through yellow to red, a vibrant subtle colour forever recalled once seen in its massed glory. They themselves had, unexpectedly, waited to see it, having postponed the voyage to England even further and lingered up here after all for some months.

Lucy sat now by the lit stove, re-reading the letters which had caused her change of plan. Clara was out on her pony. She had proved to have natural hands like her older sister Horatia, and the courage to ride; she had grown a lot, come out of her shell a very little, and enjoyed herself now nobody seized on her any more with sudden possessiveness. Luther had guided her at first with the pony and then Clara had begun to go cheerfully off by herself. Lucy gave her daily lessons as well as she could; later, the child would no doubt catch up with the rest at Fermisons.

323

Lucy thought of the prospect of her own homelessness with some despair. Among the letters which had come on their first arrival, and which itself had delayed her arrangements, had been a long one from Lucius. He said that he had been offered a curacy in the East End and had accepted it; so much for Oxford dons. He was completely involved with his work among the poor and had decided, now he was of age, that to own a great house like Aylors and keep it virtually empty, while many of these people lacked a sound roof over their heads, was sinful. Accordingly he proposed turning the Buckinghamshire house into a refuge for the deserving poor at least to come meantime for fresh air and nourishing food while they contrived to better themselves. How this last was to be done Lucius did not state; but he added that all Papa's collection of archeological finds should be donated to the British Museum as the Meggett Bequest. *I would have preferred to sell them and use the money for my project at Aylors, but there is evidently no buyer who would keep the collection intact, and I owe it to Grandfather's memory to do so*, he wrote somewhat priggishly. Lucy had written by return to tell him on no account to part with Caterina's vase; it was her property and she must keep it. Where Caterina herself was to go had evidently not been considered. Neither had Maude's wedding, which should have taken place shortly from Aylors. That had been the content of the second letter, written by the needy aristocrat hired as usual to present Maude and Horatia to an appreciative audience; Maude had, as predicted, received a suitable proposal in her first season, the bridegroom being the third cousin of an earl and desirous of entering politics. Of Horatia there was no word on that front, but Jane Ker had written lately to ask if Lucy would consider permitting the elder girl to apply for entry to Lady Margaret Hall next year, as she greatly desired. Lucy had sent permission. Horatia was evidently about to break out into a world she herself did not fully understand; it was different from the one she had always known.

The fourth letter was from Isobel O'Hara, forwarded from Boston. Lucy kept it for moments before consigning it to the flames with the rest.

As you will know, Maria will shortly give birth to her child. I would most willingly have moved again into Clonough to assist her and to be present at the birth of dear Arthur's heir. However the man Torke, whom as you know I originally recommended to Arthur, has been most insolent; he practically refused me admission. Maria's behaviour has been quite extraordinary, and not in my opinion very wise; she has dismissed the housekeeper, closed up all except one wing, and lives there alone, seeing nobody but Torke, who drives her about when necessary. He continues of course to live at the farmhouse. Maria is not yet experienced enough to know how a great house should be run or to live up to her position as Arthur's widow. I feel strongly that some of her kin should be with her to advise her, and certainly to inform me when the labour starts. There was more of it, officious and revealing in general more than Isobel herself evidently knew. Go back to Clonough while that affair continues I will not, Lucy thought grimly; and with Aylors given over to the deserving poor, that only leaves Fermisons in which to live. Welcome or unwelcome, she would have to return there; perhaps the fact that Clara would be a paying pupil would alter the temperature of her own reception. There would be Jack's window to see; it was already installed now, in her absence. After all the house was hers; she had a right to go back to it.

She thrust Lady O'Hara's letter into the roaring stove; she had already replied to say that she expected to be back in England in time for the birth, but had not committed herself about encouraging Lady O'Hara's presence at Clonough: no doubt it was the last thing Maria herself would want. Despite what the letter had implied, it seemed that that young lady was well able to manage for herself, in her own way. Nevertheless she had formerly asked Aunt Lucy to be with her for the birth, and Aunt Lucy would go.

Clara came in then, her cheeks bright with the cold which had come down. She was

326

happy; Day of Reckoning, old now, white-haired and bent, had taught her yet another hymn which Clara was still too shy to sing. His voice echoed now in her mind; he'd taken the pony to be unsaddled and rubbed down in the stable. Clara's mind felt like a casement suddenly flung wide; there was so much to see and know about that she hadn't seen or guessed before, alone constantly with poor Mama, whom Aunt Lucy said was being very well treated; one wrote occasionally, but there had been no reply. Otherwise, Clara looked forward to seeing her eldest brother and her sisters; Maria was to have a little baby soon, Aunt Lucy had told her; and Maude was to be married, and she herself was to learn to dance, the way she'd lately learned to ride. It was a long way from Five Elms, and the woman with white knitting stationed constantly outside the door.

Luther spoke, still looking out at the trees. They'd been down to the farm often, he and she, and Clara had milked a cow. 'I'd like to come back here, or some such place, when I've seen round a bit,' Luther was saying. He added that on the voyage out, he'd talked to a crew member who'd panned for gold in Australia. He'd like to do that first, then see other places, then perhaps come back. 'Let me come and stay with you,' ventured Clara shyly. It was a long speech for her to make. 'Sure, sure,' said Luther absently, not turning his head. Lucy watched him; the squat, intent form was almost like having old Luther K. back in the room. It was understandable that he had been particularly fond of this grandson. All of them, in any case, all the nephews and nieces, were doing exactly as they liked: it was pointless, as she had often told herself, to make plans for anyone.

She rose. 'You're coming first with me to Ireland,' she nevertheless told Clara. 'You will go to school there, and come and see Maria's baby when it is born.'

Clara said she would like that. Luther said he wouldn't come with them. He was going to Australia, to a place called Coolgardie. The man in the engine-room on the ship had told him all about it. Luther's thick red lips set in determined fashion; he shaved now regularly, and considered himself a man.

CHAPTER SEVENTEEN

Maude was safely married, a veiled exquisite figure in white tulle, liable to gain almost as many votes for her young husband as Georgiana Devonshire's fox muff and kisses had done last century for the Whigs. The occasion, the last to be held at Aylors before the advent of the deserving poor, had been a magnificent success: even the lilacs had

328

survived. Lucy had read somewhere that one splintered the ends and then plunged them into red-hot coals; it sounded dire, but it worked: the long pointed blooms stayed fresh and undrooping in their vases for the ceremony. She had kept more of an eye on them than on the belted earl, the third cousin who had even graced the marriage by his august presence: it was more than Maria had been able to do, but she was too far gone to travel. Everybody else was there; Lucius, assisting the clergyman; Luther, again giving a sister away and after that leaving for Australia; Horatia, tall and already severely scholarly, and Clara, her shy dark prettiness a foil for the bride as she held Maude's bouquet while the vows were taken. Afterwards, everyone drove away and Lucy, exhausted, retired to her room and a nip of Irish whiskey, then fell asleep after thankfully unlacing herself. When she awoke it was to make immediate plans to sail to Ireland, taking Clara, Caterina and the Pompeian vase. Lucius could then do his worst with Aylors and she would never visit it again, not that she had anything against the poor. It was simply that everything had changed: only Horatia, with her odd abrupt manner and snippets of suddenly revealed knowledge she must have had for years, was growing increasingly like Papa as well as, perhaps, Mehitabel.

After the wedding, it was a matter of seeing her own personal belongings crated and despatched, having written already to Fermisons to say that she herself, with Clara and Caterina, would require accommodation for their immediate future. There was no reply from Mother Felicity, and the crossing was therefore spent in some foreboding, with Caterina grimly holding on to the box which contained her precious *doario* and Clara standing at the ship's rail with her dark hair blowing in the warm breeze off the sea. Lucy sat with her cloak wrapped about her, feeling increasingly like some creature with no roots and nowhere to put them if she had. It was partly her own fault for having nothing to do with Clonough, as things were.

When they arrived they found rooms had been grudgingly allotted to them, but the presence of the crates made things cramped, and after a few days Eithne, who had already taken the child Clara under her wing in a friendly fashion, was despatched with a note to Lucy in the small careful handwriting of the Superior herself. It was not convenient to house Mrs Clifton-Turner and her companions, and their furniture, indefinitely; they were glad to have little Clara as a day pupil, but otherwise they needed the room.

Lucy was angry; Fermisons was after all her

house. 'Say that there is no reply,' she told Eithne, who stood in silent obedience with her eyes lowered beneath her postulant's veil; she was to enter the novitiate by the autumn and would take her final vows in two years' time. She had shown Clara Cathy's grave and the chapel, and had made her known to the other girls who came for daily lessons; she herself was by now a kind of pupil-teacher for the term. She went away, and shortly a second note came from the Superior asking what Lucy planned to do. This was intolerable, and Lucy made her way down to the convent parlour with a request to see Mother Felicity herself as soon as possible. She appeared after some delay behind her grille, with a silent nun in attendance.

'I would remind you that in former times, before you yourself joined the order, you were ejected from your earlier premises because the owner wanted them for his personal use,' Lucy said. 'I would not go so far, but I think that I have some right to stay here in my own house for as long as it suits me, with my guests.' She tried to keep her voice calm; it was not of course possible to discuss the present situation at Clonough, though immediately the nun began to speak of it.

'You have, I understand, living quarters at Clonough if you so desire. We have done a good deal to improve conditions here, and cannot be regarded as mere temporary

331

tenants.' The tone was smug. Lucy refrained from retorting that she would like at this moment to turn them out lock, stock and barrel; that was the kind of reply that would undoubtedly have been made in the days of Papa. 'It is not convenient to stay at Clonough at the moment,' she replied coldly.

'I am told that three of the four wings of the house are shut up out of use. Why not occupy one of those, you and your family and baggage? We are of course grateful to you for your generosity, and pray for you daily.'

Prayers will not bring me a roof over my head any more than they did for your original founder, Lucy thought, but said nothing aloud. 'My niece Lady Meggett is expecting a child shortly,' she said. 'I will go to visit her then and we will perhaps see what can be done, but I can make no promises: there are after all things you do not know of.' She rose, turned and went, hearing the grille's shutters close. The maintenance of the mediaeval habit of seclusion and calm acceptance of all charity as a right irritated her; that woman knew perfectly well what was happening at Clonough, though not perhaps the actual state of things concerning Torke.

at Fermisons, 8th September.
My dearest Maria,
I hope that you are well. As you asked me
I am here in time for your baby's birth if you

would like to have me with you. I have your little sister Clara with me, whom you have never met. She is a sweet child. Luther has gone off to Australia; as you know, he was always very adventurous; it is unlikely that his family will ever see much of him at home.

Lucius has prepared Aylors to receive a large number of poor people from the East End of London. I have brought away a certain number of things of my own, and would ask you a great favour. There is very little room here with the convent's increased activity and numbers. Would it be convenient for me to send the crates over to Clonough meantime to be stored? There is nothing of great value or importance to anyone except myself.

Lucy paused with the pen in her hand, thinking of the first thing that came to mind; a scarlet and gold musical box that had belonged to Mama and which played *Oft in the Stilly Night* when one wound a handle. She had delighted Clara with it briefly at Aylors, the child never having seen or heard such things before. She was enjoying school here now also, finding the other children agreeable after all. It would be pleasant to watch her grow up, bring her out as Horatia and Maude had been brought, and thereafter let her choose for herself what she would do; young women everywhere were

333

beginning to choose; it wasn't always a fate either of marriage to the first comer or having to turn out like Jane Ker. Jane had however been one of the successful ones; there were other governesses, still downtrodden, unconsidered, badly treated and badly paid. If one lived to be a thousand years old one might do something about everything, but now—

Eithne was at the door again. They always sent her up with notes. 'Is it from the Superior?' asked Lucy with patience; it wasn't the child's fault if so.

'No, it is from Clonough. The carriage is waiting.' The flat voice held no interest; nothing that happened in the outside world was allowed to interest Eithne any more. Lucy rose and took the note. It was brief, scribbled on an odd piece of paper and folded without an envelope.

Maria's baby has started. Will you come? Don't tell her at Liskey.

It was signed hers respectfully, B. Torke.

*   *   *

Liskey had however heard of it: as they drew up outside Clonough portico, the ancient O'Hara carriage moved away; Isobel must be inside already. Lucy hurried out and upstairs; Maria herself would be in the master chamber. As she approached it Isobel came out, her sallow cheeks turned patchy red.

334

'I advise you not to go in,' she said. '*That man* is with her alone, and refuses to leave the bedroom. I never knew of a greater scandal. I am going at once.'

'It is time you did,' retorted Lucy on the stairs. 'If Maria has a guardian it is myself. I order you to leave also, the way you did to me long ago, and little good it's done you in the end. Go back home, Lady O'Hara. I will see that you are sent word.' She made her way into the great shadowed room, not waiting for the other to reply, leaving behind any expected sounds of pious outrage. 'She's gone,' she assured Maria, who lay grossly swollen on the bed, Torke seated by her; they were holding hands. It didn't matter now. Lucy bent and kissed Maria. 'How do you feel, my dear?' she asked. She smoothed the girl's forehead; it was damp with sweat.

'It's stopped now,' said Maria. 'It started this morning. Ahhh—'

She began to writhe again, burying her face against Torke's shoulder. Lucy felt the distended body gently; the child still moved, it wasn't like her own time yet, but there was again a sponginess below that shouldn't have been there. She spoke to Torke. 'Have you sent for the doctor?' she said. He nodded.

'He's at another birth, at Leskinfere. He'll come when he can.'

Lucy spoke in a low voice, still smoothing Maria's forehead and sweat-soaked hair. 'Send

335

another servant and tell him to hurry, and to bring all his gear with him.' She didn't want to mention knives in front of Maria. How often in all the world did this condition arise, and was it, because she and Maria were almost physical doubles, aunt and niece, the same doomed inheritance? Placenta praevia. That was what they'd called it to her afterwards in Boston. If Luther K. had let them cut her open, the baby would have been saved, perhaps: perhaps not. This child, at any rate, still lived.

Lucy spoke again to Maria. 'Rest now,' she said. 'Don't try to bear down for a while; wait till the doctor comes, he'll put things right.' One had to hope that he would. She should have asked the nuns to pray for Maria, but there hadn't been time.

There was time now, more than time: five mortal hours, while it grew dark. Maria laboured despite herself and cried out, howling at last for a time like a tormented little animal; then she stopped and began to whimper. 'It won't come,' she said. Tears ran slowly down her cheeks. 'I'm tired,' she whispered. 'Ben, I'm so tired.' She turned into Torke's shoulder again. His face, watching Lucy's preventive hands, was angry, the mouth a slit.

'What in God's name are you doing?' he said. 'You're stopping it coming.'

'It mustn't be born till the doctor comes. She'll bleed too much. Try to hold on, Maria. Try to hold. Grip the sheet.' How well it all came back, and Mehitabel by her bed telling her what to do! But Maria clung only to Torke. Her cries had grown very weak, like a helpless abandoned kitten's.

'Thank God, here he comes at last,' said Torke, as the new young doctor hurried upstairs and in; they'd heard the clatter of hooves outside. He examined Maria, then looked quickly towards Lucy. 'I've never seen a case of this myself before,' he muttered.

'You know what to do.' It was not a question, but a command; she might have been his superior, and unlike most medical men he did not despise lay advice. He turned to Torke, thinking he must be the husband. He knew few people in the area as yet.

'You'd be better out of here, sir,' he said. 'We have to operate.'

'I'm not leaving her.' Torke still held Maria's hands. 'Don't fret, Maria, love. I won't leave you, not for any of 'em. You hold on to me.'

Lucy watched while the doctor unpacked his chloroform bottle and mask; thank God for chloroform. The mask went over Maria's face. The rest was quicker than Lucy had foreseen; clamps, a single cut, revealing the thinly stretched uterus, a mere transparent membrane now, with, visible inside, a feebly moving child. The doctor cut into the womb wall and brought out the child with a single deft twist, slapping it head down to make it cry.

337

It was a living boy, with chestnut hair.

Torke too was crying. He laid his shaven poll against Maria's neck, sobbing against her like a child himself. 'I never saw that happen before,' he muttered. 'Is she—'

But Maria was already dead.

*   *   *

Jane Ker, informed at once by telegraph, came across for the funeral, leaving her new term entrants meantime in the hands of a second mistress. She stood with Lucy gazing down at the dead young Maria in her coffin, her hands filled with late Clonough roses, her glorious hair combed loose to her shoulders. 'She was like a daughter to me,' Jane said softly, her face, which had grown hard and severe with the years and with her profession, briefly once again that of the plain little governess who had loved Maria's father secretly by night. 'I hope,' Jane added now, turning away, 'that she was happy in the marriage. He was so very much older.'

I should never have allowed the marriage, Lucy was thinking; and yet the uppermost thought in her mind was that she was looking down on her own dead face. Now that Maria's blue eyes were closed the likeness to herself was clear; the creamy lids, heavy as shut buds, the full lower lip blanched in death, the long rich hair. She was my double, Lucy told

338

herself, admitting after all that Maria had also been perhaps as silly, being still so very young. Perhaps she would have steadied with the years. The marriage had not been happy, scolded by Arthur and dragooned by Isobel as Maria had been: one had not of course foreseen that. The rest had followed naturally enough, and must not be mentioned to anyone.

The funeral was well attended, in the way of farewells to those whom the world has not much troubled with while they were alive. A scattering of partners had come who remembered the radiant bride at the Hunt Ball last winter; the tossing golden curls would soon be dust. Otherwise, Arthur's seclusion had ensured that his young wife knew few people beyond Clonough. Torke himself had already gone, blundering out of the house as soon as Maria was dead; he was not to be found at the farm. Lucy had contrived everything without his help. The will was to be re-read, remaining however much as it had been at Arthur's death. It would contain nothing new and only those few who were involved waited for it, among them Lady O'Hara. She had not acknowledged Lucy or spoken to anyone, sitting alone in her customary blacks in church, and now in the library. She had looked bitterly resentful when poor Maria's coffin was laid beside that of Arthur at the last; no doubt it should have been her own.

Little Clara sat there solemnly, Eithne

veiled beside her, allowed for this last time out into the world. Eithne had known Maria; Clara, her own sister, had not. Afterwards they were to talk in hushed voices about the dead girl, her golden beauty, the happy visits to Clonough in the holidays with Jane in earlier years, when everything had been kindness and joy. That was as much as Eithne knew; the notion of Maria as stepmother had hardly been allowed to become apparent to her mind. She mourned now for a childhood friend, perhaps maintaining the pious hope that Maria was in heaven now, with Papa, also no doubt Mama, his other wife; it was all slightly confusing, and there was likewise the saint.

The lawyer stood up and read the will once more. Lucy was gratified to learn that Arthur had maintained his original promise made at the time of the marriage; her own right of residence at Clonough was assured for her lifetime. She was also, Maria's possible death having been provided for, the guardian of any heir there might be. The heir lay kicking now in his pearwood cradle; she'd visit him afterwards. Not having had to endure as much fighting out into the world as most babies experience during birth, he was thriving remarkably; he would be a fine man and would live heartily and long. He did not, thankfully, seem to resemble Torke in particular; if anything he resembled his grandfather Jeremy, though with the darker hair.

Incredibly, Isobel O'Hara stood up at the end in the midst of everyone and began to speak. The company turned to stare at the tall spare figure, its face hard as ivory beneath the old-fashioned hood. 'I will contest the terms of this will,' Isobel said clearly. 'Poor Lord Meggett intended *me* to be the guardian of his widow and child, in the event; he told me as much, having trusted me with the direction of Maria herself from the time of the marriage.' She flung up her head. 'The circumstances since his death have been disgraceful,' she added. 'All year Maria chose to live alone in this house. I assumed that she was mourning her husband. However it seems evident that the man Torke, a servant, was constantly with her; he was with her even at the birth, *alone.*'

'Perhaps she required assistance,' ventured the lawyer. Isobel bridled, her false teeth shifting as Arthur's had used to do.

'I would have assisted her myself; I had in fact come to do so. She had insisted on shutting up almost all of the house and there were few servants. I take it, from what I have since heard, that she chose to hurry out, while starting the actual labour, to Torke at his farmhouse; it was raining, and he carried her back. Otherwise the child might have been born *there* instead of in the customary bedchamber. I contend that this child may not be the son of Arthur Meggett. There is no resemblance; you may see him for yourselves.'

She had, of course, already marched into the nursery uninvited.

Lucy said lightly 'I think myself that the baby resembles the former holder of the title, my late cousin Hubert Meggett, also my brother Jeremy, who was after all poor Maria's father. It remains to be seen when he grows up whom he will look like. Till then, I am his guardian by Lord Meggett's will. If he is not Lord Meggett's son—and that is no more than a malicious supposition of yours, Lady O'Hara—the property falls, with the title, in any case to my nephew Lucius, who is unable to be present today.' Lucius had sent condolences, but would not leave his poor to bury his sister. There was nobody here but women, warring amongst themselves. 'You should dismiss Torke,' said Isobel O'Hara viciously. 'He has not, at any rate, had the impertinence to be present.'

'I will dismiss whom I choose, and keep whom I choose,' replied Lucy firmly: she could hold her own these days. It was probable that Torke had decamped to the wife in Kerry. She thought no more of him meantime, but listened to the lawyer cautiously explaining that paternity was assumed as the late husband's, failing valid proof that he could not be said to possess it. There was ample proof in this instance that the marriage had been consummated; even Isobel could remember the sounds behind the door. She flounced out, defeated, to her carriage with the rest. Lucy was left alone, without Jane who had had to return at once to her school. Before leaving she had spoken up valiantly about the virtue of Maria. 'It is impossible to imagine scandal concerning her,' she had told the lawyer; and the lawyer had taken heed. Lady O'Hara was known to be a spiteful and disappointed woman; she could take the matter further if she chose, but nothing would come of it except that the county would gossip, as it always had done, about the owners of Clonough. Scandals died down: there had been something, hadn't there, about Mrs Clifton-Turner herself, long ago? Such things subsided in time, and just as well, in the name of charity.

Lucy went to see the baby presently and handed him a finger; his grasp curled round it. If he had Torke blood, Torke blood contained Meggett blood also, through the oyster-seller Hetty. In any case she herself would open up Clonough, keep the house and garden as it had once been kept, rear the baby, educate and love him. She left him meantime with the young serving-maid and went out into the garden to visit the mock orange, its blossom over now; but there would be next year, and the year after that; many, many years, while one grew old. Lucius might come over when he allowed himself a holiday; Luther could roost here between adventures and voyages; Horatia could come in vacations and take time to

343

decide what she wanted to do with her bluestocking life; Maude could come with her husband and, no doubt, children in time. Clonough would be a happy place again, and she, Lucy, the queen of it, as should have happened long ago. Everything had come full circle, in the strange ways of God.

The mock orange needed pruning. Lucy turned to go and get the shears, and as she did so observed the returned Torke, with a black band on his sleeve, coming towards her up the path. It had been tactful of him to stay away from the funeral; there might otherwise have been talk.

Lucy said nothing. Torke began to speak, somewhat in the tones of a penitent in the confessional; perhaps he had even been to one in the interim. Lucy had no idea if he had any religion except kindness. He had the air of a man who still mourned; his eyes were red, as though he had wept lately for Maria. She listened to what he had to say.

'I couldn't forgive you at first when she'd died,' he told her, 'but maybe she'd have died anyway. She wasn't well towards the end, the way women ought to be when they're the way she was, and she wouldn't have the doctor. She didn't want anyone but myself, truth to tell, and how could I refuse her? That time in the summer-house I told you of, she was crying like I never saw any woman cry. What else was I to do?'

344

Lucy stood silent, saying neither yea nor nay. The man had charm; that was certain. He was also honest. She would certainly keep him on if he would agree to stay. A little breeze stirred the overgrown garden. Torke looked round in professional despair.

'With one thing and another, there wasn't much time to keep this in order,' he said, surveying the dying weeds. 'She wanted me with her all the time, in her bed most of all; I didn't often stay at the farmhouse, I can tell you. We were together all year, and the old broomstick didn't know because nobody let her in; Maria said to tell her she wasn't at home if she should call. Maria wasn't at home to anyone but myself.'

His great face was still solemn, and Lucy suddenly smiled. 'You loved Maria and she loved you,' she told him. 'You gave her happiness. There hadn't been much, as you know, in the marriage. He altered after it; he'd been kinder to her before.'

'It was the old woman,' Torke said. 'That woman did nothing but harm all her life. I wouldn't have gone into *her* bed for the offer of a horse and a new carriage. Truth to tell, when I was in Maria's, and her lying in my arms, I often remembered yourself.'

'That matter was not to be mentioned again,' Lucy said with decision. He was incorrigible; in ways, he was like a schoolboy; in so many, she was reminded increasingly of

Luther K.

'Why may it not be mentioned? Why not now? She was a pretty thing; I'll never forget her. Do you know that on the night she started her labour, and it was raining the way it does, there was a knock on my door at the farm, in early morning, still dark, and it was herself? She'd walked down, alone in the rain, and her with the pains starting already. Her hair was all wet down her back, and I took her in soaked, and dried her and wrapped her in a blanket, then I carried her up back to the house and her own bed. They'd have talked if the Clonough heir had been born elsewhere than in the great master room. God knows whatever happened after that was beyond me, you knew more of it than I did for all I was one of eleven and often helped my old mother cut the cord and all the rest of it, and wipe the baby's nose and mouth after. But I never saw the like of that in all my life. I still don't know what was right and what was wrong, or what else should have been done except what was.'

'It was the same as myself,' said Lucy. 'They didn't cut me open, the child was born dead at last, and I was scarred inside myself so I could never have another. Would you have wanted Maria to live on so, barren all her life, and with the child dead as well?'

'It'd have been a life, at least. She didn't have much. The old man and the old woman, they should have married one another, then they could have been miserable enough together. As it was—'

The small brown eyes, calculation still in their depths, surveyed Lucy. 'Maria's dead, but my son's alive,' said Ben Torke. 'I'd not disown him if he's mine, that is. That night he was at her, the old lord, after the Hunt Ball, she'd started him already. She told me so herself. I'd like to see him.'

'You shall see him,' said Lucy, 'but if you go about saying he is your son, you are losing him his rights. He has them in any case: he is a Meggett and a Torke. Arthur Meggett-Clees was nobody; he came in from the outside.' She felt suddenly reckless, borne away on the wings of what was no doubt a wicked and most deceitful guardian devil; but the devil had already won. Torke was still looking at her intently. 'If you want me to go, and take him with me, I will,' he said. 'If you want us both to stay, I'll do what I can for you about the place, or any other service you might maybe fancy, later.'

It could not have been better put. *You'll never be able to do without a man in your bed for long.* He knew it as well as she did. It was however a little soon for the present, when they were still mourning Maria. 'I will keep the baby here,' Lucy said. 'On the face of it he is Lord Meggett's son whether or not that is the truth. What will happen in the end is not yet clear, and perhaps depends on my eldest

347

nephew; but it is unlikely that Lucius will be interested in claiming Clonough. Keep to yourself what you have told me. I have my young niece over here, as you know; later on her sisters and brothers may come as well, now and again, for a time. I expect you to behave as fits your position, which you may keep if you desire it. Otherwise you are free to go, but the child stays with me in any case.' She sounded fierce, unlike herself. 'I want him to have every chance in life and I will see that he gets it. I trust that you understand me.' Lucy's hazel eyes were full open.

'I understand you, oh, yes, I understand well enough,' said Torke. 'When none of them are here at all, and the little girl away at the convent school, maybe you will send for me in a quiet way. I will keep my silence hoping you will send. In the meantime I will get on with the garden, and the farm, and the slates on the roof. They are needing attention.'

She was being almost blackmailed, and knew it; moreover that she did not greatly mind. She must invite him to her bed now and then, in other words, or he would talk. The county would talk in the end as well; they always did. She would lose her reputation once again, having patched it up over the years. Did it matter? To be no longer considered respectable had its advantages. The O'Haras of the world would cease to call, she herself could make Clonough garden a glory again, and have it to enjoy when the young people came over. Clonough. It was hers now till she died. As for Fermisons, she'd go over from time to time, look at Jack's memorial window and think for a while of the strangeness of love. That had been the only time she'd truly known it. The rest—

The baby had begun to cry somewhere in the house; no doubt his linen needed changing. There was no taint of the doom she, Lucy Meggett, had formerly seemed to bring to young children in her time. He'd grow to be a man, would Hubert Jeremy Flaherté Lucius Meggett, eighth Viscount whether anyone liked it or not. She herself would teach him to ride, teach him to hunt, teach him to take his rightful place by inheritance from lords and, probably, oyster-sellers. Right was wrong and black was white, as it had always been for her, but it didn't matter. She knew that in Christian truth she ought to write and have poor Sabine sent over to sit and howl up in Clonough tower for the rest of her days, but she wasn't going to.

'Go now, and I will send later when I choose,' she told Torke: he mustn't think he was the master. When he had gone off Lucy turned to the mock orange and buried her face in it. It took her back to that time long, long ago, in Hubert's day when the flowers had been on the branches and she had expected soon to become Hubert's wife. If she had, she would never have known and married Jack;

and despite all bitterness, would she sooner that hadn't happened? He and she would meet again; she was certain they would meet again, and Jeremy and Hubert and Luther K. and little Alan and Papa and Mehitabel and Maria. Love didn't die; and there would be flowers next year again on the philadelphus, and old age to wait for pleasantly, unlike so many. Once in a fairy story she'd read as a child here at Clonough there had been a girl who had been offered to choose one of two sides of a strange old woman's muff. One side had been white and the other yellow. The white side had promised joyous youth, riches and happiness then and later on death in a ditch. The yellow promised tribulation first, then at last a happy old age. She, Lucy, must have chosen the yellow side without thinking. She wished she could remember the name of the story, or the book it was in; perhaps she'd find it. The long days were her own, to do with as she liked; differently from Gertrude Wint in Boston, keeping up appearances behind her aspidistra but probably not much further behind that. Gertrude would no doubt say, if she ever heard, that she, Lucy, had gone off in the end with the hired man. Let her talk, with all the rest. They always had. They always would. They could get on with it.

We hope you have enjoyed this Large Print book. Other Chivers Press or G.K. Hall & Co. Large Print books are available at your library or directly from the publishers.

For more information about current and forthcoming titles, please call or write, without obligation, to:

Chivers Press Limited
Windsor Bridge Road
Bath BA2 3AX
England
Tel. (01225) 335336

OR

G.K. Hall & Co.
P.O. Box 159
Thorndike, Maine 04986
USA
Tel. (800) 223-2336

All our Large Print titles are designed for easy reading, and all our books are made to last.